P9-CET-348

"How did you know to come?"

How did he know she would need him? That everything could be made better by his presence?

Nathan shrugged beside her. "I just didn't want you to be alone," he said like it was the most simple thing in the world.

Kate didn't say anything to that. She couldn't find the right words. Instead, her heart pounded straight against her rib cage so intensely she wondered if he could hear the thumping.

She turned to her side, enough to see his profile against the dark shadows of night. He was starlit, the dip of his brow and arch of his nose and gentle curve of his chin visible. She watched his lips part and waited for the words that sat on the tip of his tongue. She studied him so intensely she could trace him to paper from memory.

She caught her breath, caught her tumbling thoughts, lost in him somehow.

"What?" Nathan asked, turning his head slowly in her direction. "You're staring."

"No, I'm not," Kate lied ardently, even as she continued to stare.

Dear Reader,

In the small town of Hatchet Lake, you'll find the Cardiff Ranch, an idyllic place for horseback rides through the woods and nights spent listening to the crickets. It also happens to be a place for second chances, new beginnings and love.

When Kate Cardiff finds herself called home for a family emergency, she's not looking for any of those things. Burned by love, Kate is a character near and dear to my heart. At her core, she is every person who's ever wanted something so desperately that they're afraid to reach for it. And that's someone I think we can all relate to a little bit.

I am so excited to share Kate's story in my first novel with Harlequin and for you to meet the wonderful cast of characters that call Hatchet Lake home. So here's to taking the leap, dear reader, and reaching for something new! If you enjoy Kate's story, you can always find me on Instagram, @elizabethhrib, swooning over my favorite books and hunting down free little libraries.

Elizabeth

Lightning
Strikes Twice

—

ELIZABETH HRIB

HARLEQUIN
SPECIAL
EDITION

If you purchased this book without a cover you should be aware
that this book is stolen property. It was reported as "unsold and
destroyed" to the publisher, and neither the author nor the
publisher has received any payment for this "stripped book."

HARLEQUIN®
SPECIAL
EDITION™

Recycling programs
for this product may
not exist in your area.

ISBN-13: 978-1-335-72463-2

Lightning Strikes Twice

Copyright © 2023 by Elizabeth Hrib

All rights reserved. No part of this book may be used or reproduced in
any manner whatsoever without written permission except in the case of
brief quotations embodied in critical articles and reviews.

This is a work of fiction. Names, characters, places and incidents
are either the product of the author's imagination or are used fictitiously.
Any resemblance to actual persons, living or dead, businesses,
companies, events or locales is entirely coincidental.

For questions and comments about the quality of this book,
please contact us at CustomerService@Harlequin.com.

Harlequin Enterprises ULC
22 Adelaide St. West, 41st Floor
Toronto, Ontario M5H 4E3, Canada
www.Harlequin.com

Printed in U.S.A.

Elizabeth Hrib was born and raised in London, Ontario, where she spends her nine-to-five as a nurse. She fell in love with the romance genre while bingeing '90s rom-coms. When she's not nursing or writing, she can be found at the piano, swooning over her favorite books on Instagram or buying too many houseplants.

Books by Elizabeth Hrib

Harlequin Special Edition

Hatchet Lake
Lightning Strikes Twice

Visit the Author Profile page at Harlequin.com.

Chapter One

If there was one place Kate was used to being, it was entrenched in a straw-bedded pen, with her hand up a cow's backside.

It wasn't exactly where she wanted to be on this particular night, or any night for that matter, at quarter to eleven. But Mother Nature didn't exactly keep business hours. And if she'd learned anything during all these years as a livestock vet, it was that the miracle of life stopped for nothing.

And no one.

Especially not for dinner plans with an acceptably average guy from one of the numerous dating apps her friend Sarah had insisted she download upon becoming single again.

Kevin—thirty-six, originally from Grand Rapids, who liked baseball and jazz—would just have to wait another night to regale her with the wildly entertaining world of internet trading. Maybe it was for the best. Of all the things Kate would never understand, the stock market was definitely near the top of the list.

Truthfully, when Sarah had insisted that Kate make all these profiles, she hadn't prepared her to navigate what Kate liked to call the highway of red flags. Kevin from Grand Rapids had been one of the more palatable pit stops on her road trip through dating hell.

After breaking things off with her ex-boyfriend in a somewhat mutual dismissal—one where they both agreed that Cal had been a little too hands-on with his favorite barista—Kate had wanted to take a break from dating.

A two-year relationship was a long time for anyone. And at thirty years old, two years together had started to feel serious. Like something that might mean a lifetime.

Boy, did she know better now.

Sarah had insisted that she get right back on the horse as soon as it had ended.

But Kate had been on horses before. A lot of them, actually.

And she was thoroughly inclined to say that getting back into the dating world was nothing like getting back on a horse.

It was far worse.

Because even after five and a half months of closure, she still simultaneously wanted to punch Cal square in the teeth and weep into a box of double-stuffed Oreos.

Tonight, Kate planned to do neither of those things seeing as she was currently knee-deep in straw, squatting over her rubber boots, her hands laid gently along Betty's side—a heifer about as impressed with the current labor situation as Kate was.

"Good girl," she cooed encouragingly. One way or another, this calf was coming out tonight, and it was going to take both of them to do it. "How long has she been in active labor?" Kate asked over her shoulder.

"Going on two hours now," came the reply from a farmer who reminded her of her own father: broad and sturdy and graying at the temples with years of hard work worn into the pads of his fingers.

"Not unusual," Kate said, though mostly to herself. It wasn't the first time a farmer had called her out in the night for a complicated birth, and when they did, she tended to trust their instincts.

"Things were progressing nicely and then it just stopped."

Less usual, Kate mused. "It's okay, girl," she said, running her hand along Betty's haunches. "Is this her first calf?"

"Second," he said. "She had her first about fourteen months ago."

"Any complications with that one?"

"None."

"Baby healthy?"

"Yeah."

"Okay, Momma," Kate said to Betty, filing away those tidbits of information. "What's going on, hmm?" Her fingers slid across the soft coat of hair painted with spots of white and brown. The animal wasn't quite in distress yet, but Kate knew there was a fine line between a complicated birth and a dangerous one, so she worked quickly.

"I'm gonna take a look and see how she's doing," Kate told the farmer.

He nodded, leaning against the gate that separated

them from the rest of the livestock. Kate could hear the other animals chattering away.

She shifted around the pen, gathering her supplies. Part of her already anticipated what the issue was, but it was always good to have physical confirmation. As if in agreement, Betty grunted, giving her tail a flick.

From her vet bag, Kate retrieved a pair of plastic birthing sleeves and slid them over her shirt past her elbows. Then she positioned herself behind Betty, raised the cow's tail and sank one hand into the familiar pressure. To visualize the position of the calf inside, Kate felt for familiar landmarks, closing her eyes to make a mental image of what she found.

Cal had never been able to handle this part of her work, and Kate had never been able to talk about it. He was extremely squeamish, and the late hours, manure-covered boots and a truck that constantly smelled of wet straw had started to irritate him more, the longer they were together.

But this part of the job was what most exhilarated Kate. Guiding a new life into the world…there was literally no better feeling than that. Even as a girl, growing up on her parents' ranch, these middle-of-the-night births were always her favorite.

"Are you backward in there?" Kate asked no one in particular as she continued her exam. A breeched calf would make this a potentially deadly delivery, but thankfully Kate's fingers brushed over a soft nose and the edge of one hoof. Her hand grappled around for the other. When she couldn't find it easily, a flutter of recognition exploded in her gut.

She'd seen this before.

"Carpal flexion," she told the farmer. "One of the calf's legs is bent back in the birth canal."

"Is she gonna be able to give birth on her own?"

Kate shook her head. "She can't deliver like this without some help."

"What kind of help are we talking about?"

Kate retrieved her bag once more and located a thin rope. "I'm going to have to change the position of the flexed limb. Until I do, the calf will be stuck."

"Hang on, Betty-girl," the farmer said sympathetically.

Kate looped the rope over the leg that was presented properly in order to maintain its position. She took a second rope, then reached back inside and shoved the calf down the birth canal. Freeing up some space to work, she slowly shifted the calf's other leg, bending it at the highest joint. When she finally reached the hoof, she slipped the second rope on and extended it outward.

Betty made a disgruntled noise and Kate agreed. They were both sweating, but Betty began to shift, eager to have this entire process over with.

Kate took the ends of both calving ropes and attached them to a pair of handle grips. "All right, girl," she said. "Time to push this little one out."

Kate stood to give herself more leverage.

"Do you need any help, Doc? You're not a very big thing."

"I've delivered my fair share of calves on my own," she assured him. Complications with calving were far more common than most people thought, and this would not be the last calf she had to literally pull into this world.

He nodded and let her work.

Kate timed her pulls with the contractions. Her boots slid against the ground as she gave a great, heaving tug, watching the hooves slip out, followed by the nose and then the head. The shoulders slid free next, and Kate caught her breath.

"Just those hips now," she said.

One more tug and she felt the moment the entire calf slipped free, sprawling onto the straw-packed ground.

"Well, that's certainly an introduction to the world," the farmer said.

"I'll say," Kate agreed, dropping to her knees to inspect the calf. She rubbed straw over its coat, clearing the birth from its face, making sure it was breathing. "Got a name picked out?" she asked the farmer.

"You want a namesake, Doc?"

Kate laughed. "She can join the rest of the little Kates running around farms all over the county."

"And here I thought I was being original."

Kate just smiled at him before moving out of the way. Betty perked up, shuffling to inspect the new addition to the pen. Kate waited for the mothering instincts to kick in and for Betty to start grooming the baby before she removed her gloves and collected her supplies.

The farmer reached out for her hand as she left Betty and little Kate. "I do appreciate you coming out this late."

"Just happy I could help." She shook his hand.

"Can I get you anything before you go?"

"Thanks," Kate said, "but I should be getting back home. I've got early calls tomorrow."

Kate said farewell to her two patients and made her way back to her truck. She tossed her bag into the back and climbed in, cranking the music while she drove to keep herself from falling asleep. Luckily, she was still buzzing from the thrill of the birth.

By the time she got home, all she wanted to do was fall into bed, but that was absolutely not an option in her current state, so she dragged herself to the bathroom and stripped her clothes into a neat pile to contain the muck. When steam rose from the shower, Kate climbed beneath the spray, her entire body sagging with welcome relief.

For a few minutes, she simply stood there, letting the heat seep into her muscles. She didn't want to think about what each new ache meant. She was too young to be getting old, but too old not to be mindful of every creak and crack of her joints.

Of what it would mean twenty years down the road.

She washed and scrubbed until her skin was pink. Leaving the warmth of the shower was a terrible feeling, but it had to be done. In front of the mirror, Kate wrapped herself in a soft cotton towel. With the heat of the shower still etched into her skin, the flush made her otherwise unremarkable self seem a little more interesting. Her hair sat in a tangle around her shoulders, darker than it would be until it dried to her usual blond. The color highlighted the flush across her cheekbones, which were often painted with grease or dirt or some other manner of mystery smear. Taking care of livestock always came with its share of surprises. Her green eyes glistened, and her long eyelashes curled to frame them. Kate was only ever exactly herself in this world. No makeup or products would change what the animals thought of her. Frankly, they didn't care for those sorts of things, and neither did she.

She moved to her room, sitting on the edge of her bed

in only the towel until she spied a blue dot blinking on her phone. A notification. She had half a mind to just leave it. To let it go until morning. But something stirred in her gut, and she reached for it.

It was a text from her mom. Their last communication was more than three weeks ago, and a flash of guilt filled her.

But before she could even consider why her mom would be texting her this late, the phone started to buzz in her hand.

Brows drawn together, she answered. "Hello?"

"Kate, honey—"

"What's wrong?" she croaked. There was only one reason people ever called in the middle of the night, and it was never to deliver good news.

"I'm sorry. I didn't mean to wake you."

Kate stood, already pacing the floor on the hunt for clean socks and underwear. "You didn't, I just got in from a call. What's going on?" There was a beat of silence in which Kate's entire body shivered with dread. "Mom?"

"It's your dad," she said. "I think you should come home."

Chapter Two

Heart attack.

Funny, how those two little words meant absolutely nothing one minute and everything the next.

Kate had spent most of the plane ride home contemplating the weight of those words. Trying to rationalize the why and the how, but mostly what it all meant.

What happened next?

It was all she could do to hold herself together during the flight. The unknown made her antsy, made her want to shout at the people around her out of sheer terror. How could they sit there, right next to her, eating and laughing and joking, completely oblivious to the way her world was crashing and burning?

Kate had wanted to crawl out of her skin. Wanted to do something, anything, to alleviate the weight she felt pressing down on her. But all she could do was clench her teeth and run her hands over her knees. Back and forth. *Back and forth.* Finally, the plane had landed, and she'd raced out of the terminal and to the hospital.

It was an exhausting way to exist, quiet panic. It took all her energy to keep the worry contained. She didn't know how her mother did it.

Even now, as they sat side by side, her mom ran a gentle hand over Kate's arm, sitting patiently.

Waiting.

Waiting.

Kate wanted to scream.

Instead, she looked out the window, the streaky glass dotted with the first beads of rain, and considered what she would say to her dad when she saw him.

If she saw him.

Kate shook her head, brow furrowed.

Don't think like that. Don't even put it out into the universe.

"Kate," her mother murmured. "You're shaking."

Kate took a deep breath, sinking into the hard-backed plastic chair in the small waiting room they had been directed to. A nurse worked tirelessly at a desk by the entrance of the unit. Others roamed the halls with medication cups and binders filled with charts and orders. The halls were a muted shade of beige with a railing of burgundy running along their length. She could see the dings and scratches on the railing where stretchers or wheelchairs had bumped along. She heard the ring of call bells as they lit up outside patient rooms and the shuffle of socked feet along the floor. This was the cardiac recovery unit. Her dad wasn't here yet, but it was where they would bring him.

If everything went well.

She shivered.

"Why don't you go get a coffee?" her mother said.

"I'm fine," Kate answered immediately, barely letting the suggestion pass her mother's lips.

Her mother's hand tightened on her arm, squeezing gently, pulling Kate from the panicked thought spiral she'd entered. "Why don't you go get *me* a coffee?"

Kate stilled for the first time since she'd sat down. It was less of a request and more of a task. Even when Kate was a girl, her mother used to do this. Panic, worry, anxiety—she would ease it with a task like watering the horses or stacking hay bales. This would give Kate something constructive to do and a quiet moment to understand all the complicated emotions she was feeling.

Did her mom really want a coffee? Not likely.

But did she want Kate to stop vibrating with anxious energy? Absolutely.

"Okay," Kate conceded, climbing to her feet. The ache in her limbs caught up with her as she stood and stretched. She'd sat in the truck, sat in the plane, sat in the cab on the way to the hospital, and then she'd sat in this awful chair waiting for awful news. It was a wonder she could stand straight at all. Even more so that she walked without stumbling or wincing.

Kate headed down the hall, wandering until she found a sign for the cafeteria. She followed the faded green arrows to a small food court. The entire room smelled like coffee. Dark and burnt. She doubted anyone ever complained.

If you were here long enough to need a coffee, you obviously had bigger things to worry about.

Kate waited as a man in an apron poured two cups of black coffee. He handed them to her with half a smile.

How many times a day did he do this? How often did he stare down the panic and worry and terror that accompanied most of his customers?

How did he bear it?

Kate turned away before her jaw began to tremble, stuffing milks and sugar packs and stir sticks into her pocket.

She found some change in her wallet and paid the woman at the cash register, making as little eye contact as possible, wondering if she could tell why Kate was here.

If she knew that Kate was waiting to hear whether her dad had survived not just his heart attack, but also the procedure meant to save his life.

Heart attack.

She never wanted to hear those words again.

As Kate wandered through the seating area, her pocket began to buzz. She reached for her phone, almost dropping both coffees in the process. She managed to set them down on a table at the last second before flipping her phone over, her heart in her stomach as she expected to see her mom's face light up the screen. Only it wasn't her mom. It was Sarah.

The instant panic faded, sinking back down to her toes.

Kate had almost forgotten that she'd sent off that half-coherent text at the airport, telling Sarah she was flying to Hatchet Lake. She'd been so scatter-brained in that moment, trying to get through security and to her gate, that she now realized she'd completely forgotten to say why she was traveling.

"Hi," Kate said as she answered the call.

"Okay, so I googled Hatchet Lake, and do you know

what shows up? Nothing. Not a damn thing except one gas station and a bunch of corn and maybe a weird bed-and-breakfast. It might just be my night shift stupor, but I'm pretty sure this is the kind of place where people go to get murdered." Sarah yawned into the phone. "What the hell are you doing out there?"

Part of Kate wanted to laugh as Sarah launched into her tangent without even a hello, though she supposed that was what best friends did best. Her flickering smile faded. "I had to come home."

"Like *home* home?"

"Yeah," Kate sighed. Sarah knew her parents lived on a ranch in a tiny town in Southern Michigan, she just hadn't known which tiny town. "My dad's in the hospital."

"Oh, Kate," Sarah breathed, sobering on the other end of the line. Her tone shifted slightly. "What happened?" she asked, forever the assessing nurse.

"Heart attack. It just came on suddenly in his sleep. Mom got him to the hospital, but it was a long drive, and they're not sure how much damage was done."

"Did they take him to the cath lab?"

"Yeah."

"Good. That's good."

"Hmm," Kate agreed quietly. She supposed so. The fact that he made it to the cath lab was the best they could hope for in this situation.

"It is," Sarah assured her. "They'll take a look at his arteries, at the chambers of his heart. See where the damage is and figure out how to fix it. They'll probably throw a stent in, and he'll be home in a few days, good as new, ordering the horses around or whatever happens on a ranch. Don't worry."

Kate laughed then, the pitch all wrong. It was fear, mostly, but she'd take Sarah's platitudes right now, even if she ended up being wrong. Sarah had been by her side through a lot, and if there was anyone in the world Kate would believe right now, it was her.

They'd spent exactly one undergraduate class in microbiology together when they were both studying at Michigan State University, and that was enough to seal the friendship. Even though life had taken them in completely different directions, Sarah into nursing and Kate to veterinary college, the friendship had persisted. And despite the fact that Sarah had spent the past several years working as a travel nurse, taking her from one side of the country to the other, Kate had never wondered when that next phone call would come. It just always did.

"Are you doing okay?" Sarah asked. "Eating, sleeping, drinking enough water?"

"I'm running on about twenty-four hours of no sleep. And I'm about to be heavily caffeinated, so…you know."

"You should have been a nurse, you'd fit right in," Sarah remarked. Then, on a more serious note, she said, "Keep me posted on how it goes and call me if you need anything. I mean it. *Anything.*"

The way Sarah said *anything*, Kate imagined that the word was underlined, with five exclamation points following it. "I will."

"Try not to worry, though I know you will. I'll talk to you later?"

"Yep," Kate said. "Later."

"Okay, bye."

Kate hung up the phone and stuffed it back in her pocket. She grabbed the two coffees again, taking a sip of hers. She hated it black, but she didn't have the patience for anything else. Sarah's reassurance had sounded great on the phone, but now that the call had ended, Kate was less sure and the same worries started to creep back in. She made a beeline for the cardiac floor, hardly stopping to move out of the way of a group of residents on their way to a call.

When she found her mom again, nothing had changed, though Kate felt like she'd been gone long enough for that to be an affront. Or maybe a gift, she wasn't sure. Her mom sat there, perusing a magazine like she was waiting for an oil change at the mechanic's and not for her husband to be rolled out of a procedure meant to save his life.

Kate sank down in her own chair, handing her mom the second coffee. She dug the milk and sugar and stir sticks from her pocket.

"Feel better?" her mom asked.

Not really, Kate wanted to say, but she also didn't feel like being sent on another errand around the hospital, so she nodded vaguely. "Sarah called."

"How is she?"

"Good." Kate frowned. "Have they… Has the nurse said anything?"

"No news yet."

Kate couldn't contain it anymore. "How are you so composed?"

"They say no news is good news."

"Mom," Kate complained.

Her mom sighed, laying aside the magazine. "There was nothing I could do, Katie. If it's his time, then it's his time. But I know it's not. Your father is stubborn, and he's not ready to go anywhere yet."

Kate traced her finger around the rim of her coffee cup.

"Though that had to be the most terrifying drive of my life," her mom said after a moment. "It was only after we were halfway to the hospital that I realized I should have called an ambulance instead of driving. And then I was furious with myself."

"Waiting for an ambulance to get to the ranch would have taken longer," Kate said. "You did the right thing."

Her mom nodded. "And I'll be sure to tell your father that when he's moved up to his room. Somehow that man still managed to critique my driving while having a heart attack in the passenger seat."

Kate snorted into her coffee, the image of it catching her off guard. If that wasn't exactly like her parents, to be arguing over something as inane as driving in the midst of a medical emergency.

It was so ridiculous that Kate started to laugh, and then she couldn't stop. She laughed until her eyes watered and she had to wipe the tears away on her sleeve.

Her mom leaned over, wrapping her arm around Kate's shoulders, pressing a kiss to her temple. "I'm glad you're here. I wish it wasn't *here*, but I've missed you. We've both missed you. It's nice to have you home."

Home, Kate thought, wondering what that meant.

After everything with Cal fell apart, Kate had relocated to Northern Michigan and found a job covering shifts for an established large animal veterinary practice. Home was technically the furnished one-bedroom apartment she'd rented from her boss.

So, what happened now? Did she go back to the ranch? Take an extended leave of absence from her job? Her boss had been great about her last-minute family emergency and had even promised not to charge her rent until she returned, though Kate knew a longer conversation was needed. One way or another, Kate suspected she was probably going to be here for more than a few days.

"Mrs. Cardiff," a voice called suddenly. Both Kate and her mom were up and out of their chairs in an instant. A nurse stood there, clad in blue scrubs, a clipboard in hand. "Your husband is on his way up to the floor. We can show you to his room now if you'd like."

Before either of them could say anything, the elevator door opened and a stretcher was wheeled out by a porter. Kate recognized the man in the bed instantly. He wore a speckled gown and was covered in a heap of blankets, but Kate would know that nose anywhere. Crooked from the time a horse kicked him as a boy—if you believed the story.

Somehow he seemed smaller now. More feeble.

Kate hurried to his bedside. "Dad?"

His face melted into a dopey smile. "Hi, baby."

"How are you feeling?"

He gently tapped his chest. "Good as new. Got some brand-new parts in me. Your mother will have a hard time getting rid of me now."

"We'll see," her mom said, though there were tears in her eyes as she smiled down at him from the other side of the bed.

"That's not funny," Kate said. "Don't even joke."

He grinned, his eyes barely open now. "I'm glad you're home."

And that was the last thing he said before drifting off to sleep.

Chapter Three

Home was a two-story whitewashed farmhouse on a sprawling acreage that Kate had only visited once in the last five years. Between her work schedule and the relationship with Cal imploding, she'd left it too long between visits. Too long between phone calls and texts.

But that was yesterday's problem.

Today she was back because there were things that needed to be done, and her mom couldn't possibly handle it all herself. Not while her dad was laid up in the hospital. As it was, her mom would spend half her day driving back and forth from the city.

Sarah had joked that Hatchet Lake was the equivalent of an abandoned wasteland when she'd googled the town, and although that wasn't exactly true—the town had been built up since Kate had snuck away as a teenager—it certainly wasn't a bustling metropolis. The same people from the same old families, who owned and ran the same shops and businesses, still lived here. Kate knew she'd find Diane Hostetler running Sunnyside Diner on Main Street and Old Joe, who had been old when she was a teenager, serving at the local pub. She'd grown up in the kind of small town that never seemed to change. And though the place always had an influx of tourists in the summer, seeking the solace of the prime campgrounds around the lake, when they were done and gone, everything was just the same as it always was.

Kate wasn't sure now if that was eerie or comforting.

"I'll put a pot of coffee on," her mom said as she climbed out of the dusty pickup truck. "And start on some breakfast."

Kate followed slowly, inhaling so deep her lungs felt like bursting. Honeysuckle and hay filled the air, while wild green fields disappeared into thick deciduous forest as far as the eye could see. It was the kind of forest that turned the color of fire in the fall and stood naked in the winter.

Kate had always loved the forest.

Loved the adventure that began the minute she set foot beyond the trees.

Trails used to crisscross between the oaks and maples, and Kate used to ride them for hours as a girl.

She wasn't sure if they'd been maintained in her absence.

As she glanced around, she started to notice other things that hadn't quite been kept up.

The porch railings were peeling, flaky blue paint scattered among the grass. There was a tear in the screen door at the front of the house and new rust spots on the truck they had just climbed out of. Even the grounds weren't exactly the way her dad used to keep them. She remembered pristine lines that used to be cut into the fields with the mower when the grass grew too tall and reinforced fence posts that would stand proudly, running the length of the property. The fields now grew with wild abandon, and the fence posts leaned like old men pained by arthritis. Kate supposed some of those things were to be expected. Only in her memory would everything look shiny and new.

A faint whinny carried across the yard, and Kate looked out toward the stables. The large ochre structure rose up against the horizon, towering and majestic. A lonely mountain in the middle of the property.

Coffee sounded wonderful right now. As did a shower and eight hours of uninterrupted sleep. The nurses had finally convinced Kate and her mom to return home for some rest now that they'd laid eyes on her father. The hospital had said they would call if there were any changes. But coffee and rest and food would have to wait—at least until the horses were tended to. They would need to be turned out for the day, and the stalls would need mucking.

"I'll be there in a minute," Kate called after her mom, who had trudged up the porch steps and was fumbling with the key at the front door.

Kate didn't hear what her mom said in reply. She was already half jogging to the stables, wondering how many horses were housed on the property right now. There used to be a time when this place was overrun with horses, some of them belonging to her parents but mostly to the boarders who would come up on the week-ends for lessons or to visit their champion show horses that needed good care in between their trophy wins.

It wasn't the same now. Kate knew that.

It couldn't possibly be.

But she was still taken aback when she slid open a large, weathered door to find the stables eerily quiet.

For a moment, her breathing was the loudest thing in the building. Kate squinted, adjusting to the dim lighting. And then, suddenly, there was a snort and a dark muzzle appeared over the door of a stall about halfway down the main aisle.

Kate grinned, though the smile faded as she walked by empty stall after empty stall. That was a sight she wasn't used to, and something uneasy settled in her bones.

When she reached the stall where the horse waited, she ran her hand along a soft muzzle. "Hello, Shade," she said to the mare, lowering her head to feel that smooth coat along her cheek. Shade had been a baby born on the property to Shadow, the first horse Kate had ever ridden. When the baby was born, she'd had similar coloring to Shadow, but Kate had always maintained it was just a shade different, and somehow the name had stuck. Kate and Shade had grown up together, and though she could be a skittish and timid horse, in the right hands, with the right amount of trust, Shade would fly beneath you.

Kate could almost feel the ground tremble and the wind wrap around her. She was suddenly itching to be on a horse again.

Kate unlocked the gate and stepped into the stall to greet her old friend, scratching the mare along the neck in a hearty hello.

Shade was one of the reasons Kate had wanted to

become a vet. Working with this animal and earning her trust had created a feeling of accomplishment that Kate had yet to replicate in any other capacity.

"You've grown," she said to Shade.

As if she understood, the horse neighed and jerked her head. Kate wondered if Shade could see all the ways in which she had also grown. If she seemed different to the horse? Or if she simply looked older? They'd both changed and yet, for a second, it felt as if nothing had.

Then midnight phone calls and heart attacks surfaced in the back of her mind, and Kate remembered that everything had changed. She didn't know what her dad's ill health meant for the ranch. She didn't even know what to expect today, never mind next week or a month from now.

Kate leaned into Shade, feeling the velvet of the fine hairs against her skin. She waited until her heartbeat slowed, letting the panic of the moment subside. Horses were good for that. Good for anxiety and worry. They could hear a human's heartbeat from four feet away, and in the wild they would sync their heartbeats with the rest of the herd. Kate liked to think that they did that with people, too.

"What are you doing to my horses?"

"*Your* horses?" Kate said, whirling around so quickly at the unfamiliar voice that she stumbled against the gate. Shade whinnied, shifting from side to side at the sudden intrusion. Kate felt a hand wrap around her upper arm, pulling her from the stall before Shade could accidentally crush her against the gate. Spooked horses were unpredictable, and if Shade attempted to bolt or charge, there was only so much space inside the stall for the two of them.

Kate and the stranger both reached for the gate, hands fighting over the latch as they secured Shade in the stall.

"What are you doing?" Kate demanded, staring up into a pair of steel gray eyes.

"She spooks easily," the stranger said, and Kate caught herself looking at the shape of his lips before she could break from the spell. A tone of annoyance filled her voice.

"I know. She's *mine*."

"Yours?" he said, his face shifting. He had a nice face, Kate found herself thinking before she could stop it. Dark hair, as black as a starless night and just long enough to fall across those gray eyes, covered his head. He wore the shadow of scruff along his cheeks and chin, and with his teeth clenched, she could see a strong jawline and prominent brows.

They furrowed instantly, looking at her like she was a bold-faced-liar.

Kate disliked his assumption, and the fire of frustration flamed beneath her cheeks.

Then, he surprised her by saying, "Little Katie?"

Her mouth fell open. "What?"

"You must be Katie." A grin replaced the hard lines on his face. "Your parents talk about you all the time. The way they do, I always envisioned someone who was eternally twelve years old."

"It's just Kate now," she said firmly, because the last thing she was about to do was let this man call her Katie like he was some old friend. She hardly liked it when her parents called her that. "And who are you?"

"Nathan Prescott." He held his hand out to her. "Hired ranch hand."

"Right. Well," she said, shaking his hand for a brief

second before she pulled away. Ignoring his hand would have been rude, but considering he'd just dragged her out of Shade's stall like a sack of cornmeal, he was lucky she didn't curl her fist and punch him instead. "You can just carry on with whatever you were hired to do. I'm good here."

"Good?" he scoffed. "You were about to get yourself taken out by your own horse."

"I was not."

"I'll kindly disagree. I'm pretty sure I pulled you out of the stall before the horse could trample you."

"Trample me?"

"You know, this is why we don't let the riders around the horses without a helmet. Not that we've been getting many riders lately." He veered off topic, glancing at the wall of riding gear before he looked back at her. "Either way, you should definitely be thanking me."

"Thanking you?"

"For saving your life."

"For unnecessarily manhandling me out of the stall and probably scaring Shade even more? Do you even know anything about properly handling horses?"

"I…have the basics down." His tone was thoroughly unconvincing.

Kate's face fell. "You're completely inexperienced."

"What I lack in experience, I make up for in common sense. And do you think I could have looked your parents in the face if I let their only daughter get crushed by her own horse?" Nathan raised both his eyebrows. "How is your dad, by the way? Your mom texted me earlier saying he's out of the cath lab."

"He's fine," she said, trying to keep up with his non

sequitur. "And I did not need your help. So I will *not* be thanking you."

He smiled at that, and it irked her more.

"If anything I should be blaming you," Kate continued, not quite ready to let this die. All she had wanted to do was visit peacefully with Shade and here she was instead, arguing with a stranger whom she was mildly attracted to—not even mildly, there was just barely a hint of attraction there—and whom she simultaneously wanted to punch in the mouth for being so obtusely annoying and entitled. How could he possibly think that he knew more than she did about the horses she was raised with?

Then he laughed. Laughed! "You're blaming me? For what?"

"Because *you* startled us both. This is your fault."

"Because I thought you were some entitled tourist who just waltzed into the stables to browse. No one gave me the heads-up that you were going to be here. I'm just doing my job."

Kate scoffed. "When does that ever happen?"

"You've been gone for a while, from what I've been told. Things are a bit different around here. We're always running some teenager or another off the property." He wrinkled his nose. "They like the aesthetic for their Instagrams."

Kate frowned at that entire sentence but chose not to say anything. Nathan's comment, the one about her being gone, prickled unpleasantly inside her. The fact that her parents had clearly been talking about her to him annoyed her more than anything. She looked him up and down, from his worn jeans to the black shirt already dusted with grain from the horse feed. It was a mistake, she realized, looking at him like that, because he noticed and quirked a brow in her direction, curious and maybe even a little amused.

The flames inside her fanned out, and she crossed her arms. Perhaps it was just the exhaustion or the uncertainty of her dad's condition that was making her lash out, but it equally might just be Nathan. She did *not* like him. Whatever instant spark of attraction she felt fizzled out completely, and Kate chalked him up to a pretty face and an empty head with a side of arrogance. "Well, I think I know enough about my own horses. So, thanks for the unsolicited advice, but I'll be just fine."

"Just keeping everyone safe," he said, "like I was hired to do."

"I don't think that's what you were hired to do." She took a pitchfork from the hook on the wall and shoved it at him. "Hired hands normally need one of these."

With that, Kate turned and walked away, marching straight out of the stables and back toward the house, fists clenched.

First, he had the audacity to insult her capabilities with the horses. Animals were the one thing she was good at. The one thing she actually understood. And then, just to add a little insult to injury, he practically called her a child. A twelve-year-old child that apparently needed a helmet to enter the stables.

Kate stormed into the house, throwing the screen door open. It rattled and slammed behind her. Her mom looked up from the newspaper.

"Do you know there's a man in the stables?"

"What?"

"There's a man in the stables!" Kate said again. It felt like she was spitting fire.

Her mother slid a mug of coffee across the counter, sharing absolutely none of Kate's concern. "Nate?"

"Nate," she said, grinding her teeth together. The fact that they already called him Nate irritated her. She took a sip of the coffee, and the disdain she felt tasted like dish soap on her tongue.

Something in her face startled a laugh from her mother. "What, you thought your father was single-handedly running the ranch at almost sixty?"

"Well, no," Kate said, and the thought was as ridiculous as it sounded. She had just finished observing how things had changed since she'd last been home, so she certainly didn't expect that her parents were doing it alone. They'd had ranch hands in the past, hired for short contracts during their busy seasons.

But Nathan Prescott?

"I take it you don't like him." Her mom frowned and tilted her head. Something that silently said, *Already, Kate?*

"He knows nothing about horses!" she argued, defending her position.

"He's a hard worker. And he's learning."

"Barely," she muttered. How could anyone possibly teach that man anything?

Her mom sighed. "You always were better with animals than people."

"Gee, thanks."

"That's not an insult, Katie. Just maybe give Nate some more time. Don't be so quick to judge him."

"It was deserved. Trust me." At the look on her mom's face, Kate relented. "Fine, for your sake, I will tolerate him. Maybe."

Her mom threw her hands up in mock relief. "That's

all I ask. Besides, you two will probably be seeing a lot of each other."

"Why?"

"He's staying on the property."

Kate gaped at her mother. "You gave him the guest house?"

"I can't do it," Kate said, lying on the twin mattress and quilted comforter of her childhood bedroom. She stared up at an inaccurate array of hand-glued glow-in-the-dark stars that were scattered across the ceiling. Her phone was wedged between her ear and a pillow that smelled like her mom had hidden an entire jar of potpourri inside it.

Sarah was on the other end of the call, prepping for another night shift.

Even after a four-hour nap, Kate still felt like she'd just crawled out of a swamp. A shower would probably help that, but the idea of moving was entirely unappealing.

"I'm really failing to see the problem here," Sarah said.

"I told you. His name is Nathan Prescott and we hate him."

"The ridiculously attractive, presumably unattached man in your barn?"

"It's a stable. And stop saying it like that," Kate said between gritted teeth. Of course Sarah would cling to that part of the story—how attractive he was. "You're supposed to hate him with me by default. That's your one and only job."

"Rancher Hotstuff? I think I'd rather keep him for my fantasies."

"Oh my god."

"And you should, too. Or better yet, go make that fantasy a reality. It's basically been delivered to you on a silver platter at your doorstep."

"Oh, sure, when you say it like that, it all makes so much sense," Kate said sarcastically. "Why didn't I think to ask out the man who just insulted me? Missed opportunity."

"I could hear that eye roll," Sarah said. "And okay, maybe you two got off on the wrong foot, but admit it, Kate. You're still hung up on Cal—"

"Excuse me, I am definitely not still hung up on him! I do not even like the guy anymore. As far as I'm concerned, that part of my life no longer exists."

"You might not want to be with him," Sarah explained, "but you're still angry at him. And that's just as bad as pining after him. You have to let it all go. Cal was a bump in the road. We're over it now, time to move on. A hot rancher seems like the perfect place to start."

"Is that what *we* think?"

"That's what *you* should be thinking. What *I* think is that you're just afraid of trying again, and being mad at Cal gives you an excuse not to."

Kate's entire face scrunched into a grumpy wrinkle. "I don't think I like talking to you anymore."

Sarah laughed. "You love it because I'm cheaper than therapy."

"Put Parker on the phone. At least he loves me." Parker was Sarah's two-year-old son. He was the product of a one-night stand and even though Dad was not at all involved, Sarah had been absolutely enthralled with the boy from the moment he was conceived. And

Kate was proud to call herself the favorite of all his surrogate aunties.

"He's a toddler. He loves everyone."

"Well, now I'm feeling great about myself."

"Look, take your mom's advice," Sarah continued. "I can tell you from experience that moms are usually right."

"You've only been a mom for two years."

"And I've been right about everything so far. Parker has no complaints. Five-star review every time."

Kate made a vague humming noise in the back of her throat, dragging herself from the nap nest toward the window where she fiddled with the blinds, squinting at the sun that peeked in through the slats.

From there she could see clear across the property to the fenced pasture that the horses now roamed. There were only six of them out there, three belonging to the family. Shade was there, her coat like charcoal against the green of the pasture; Tully, a rich brown mare; and Samson, a younger pinto with white speckled patches that scattered down his back. The other three were unfamiliar, most likely belonging to boarders.

Something in her chest sank, and Kate couldn't quite place it. She spotted Nathan seated on the wooden fence that surrounded the pasture, arms held up to his face as he cradled something between his hands.

Kate focused. She thought it might be a camera.

"What are you doing?" Sarah asked. Kate could hear her clattering around the kitchen, most likely preparing food for the world's pickiest toddler.

"Spying."

"On Rancher Hotstuff?"

Nathan sat there, raising and lowering the camera.

"You're going to have to stop calling him that."

"Hey, you're the one watching him through the window." A pause. "It's just through the window, right? You haven't got the binoculars out yet?"

"Hilarious."

"I'm just saying."

"I can't believe he's staying here," Kate grumbled, letting her eyes drift farther across the property to the small guest house. It was a muted shade of blue, like the sky just before a twilight sunset, with two wicker chairs on the porch and one of her mom's homemade wreaths hanging on the front door.

When Kate was younger, they'd let boarders stay the night so they had easy access to their horses. When she was a teenager, she would hang out there, sometimes on her own, sometimes with friends. As an adult, the few times she'd been back to visit the ranch, she'd always stayed there. The house was completely self-sufficient, and it let her be close to her parents without actually having to live on top of them again.

Even now, listening to her mother putter around the kitchen downstairs made Kate feel like a preteen with a curfew.

She frowned, turning away from the window as she remembered the look on Nathan's face when he had dragged her out of Shade's stall like a child. Frustration bloomed in her chest once more, and she crossed the room toward her suitcase, kneeling to angrily rifle through her clothes.

"It could be worse," Sarah reasoned.

"How could it be worse? My dad's still in the hospital and the world's most annoying hired hand is literally living next door."

"You could have all of that and a two-year-old that likes to wake you up at three in the morning by shoving his sticky fingers in your ear."

Kate snorted, finding a pair of sweats and tucking them under her arm on her way to the bathroom. "You're loving that big-boy bed, aren't you?"

"I miss the crib every day."

"Well," Kate said, standing in front of the mirror in the bathroom. "Any time you want to trade, let me know."

"I could exchange Parker for Rancher Hotstuff for a weekend," Sarah mused. "Take him off your hands."

"This is why we're friends," Kate agreed.

"Because I let you avoid situations that will inevitably help you grow, instead letting you wallow in a heartbreak-shaped fantasy world?"

"No," Kate complained loudly. "And though I feel like that was supposed to be a jab at my inability to let things go, I'm going to choose to ignore it. Tell Parker I miss him."

"I always do."

"Have fun at work."

"Have fun with Rancher—"

"Don't say it."

"—Hotstuff." Sarah cackled and hung up.

Kate shook her head, stripping out of her clothes while she waited for the water in the shower to heat up to a reasonable temperature. When it did, she climbed underneath, letting everything fade until it was just the light pressure of the water tapping against her skin. She waited for the heat to seep into every part of her and for the steam to drown out all thoughts of her dad and the ranch and Nathan.

She couldn't keep thinking about what it all meant.
What it meant that she'd finally come home.

And what it meant to admit that she really had missed this place.

Because if that was true, why did she want to run so badly?

Chapter Four

She woke with the dawn the next morning, watching a yellow sunrise spill across the horizon and turn the fields to dewy gold. Kate marveled at just how quickly she'd fallen back into the routine of the ranch.

Maybe it was just jet lag and a broken sleep schedule.

Or maybe it was a childhood of dawn wake-up calls, of racing out to the stables to greet the horses in the morning. These things were ingrained so deeply in her that she couldn't shake the call to rise and fall with the sun, no matter how long she'd been away.

When she'd flown home to her dad's bedside, she'd expected to be thrown into the chores, helping to keep the ranch afloat while her dad recovered. She'd not expected a brand-new ranch hand to be living in *her* guest house. Nor had she expected Nathan, a man who could hardly *call* himself a ranch hand. But the fact remained that he was here, in her space, doing the things she thought she would be doing. Truthfully, she felt oddly usurped.

Like she'd been replaced without anyone telling her.

And that was the worst way to be supplanted.

Of course, she could go out and help him. Kate knew well enough that more hands were always welcome in the stables.

But after yesterday, that was the last thing she felt like doing. Considering she had just promised to give Nathan a chance, her mother would be terribly disappointed.

Frankly, Kate wasn't sure which was worse: clenching her teeth as she worked side by side with Nathan or enduring the pointed stare of her mom over cornflakes. Her stomach grumbled in answer, and Kate took that as a sign to chance breakfast and reevaluate her options.

She slipped on a pair of jeans and a worn gray sweater before heading downstairs. She expected to find her mom in the kitchen, puttering around with breakfast at this hour, but the lights were off, the room empty. Maybe her mom was finally catching up on all the sleep she'd missed.

Kate padded around quietly, searching out a mug and turning on the coffee maker, finding everything exactly where it always was. Through the kitchen window, she watched Nathan trudge across the field. He hopped the wooden fence of the paddock easily, and the fact that he didn't just use the gate amused her for some reason.

When black coffee started to *drip*, *drip*, *drip* into the bottom of her mug she turned away, popping a couple slices of bread into the toaster. She busied herself with butter and jam and creamer, wondering why she had been relegated to the status of useless. Her dad was being taken care of by some amazing nurses, leaving Kate little to do in that department. The horses didn't need her to muck their stalls because they had Nathan. And her mother was as independent as she'd always been.

She plopped down on a stool at the island, pondering this and her mother's homemade raspberry jam as she sipped her coffee.

It wasn't as if she *was* actually useless. She had a very specific skill set.

The horses may not need her to feed them or turn them out to the pasture or to muck out their stalls, but what did Nathan know about yearly vaccinations or blood work or hoof testing? Nothing. That's what.

This new line of thinking elevated her mood considerably as she finished her breakfast. Her dad had always kept records of the vet exams in his office. She could review this year's exams and see how Shade and the others were doing. See if there were any preventative measures that should be put in place for their health now that some of the horses were getting much older. At the very least, she should be familiar with their care if she was going to stick around for a bit.

Kate deposited her dishes in the sink to be dealt with later and wandered through to the back of the house, where two mahogany-and-glass doors contained over thirty years' worth of information pertaining to the ranch. There were trophies and medals adorning the shelves from Kate's various riding competitions over the years.

On the walls, photos of favorite clients, favorite horses, favorite summers spent out in the fields stared back at her.

A giddy rush of nostalgia filled Kate's chest, her memories tinted with the rose colors of childhood. She'd had a great childhood here. So great that sometimes she still wondered what made her think she'd be better off leaving.

She ran her fingers over the leather of her father's chair. It was positioned behind a massive desk, kept neat and dusted, telling Kate her mother had been in here recently to straighten up. A picture of Kate in her graduation cap and gown sat on the corner of the desk, along with a photo from her parents' wedding day.

There was also a calendar with delivery dates etched into the squares, receipts for payroll and a sleeping laptop. Kate opened one of the drawers, retrieved a small silver key and unlocked the large filing cabinet set against the wall of the office.

It rolled open to reveal a dozen files, and Kate flipped through them, looking for something familiar. She'd spent many summers in here filing paperwork for her dad, so it didn't take her long to find the folder dedicated to the veterinary exams.

She slumped down in the chair, letting the file fall open on the desk, scanning the dates. There were records for every year but the current one. According to the paperwork, the horses would have been due for their annual check-ups at least three months ago.

Kate scanned the loose documents on top of the desk, wondering if the paperwork was sitting there, waiting to be filed.

"Katie?"

Her mom's voice lingered in the hall, her footsteps soft.

"In here," Kate called back.

Her mom appeared a moment later, glancing around the office. "What are you doing in here?"

"I was just searching for the vet records. Thought I might as well take a look and see how the horses are doing." She trailed off for a second, brows furrowed as she flipped through the stack of papers in her hand once more. "I can't find the records for this year."

Her mom gently took the papers from her hands, tucking them back into the file they'd come out of. "They're not done yet."

"What do you mean they're not done yet?"

Her mom smiled, dismissing Kate's question. "We just haven't gotten around to it yet. We will. Don't worry."

Kate found that odd. She'd never known them to be late with this kind of thing. "It's been more than a year, Mom."

"It'll get done, Kate."

"I know, I just…" She shook her head, not quite sure what she meant to say. "I brought my supplies with me. Just in case. I can do the exams."

"You don't have to do that," her mom began to say.

"But I want to. It'll keep me busy. Give me something else to think about other than Dad. Besides, what's the point of having a vet for a daughter if you don't get to take advantage of it every once in a while?" Kate squeezed her mom's hand as she passed.

"I didn't want to put you to work."

Kate shrugged. "Guess that's the good thing about loving your job. Never really feels like work."

She headed back up to her room to grab her bag. The black one with her supplies. It was only filled with a portion of what she normally carried with her, but it was enough for a basic exam. If the horses needed something more in-depth, she could drive out to the valley for more.

Kate made a pit stop in the kitchen, pocketing a couple apples. Then she pulled on a pair of work boots that probably belonged to her dad and mucked out to the stables once more.

It was still early, but the heat of the day was starting to set in, and Kate regretted the sweater she'd pulled on that morning. The stables were empty when she arrived, the horses already fed and watered and roaming the pasture.

Kate set up in Shade's stall before marching out to the fence line. She held her hand up to her face and called for Shade. It took a few moments but the horse responded, and Kate was glad she didn't have to march out across the pasture to retrieve her.

"Hey, girl," Kate said as Shade trotted over, throwing her head up and down in greeting. Kate ran a comforting hand over Shade's back before leading her into the stables. Shade nudged at her playfully and Kate laughed, wrapping her hand around the horse's head to kiss her on the muzzle.

Once inside, she settled Shade in her pen and began the physical exam by retrieving her stethoscope to listen to the horse's lungs. An airy whooshing sound filled her ears, and Kate closed her eyes, honing in on the sounds, listening for any kind of unexpected deviation to what she expected. There was nothing of note, so she moved on, stilling the stethoscope over Shade's abdomen to listen to the horse's gut sounds. After everything gurgled the way it should, Kate took some digital pulses, then checked the horse's gums and eyes and all the other little things that were needed to determine a general body condition score.

She gave the hooves a good once-over, then made a mental note to inquire with her mother when the farrier was supposed to be on-site next. Though Shade's hooves didn't look terrible, they were definitely close to needing a trim.

"Good girl," Kate said, enticing Shade with one of the apples she'd snuck from the kitchen. "Just some blood work and we'll call it a day."

Shade made an agreeable noise as Kate pulled the supplies from her bag, prepping gloves and a syringe and blood collection tubes.

A shadow passed behind her, and she glanced over her shoulder to see Nathan leading Tully back to her stall. He settled the horse in there, then turned around, flashing Kate what might be a sheepish smile.

"Thought I'd save you having to chase Tully around the pasture."

Kate inclined her head but didn't say anything, just took her supplies, pulled on her gloves and gently palpated for the jugular vein in Shade's neck before taking her blood samples. She rocked the tube gently when she was done, dispersing the anticoagulant. There was a fridge in the feed shed that she could use to keep the samples cool until she could get them in the mail to be shipped to the lab for analysis.

When she turned around, Nathan was still there, leaning over the gate, head resting on his arms as he watched her.

"Can I help you?" she said pointedly.

"A livestock vet, huh?"

She nodded, pushing against the gate. It met a little

resistance from him, but not enough to stop her. Shade followed her out, and Kate watched as the horse walked the same worn path out of the stables and into the pasture.

"When your parents told me you were a vet, I assumed they meant dogs and cats. They never mentioned it was, like, horses and cows."

"Because they tell you everything about me?" she said with just a bit of edge as she collected her things, carrying them over to Tully's stall. Nathan walked ahead and held the gate open for her.

"Okay," he relented. "I get it. I was a bit of an ass."

"A bit?"

"I overstepped the other day." He touched his hand to his chest. "Terrible first impression."

"That's putting it mildly." Kate strung her stethoscope around her neck, giving Tully a firm rub behind the ear as Nathan tilted his head to regard her.

"You're one of those people, aren't you?"

Kate narrowed her eyes. "One of what people?"

"The ones who make it agonizingly difficult to apologize."

"Oh, is that what you were doing?"

Nathan opened his mouth to respond, but before he could say anything, Kate stuffed her stethoscope in her ears and placed the bell over Tully's chest, waiting for her lungs to expand and deflate.

She listened to the lung fields for a while—*inhale, exhale, inhale, exhale*—getting lost in the rhythm and secretly hoping Nathan would get bored and leave. Unfortunately, he was still standing there when she moved to listen to Tully's gut and when she put her stethoscope back in her bag before checking Tully's gum line.

"Don't you have work to do?" she asked. "You know, the whole reason my parents hired you?"

"Of all the things your parents failed to mention about you, this one takes the cake."

"What," she said, taking the bait.

"How bossy you are."

Kate clenched her teeth, wanting to shout, *Excuse me?* Instead, she bit the inside of her cheek. She wouldn't give him the satisfaction. "You know, for the life of me, I can't figure out what my parents saw in you."

Nathan listed off qualities on his fingers. "My charm, devilish good looks, work ethic. The fact that I can muck out a stall in ten minutes flat."

Kate stood before him, hands on her hips, judging him in a way that would make her mother shake her head disapprovingly.

"Okay, fifteen minutes," Nathan relented. "But I'm getting faster."

"Sure you are."

"Look, I might not know everything about horses, but I know more than I did when I started, so that has to count for something." He flashed her a toothy grin.

"My mother likes you," Kate said suspiciously, more to herself than to him because she just couldn't figure that one out. What was it about him that had her mother so enthralled?

He laughed in response. "You don't sound pleased about that. I do make quite the impression on parents. It's one of my better talents."

Kate stopped what she was doing. "And how many parents have you had to meet?"

Nathan lowered his voice to a whisper. "Are you asking how many girlfriends I've had, or how many of those relationships were serious enough to warrant bringing me home?"

"Neither," Kate said at once because she really didn't care, and she told him as much. "I take it back. I don't want to know."

"Well," he said, leaning over the stall and completely ignoring what she said. "For the record, Anne and Dale are definitely on the top of my favorite-parents-of-all-time list. The daughter, though, she's going to take some getting used to."

By the time she spun around to glare at him, Nathan was already strutting out of the stables, *whistling to himself*, leaving Kate to her exam, more frustrated with him than ever.

Chapter Five

If there was one thing Kate didn't expect to find the next morning, it was Nathan sitting at the island counter, nursing a fresh cup of coffee and one of her mother's homemade biscuits dolloped with butter and jam. Yet, as she reached the bottom of the stairs, that was exactly where she found him.

Eating breakfast.

In her parents' kitchen.

Like it was normal or something.

She crossed her arms, glad she'd decided to put on a bra before coming downstairs this morning instead of dragging herself to breakfast in her pajamas like she'd originally planned. If this was to be a regular occurrence in the Cardiff house, Kate was definitely going to have a chat with her mother.

"Oh, good, you're up," her mom said, spinning around

with a muffin tin in one hand, wearing an oven mitt over the other.

"I didn't know there was something to be up for," Kate said, awkwardly accepting the mug that Nathan pushed in her direction. She took the stool at the end of the island, making sure to leave an empty one between them. "Am I late?"

"No," her mom said, "just trying to sort some things out. I asked Nate to come by this morning. Figured it would be easier this way."

"And I never turn down a hot breakfast," Nathan said, grinning at her mom in a way that made her mom positively beam. Kate had the sudden urge to push him off his stool. She'd probably give it her best shot if it wouldn't reduce her to exactly five years old in her mother's eyes.

"What things are we sorting out?" Kate wondered, sipping her coffee. She kept her eyes firmly on her mom, though she could feel Nathan's gaze traveling across her body. Warmth burned through her.

"We need to go pick up the feed for the horses."

Kate tilted her head with a frown. "Don't they usually deliver that?"

Her mom busied herself at the sink. "We've only got a few horses here right now. Doesn't make sense to pay extra for delivery."

"On that note," Nathan said, "I'll go get the truck ready."

"Right." Kate watched him go, her brows pinched. Why did it sound like her mother was about to ship her off with the ranch hand?

Her mom turned around, leaning against the sink while drying her hands on a towel. "I'm going to run up to the hospital this morning and visit your father. Hopefully I'll make it before the doctor rounds."

There it was. Kate made a face, anticipating the terrible request that was about to come her way. "I should go with you," she tried, knowing it was already hopeless.

"It'll be a short visit," her mom insisted. "Today I could really use your help here. Your father usually goes with Nate to help supervise. Make sure it's the right feed and all that. Help load the truck if Steele's is short on employees."

"Nathan's a big, strong guy. I'm sure he can handle it."

"I'm sure he could, too. But he's also picked up all your father's chores since the heart attack without so much as one complaint." Her mom gave her a look. "Please."

How could Kate possibly say no to that? "All right. Fine. I will supervise. Give dad a hug for me. Tell him I'll come visit later."

"Thank you."

Kate gave her a thin-lipped smile, somehow knowing she got the raw end of the deal. But she *had* flown home to help out her parents. If this was what her parents needed her to do right now, how could she begrudge them that? No matter how frustrated Nathan seemed to make her, Kate could suck it up for one morning.

She took her time with breakfast, letting Nathan clear out the back of the work truck they used when they had larger pickups to make. When he was done, he pulled up in front of the house, beeping the horn once.

"That'll be my cue," Kate said, standing and depositing her coffee mug in the sink.

"Be nice," her mother whispered as she placed a kiss on Kate's cheek.

"When am I not nice?"

"I can see how unimpressed you are by the way you're pursing your lips. You always do that when you're annoyed."

"I'm not annoyed. And I *don't* purse my lips."

"You're very easy to read."

"Well, you've had, like, thirty years to practice," Kate scoffed. "That doesn't count."

Her mother hummed as Kate shoved on her shoes, waving on her way out the door. The day was warm, the sun already leaving patches of yellow on the porch as she made her way down the stairs and to the passenger side of the truck. She climbed into the seat and buckled her belt, all while Nathan stared at her, one brow peaked with interest.

"What?"

"You're not going to fight me for the keys and demand to drive? Seems like the kind of thing you would do."

"I would have," Kate noted, leaning forward enough to see the kitchen window, "but my mother's watching us right now to make sure I'm nice to you."

"Is that what it's already come to?"

"That's what it's come to," Kate said, reaching out to adjust the radio. If she was going to be stuck with him for the rest of the morning, she didn't necessarily have to talk to him.

"You know," Nathan said, "I'm pretty good at reading people."

"You and my mother both," Kate muttered, folding

her arms across her chest. Apparently she really needed to stop pursing her lips.

"It's almost as if you've already decided not to like me."

"No," Kate said sarcastically. "Really? Am I giving you that impression?"

Nathan snorted, pulling onto the road that led off the property. With one hand, he swept his hair back and out of his eyes before grabbing a ball cap off the dashboard and sticking it on his head. From this angle, all she could see was the strong line of his jaw and the way his cheeks dimpled when he was trying not to smile. Kate turned away, staring out her window instead. The last things she needed to be thinking about right now were strong jawlines and dimples.

"Honestly," Nathan continued, "you're giving more of the perturbed-princess vibe."

"Excuse me?" Kate said. "You can just take back that entire sentence and start again. I am most definitely not a princess."

"Please. Only child—*only daughter*. Who grew up *here*," Nathan said, gesturing as they turned onto the main road and got a look at the dips and valleys and green spaces that made up the ranch. "Your parents are absolutely enthralled with everything you do. There is no way in hell you weren't doted on as a kid." He turned his head just a fraction to glance at her. "Tell me I'm wrong."

Kate opened her mouth, closed it. She sighed.

"That's what I thought," Nathan said. "The princess and all her horses."

She was loath to admit it, but when Kate thought about it...when she *really* thought about it, he wasn't exactly wrong. It wasn't that she was spoiled growing up. Living on a ranch came with its fair share of responsibilities. She learned the hard work that came with the territory of loving and owning large animals. But as a kid, it had never felt like work. It was fun. And because of that, she'd never wanted for anything. As a girl, she'd been completely content with her horses.

"So the fact that you don't like me makes sense," Nathan continued.

"How?"

"You, the horse princess. Me, the lowly ranch hand. It's a tale as old as time itself."

"That is, one, ridiculous. Two, I'm concerned about the number of children's books you're apparently reading, and three, not at all why I don't like you," Kate clarified.

"Ha!" he said. "So you admit it."

"Dislike is probably a strong word," Kate admitted, if only for her mother's sake. "Maybe you just really irritate me."

Nathan nodded like he'd heard it before. "I can work with irritate."

"Frustrate?"

"Still okay."

"Exasperate?"

"Now you're just spitting out synonyms."

Kate chuckled despite herself. Nathan turned down a side road, kicking up dust as he did. He was comfortable, she noted, one hand on the wheel, the other lounging on the center console. There was no other traffic, and they flew down the country road.

"You know," he said, "I hate to break it to you, but in

every story, the princess and the lowly ranch hand end up becoming friends. It's sort of inevitable."

"Is that right?"

He nodded. "So if you're just going to end up liking me, you might as well start now."

Kate pretended to consider, then said, "I think you'll be surprised at how long I can hold out."

Nathan's smile cracked into something toothy. "That sounds sort of like a challenge to me."

"No," Kate said, shaking her head. "Just setting the expectation. I wouldn't want you to lose sleep over it."

Nathan looked between her and the road. "I'm pretty sure you just issued a challenge. And I'm super competitive."

He stared at her for a moment that felt like it went on forever. Her heart fluttered, racing so fast she thought it could outrun the truck. It only eased when he jerked the wheel to avoid a pothole, sending them both crashing against their seats.

"The end of summer," he said after a moment.

"The what?"

"You issued a challenge and a challenge needs terms. Give me until the end of summer. By the time autumn hits, I guarantee you'll like me. You'll even be calling us friends."

Kate burst out laughing. She had no idea if she would even be here by the time summer ended, but she was intrigued. "And what do you get if you win?"

Nathan seemed to consider for a moment, and Kate wondered what he could possibly want out of this. "All right," he said. "If I win, you have to tell your parents that I'm the greatest ranch hand they have ever hired."

Kate could barely keep the exasperation off her face.

There was no way in hell she was going to admit that to her parents. He must have known that by the way he was smirking at her. "And if you lose?"

Nathan grew quiet. A cloud crossed the sun, casting them both in shadow. Kate watched the way his jaw worked, the scruff along his chin painting him like some kind of old Western portrait.

"Name your terms," he finally said.

Her first thought was that he should quit and go find a job he was more suited to, but when she considered the reality of that, all she would accomplish was losing the help that her parents obviously needed around the property. "Fine," she said. "If I win, you have to move out of the guest house."

His head snapped toward her, his brows arched in surprise. "For how long?"

"It'll depend on how badly you lose."

"And how exactly do we determine that?"

Kate smirked. "Well, like all super scientific things that can be measured, there is obviously a friendship scale. My side of the scale tracks how much more I could actually end up disliking you by the end of summer."

"I'm already working in a deficit, am I?"

Kate held her fingers up, measuring. "Just a little one."

"Okay, so we've got a like-to-loathe scale that we're working off of. And if you loathe me, I'm being evicted."

Kate smirked. "Don't look so sad. If you lose, it'll give you plenty of time to reflect on all the ways you failed to cement this friendship."

"And where will I stay? Your parents sort of promised room and board as part of my contract."

"We can get creative," Kate said. "Some of the stalls

in the stables are clearly empty right now. There's even an old canvas tent in the attic. I hear sleeping out under the stars is nice this time of year."

"All right, Princess," Nathan said, sticking one hand out toward her. She took it and they shook. "You have a deal."

Steele's Supply Depot was the same old rust bucket it had been when Kate was a teenager. She was pretty sure the same stalled tractor was parked on the front lawn, only now it was sunk about half a foot into the earth, decomposing into a rusty grave marker. The yard was now marked with dozens of metalwork sculptures, creating a funnel to the side door of the warehouse where they entered.

The inside of the warehouse was familiar, smelling of grain and salt and wet cardboard. It brought back memories of accompanying her father and playing hide-and-seek among the towering shelves that ran the length of the building. Each one was piled high with farming supplies reaching to the skylights in the roof.

Kate wandered the aisles, each shelf she passed weighed down with bags of feed for various livestock. Everything was coated in a fine layer of dust. There was something oddly comforting about knowing this place hadn't changed at all. The old quarter gumball machine was probably still sitting right beside the cash desk.

As Kate explored, Nathan strolled away to track down Randy Steele's son, Patrick, because that was one thing that had apparently changed since she was a girl. Randy had retired and his son had inherited this supply depot.

Kate's recollection of Patrick was fuzzy at best, probably because he was a few years older than her. She knew they'd ridden the same school bus at one point, because she distinctly remembered that he once got in trouble for throwing rotten eggs out the bus window. Boys made no sense back then.

Honestly, they still made no sense. Once again, Kate felt the sting of Cal's betrayal and the ache that came with repeatedly tearing apart and stitching together her adult love life. The moments where Cal crept into her thoughts were fewer than they'd been months ago, but the fact that he was still there, in the back of her mind, was frustrating.

It was even more frustrating because, without a doubt, Kate knew Cal wasn't dwelling over their past the way she was, however infrequently. He'd probably moved on. Multiple times by now.

Kate came to the end of the aisle, broken from her thoughts as she spied Nathan and a man she guessed was Patrick. They walked toward her, and Patrick's face split into a smile.

"Kate Cardiff. What's it been, twenty years?"

To her surprise, Patrick hugged her, almost sweeping her off her feet. The movement startled a laugh from her. "Neither of us are that old," she said as he let her go. "More like ten."

"That's true. I think the last time I saw you was that going-away party your parents held for you right before you went off to university."

Kate was surprised he remembered that. She'd certainly been too eager to get out of Hatchet Lake at that point to dwell over all the things—all the people—she was leaving behind. "That's probably about right."

"Hey," he said, tone sincere. "I was sorry to hear about your dad."

Kate nodded her thanks. "He's doing better now. They're taking great care of him at the hospital."

"If there's anything you guys need, just let me know."

"Thanks, Patrick."

"Of course." He clapped Nathan on the shoulder then. "Let me show you to the skids. I've got everything wrapped up, if you want to just back your truck up beside the loading bay."

The two of them walked away, muttering about fork-lifts and weight restrictions while Kate wandered toward the office to settle the bill. There was a young woman behind the glass. She looked up as Kate approached. Before she reached the door, Kate was jostled by someone coming around the corner of an aisle.

"Sorry," she said automatically, reaching out to steady the man she'd run into. She frowned, knowing the face but taking a long time to connect it to a memory. The face was older now, spots and wrinkles filling up the space around the eyes and lips. There was a hollowness near the cheeks and wispy gray hair beneath an old cowboy hat. "Doc?"

"Katie Cardiff," he said with the same tone of surprise. "I heard you had come home."

She wanted to ask how but nothing stayed a secret long in Hatchet Lake. There weren't enough of them to go around, so they spread like wildfire.

"I haven't seen you in a good—"

"Ten years," she supplied. The last few times she'd visited her parents, she'd hardly been there long enough to visit anyone in town, and apparently they were all rubbing it in today.

"About that, yeah." He wrapped an arm around her shoulders, walking Kate toward the office. "Come to take over from me?"

Henry "Doc" McGinn had been the livestock vet in Hatchet Lake for as long as she could remember. His practice incorporated all the local farms and ranches, including their own.

"I don't know about that, Doc."

"We could sure use you," he said. "I don't know if you've noticed because of my rugged good looks, but these old bones are getting ready to call it quits soon."

"Already?" Kate teased. When they reached the office, Doc leaned against a counter, more for support than anything, and the young woman began loading up an order for him.

"It's just about time. I was sorry to hear about your father, but I'm sure glad it's brought you home for a while. Those horses need someone good looking after them."

Kate's eyes widened, suddenly curious. "I saw you hadn't been by the ranch yet this year."

He sighed heavily. "I told your parents not to worry about it. That I'd take care of it this year, but you know your dad. Stubborn and proud to the core. He doesn't like to owe anyone anything. Especially money."

"Yeah," Kate said as a million different things filtered through her mind. Money? Was that why her parents hadn't had the vet out yet? Were they struggling financially? She started to piece things together. The late vet visit. The canceled food delivery. The fact that the ranch was only housing three outside horses right now.

Doc paid for his supplies and scooped them into his arms. "I'll see you around, Katie."

"Sure, Doc. See you." She forced a smile as he walked away. The girl in the office brought her a clipboard with a sheet to sign.

"Should I put it on your business account?"

Kate nodded. Was there even room on the business account? How should she know? Her parents hadn't mentioned one word about possible financial troubles. And now with her dad being laid up for the foreseeable future and medical bills, what would that mean for the ranch? Would they have to sell and move somewhere closer to the city?

"Actually," Kate said. "I'll put it on here."

She pulled out her personal credit card, handed it over and waited for the girl to ring her up again. Then Kate scribbled her name on the bill and turned to go find Nathan. She couldn't even imagine a world where she couldn't return home to the ranch. The idea of them selling it felt like a bad fever dream. Though what should it matter to her? What influence should Kate have when she couldn't even bother to visit more than once in five years?

She reached the truck to find the feed loaded into the back, the forklift abandoned by the wall.

"All settled up," she said. "Are we good here?"

Nathan shoved the door at the back of the truck closed. "Yeah."

"See you next month," Patrick said, waving them off. "Or sooner. I mean it, Kate. If you need anything at all don't hesitate to reach out."

"Thanks again," she said, finding that she genuinely meant it, before climbing in the truck and closing the door behind her. She leaned her head back against the seat, letting her eyes close for a second.

"What's wrong?" Nathan asked. He started the truck

and pulled away from the supply depot, onto the country road that would take them back to the ranch.

"Nothing."

"Did something happen?"

She shook her head.

"Kate?" There was a brief pause. "It doesn't seem like nothing."

Kate opened her eyes and glared at him. Nathan held a hand up in silent apology before focusing on the road again. It was quiet for a long time, not even the radio on to fill the void. Her thoughts stewed and festered until they felt too big to be contained.

"Have my parents mentioned anything to you about finances?"

That clearly surprised him. "What?"

"I just wondered if you'd heard anything since you've been here. They just seem to tell you everything else."

"I… I don't know," he mumbled, brow furrowed like he was trying hard to remember. To replay conversations, looking for meaning where there used to be none. "They haven't said… Are they having trouble?"

"I don't know," Kate muttered. "Forget I mentioned it."

And for the first time since she'd met him, Nathan did the least aggravating thing possible and just drove.

Chapter Six

"Where are you going?"

"Into town," Kate said the following morning, taking one last sip of coffee before dropping her mug into the bubble-filled sink. A lazy stream of light cut through the window, painting her hands in shades of gold as she turned to her mom. "According to the lab, the results from the blood work I sent off for the horses were supposed to be in this morning. I'm gonna go pick them up."

"Doesn't that usually come in an email?"

Kate nodded. "But I don't have an online account set up for the lab that processes Hatchet Lake yet. I'm locked out until they can verify my remote access." Though it was more inconvenient, Kate was impressed at how quick the turnaround time had been. Even at her day job, the online results took about the same amount of time to populate. Unless there were critical results, when labs usually called vets or offices directly. "The best they can do is mail me a hard copy since Dad apparently left the sixties behind and finally got rid of the fax machine in the office."

"It was bound to happen eventually." Smiling fondly, her mom glanced at her watch. "It's still early. The post office won't be staffed until nine."

"I know," Kate said. "I was gonna walk over."

"You can take the truck. I wasn't going up to the hospital until later to visit your dad."

"It's okay." Kate flashed her a brief smile. "It's good for me." She took half a second to consider the comments Doc had made yesterday and if she should just outright ask her mom what was going on. Ask her if the ranch was going under. If they needed help. But if she knew anything about her parents, the first thing they'd do would be deny it. They wouldn't want to worry her, so even if she asked, her mom was likely not to commit to anything. Kate knew better. She'd have to let her parents tell her in their own time, regardless of what was going on.

"I'll be back in an hour or so," she said.

Her mom made a sound, something between a scoff and a laugh. "I think you underestimate how far it is to walk into town."

"I remember being able to get to the convenience store and back in under an hour."

"That's when you were ten and used to run the whole way."

"My legs are longer now," Kate teased. "It'll even out." Her mother simply shook her head as Kate collected her things and went outside. She skipped down the porch steps, following the worn trail across the property. If she cut through the pasture, it would save her about fifteen minutes.

As she picked her way across the ranch, she passed Nathan leaning up against the wooden fence surrounding the pasture, one leg braced upon the lower beam, his elbows on the upper one.

"Where are you off to?" he asked.

"The post office. The horses' lab results came in."

"You want a ride?"

"No, I'll walk, thanks."

"That's what friends do, you know. Offer each other rides."

"Nice try," she said, and to that he just shrugged, turning back to the paddock. That was when she noticed the camera in his hands. The same one, she presumed, that she saw the other day from her window. She paused, hands in her pockets, stopping to stand with him at the fence where he watched the horses graze and roam.

"The lighting right now is great," he said, more to himself than to her as he focused the lens and snapped a photo of Shade trotting past. "I'm a photographer by trade," he added.

"Ah," Kate said. "We finally uncover the secret life of the ranch hand. What kind of photography do you do?"

"I usually favor nature."

"Like wildlife and landscapes and things?"

He nodded. "I pick up contracts, travel around. Been to some pretty amazing places."

"I'll bet," she said, envisioning the things he'd probably seen. Mountains and glaciers and waterfalls. None of which he would find here. It was all the more reason to wonder how he'd ended up on this ranch in the middle of nowhere. "So, what? You figured you'd settle down, take up the rancher life?"

He laughed at that, the sound just a puff of air. "I'm in between contracts. A couple of photographer buddies and I drove out here to capture the wicked storms you get in the summer."

Kate considered the thunder and lightning that so often plagued the area in the hot summer months. Never once had she thought to grab a camera when those dark clouds started to pile on top of each other. "So now you're a weather photographer?"

"I like to diversify. You know, do weddings and those cute photos of newborns dressed like acorns," he joked.

"People always want pictures of their newborns looking like an acorn on a bed of wildflowers," Kate agreed.

"Right! I picked up this job for some extra cash and a place to stay. I didn't think it would be a long-term thing, but I'm not unhappy with how it's turning out."

He lifted his camera and snapped another photo, this time of Tully shaking her head back and forth, throwing her mane into the wind. He took his phone out of his pocket and scrolled through it, then he handed it to her. The screen was open to an Instagram profile.

Kate scrolled through the page, her eyes going wide. The entire page was full of storm clouds. Big, bright, angry, colorful, dark, exploding clouds. He was *really, really* good, though she was hesitant to admit that out loud because that felt exactly like something a friend would say. And they were most definitely not friends.

Nathan leaned over her shoulder, close enough that she could feel the breath of his words along her neck. The sensation sent a shiver down her spine. "I love how angry the clouds can look in the moment," he said. "A complete mess of power and anger and rage—and then, suddenly, it's like nothing happened at all. It reminds me that everything passes eventually."

"The calm after the storm," Kate said. She thought about her dad. About the mess of emotions she'd been filtering through these past few days. Fear and anger and denial and anxiety. It was so much that she'd hardly had the time to name them properly. It felt like a storm. Just like the mess of clouds that he'd so aptly captured on the screen. To think that it all passed eventually gave her a modicum of comfort she didn't even realize she was searching for.

"Exactly," he said softly.

She swiped through to another photo, clicking on it to see a larger image. A cascade of pink-and-orange clouds tumbled across the screen. She handed the phone back. There was real talent there. It was no wonder he spent his life chasing moments like these around the world through his lens.

"I think it's supposed to storm today," he said, glancing up at the sky thoughtfully.

She watched the stretch of his neck and the bob of his Adam's apple before she realized she was staring. "Looks clear to me."

"We'll see. You sure you don't want that ride?"

"I'm sure."

He picked the camera up and faced it in her direction but before he snapped the photo, she reached out and blocked the shot. "Save it for the horses."

"Right," he said. "Maybe when we're friends."

She rolled her eyes, turning away. There was something there. Some small, twisted thing in the pit of her stomach. She tried not to think too hard about it. Or about the fact that although he still annoyed her, he was growing on her. It was slowly, sort of like the way mold grew, just there in the corner. Not really tolerated but no matter how many times you wiped it away, it just came back. "Goodbye, Nathan."

Without waiting for a reply, she slipped through the gate to cut across the pasture. As she walked away, she did her best not to look back, not to stare at him, though that was what she wanted to do. She didn't even want to be thinking about him, but somehow he was there, at the forefront of her mind.

Maybe it was her way of coping. He made for a decent distraction.

Though she didn't know whether he was a good or bad distraction. Sarah would tell her that he could be a *very* good distraction.

When they'd finally gotten back to the ranch yesterday after retrieving the horse feed, they'd spent the better part of an hour unloading the truck and stacking the bags of feed in the shed. They'd both been sweaty and exhausted by the end of it.

He'd looked at her then, brow arched. "Does this make us friends yet?"

"Not a chance," she'd said, to which he'd just grinned before collapsing onto a bale of straw. A very good distraction indeed.

Still, Kate couldn't quite figure out what he was doing here. If all he was after was a little job to make some spare cash while he chased storms, then he'd come to the wrong place. The ranch was the opposite of an easy side job. It was work. Hard work. Laborious, dirty work.

She certainly wouldn't do it if she didn't love it and the animals.

By the time she'd crossed the field and hiked up the short ditch to the road, she was in a tangled mess about the whole thing and did the only sane thing she could think of.

She called Sarah.

The phone rang twice before Sarah answered. "Hello?"

"So, I'm pretty sure my parents are broke and maybe the ranch is in trouble. But it's just an inkling. And I'm not sure I want to dig at it right now when my dad's still in the hospital and clearly won't be coming back home to run the ranch full-time and my mom's probably super stressed. And Nathan is just everywhere and now he thinks we're going to be best friends because of a stupid bet and—"

"Okay, okay," Sarah said, interrupting her. "That was a lot. That's like when Parker tries to explain his weird, animated TV shows to me." There was a babble of toddler agreement in the background. "How about we take a breath and start from the beginning?"

Kate did, realizing she was nearly breathless after hiking across the pasture and up the ditch. She exhaled and started again. "I'm afraid my parents are going to have to sell the ranch."

"But they haven't said anything?"

"No."

"So, this is just you projecting?"

"I am not projecting. This is based on solid facts."

"Do you think you're maybe just worried about your dad and what it means for him coming back home and adjusting after the heart attack?"

"Well, of course I am. But this feels like something more."

Parker shrieked in the background.

"What was that about?" Kate asked.

"We just passed a McDonald's and I didn't pull in."

"Poor kid."

"That's not helping."

"You know I'm always team chicken nugget."

"You're team avoidance. Back on topic. Why do you think the ranch is in trouble?"

Kate considered that feeling in her gut. About what put it there in the first place. "I couldn't find the vet reports from this year. I thought maybe Dad had just filed them away somewhere different, and then mom said they hadn't had the vet out yet to see the horses for their annual checkups."

"Which is unusual?"

"Very. It's been over a year since their annuals. I've done them since I've been here, but that's beside the point."

"Okay."

"And then I ran into Doc at the supply depot in town— he's the vet we've used at the ranch since forever—and he offhandedly mentioned something about being glad I was here because he hadn't been out to the ranch yet this year because my dad is stubborn and proud. *Especially* when it comes to money."

"That hardly means the ranch is going under," Sarah said.

"They've also canceled the food deliveries for the horses. And I'm pretty sure it's because they can't afford it. So Nathan and I went to pick the order up yesterday." Kate sighed. "There's only three horses that are being boarded right now, and I don't even know if my parents are making any money off of them or if they are doing people a *favor*."

"Kate, if it is happening and your parents didn't tell you, it's for a good reason."

"Yeah," she muttered, "because I haven't been around."

"No, it's because they want to protect you. This is your childhood home. Where you grew up. If they really are having financial trouble, the last thing they would want to do is ruin your memories of that place by making everything about money."

"That's exactly why it's so frustrating! I could help them."

"Would they want that, though?"

Kate grumbled. "No. Doc was right about that. My dad is stubborn. He'd never accept money from me."

"Maybe you're looking at this the wrong way," Sarah said. "Maybe it's not about the ranch going under but your parents just slowly stepping away from it."

"You think they're done?" Kate asked, blinking as if it was the most shocking news she'd ever heard. She'd never considered that her parents might *want* to sell.

"Your dad just had a heart attack, Kate. Maybe it's time they close up shop and move closer to the city."

Kate couldn't even fathom it. In her mind, her parents were synonymous with the ranch. She had never once thought that they might be done with it one day. That they might want to pack up and leave. "Guess everyone wants to retire, huh?"

Why did that make her so sad? She hadn't thought about this place in any great capacity in years. Why now did it bother her that she might be losing it?

"Okay, let's circle back to the Nathan thing."

"What Nathan thing?" Kate said, still distracted by the vision she'd conjured in her mind of a For Sale sign posted at the edge of the driveway.

"Something about a bet and being best friends? Last time we spoke you loathed the man. You went from loathing to friendship awfully fast. Did something else happen?" Sarah said. There was teasing in her voice. "Sounds like maybe you two were playing building blocks together."

"God, no! Nothing like that."

"Well, that's disappointing. I'd personally like to hear more about this bet, please."

Kate resisted the urge to roll her eyes, because what good was that when Sarah couldn't see it? "It's stupid. Nathan said since he was going to be around I was just going to have to start liking him. I said that I could hold out surprisingly long. I guess he took that as a challenge. Now he has however long I'm here this summer to convince me that we're friends."

"And what happens at the end of the summer?" Sarah wondered.

"Either I have to grovel to my parents about how wonderful a ranch hand Nathan is, or he has to move out of the guest house."

"You know, this does sound like a friendly sort of bet."

"Oh, don't you start, too. I hardly know the man. And what I do know of him still mildly irritates me."

"But only mildly," Sarah said in a singsong voice. "That sounds like an improvement."

"We're not friends," Kate insisted. "But he's also doing a lot on the ranch in my dad's absence, so I'm try-ing to curtail the side-eye. Mostly for my mom's sake."

"How kind of you. If I had an attractive cowboy trying to be my friend, I wouldn't be making him work so hard."

"One, he's not a cowboy. He's actually a photographer. So ask me again why my parents hired him to take care of horses." Kate shook off that train of thought. "How do you even know if he's attractive or not?"

"Rancher Hotstuff is attractive in my mind, okay? Do not ruin the illusion for me. You could send a picture, though. Just to confirm what I already know."

"Yeah, not gonna happen."

"A girl can dream."

Parker shrieked in the background again.

"Just get the kid some chicken nuggets already."

"We just passed a construction site. The child has an obsession with trucks."

"Bring him to the ranch. We'll let him drive around in the old farm vehicles."

"Don't tempt me. Speaking of visits. How long do you think you're going to be out there? Have there been any updates on your dad?"

"Not many since we last talked. Hopefully, he'll be able to come home soon. I know my mom would feel better having him back in the house. Makes it easier for her to dote and fuss and all that. She's dealing with all this better than I would if I was her, but I know going back and forth to the city is going to wear her out eventually."

"Well, all I can say is listen to those nurses when they tell you to go home and get some rest. We usually know what we're talking about."

Kate sighed. "I miss you. Phone calls are nice but it's been too long. Parker's going to be a teenager soon."

"Please, no. I'm not ready. I'm barely surviving *Co-Comelon*."

"I don't even want to know what that is." The road evened out over the next three hundred meters and Kate could spy the gas station that housed the town's only post office. There was a single pickup parked at the pump and a pile of firewood stacked in orange bags at the corner of the lot. A signpost bore old markers with faded letters reading FARM-FRESH EGGS and BLUE-BERRIES. Marked arrows pointed down the road to the farms just outside of town. Another sign pointed to HATCHET LAKE CAMPGROUND.

"I better let you go," Kate said. "Give Parker a hug for me."

"Yeah, you do the same with Rancher Hotstuff."

"Not gonna happen."

Sarah laughed, and Kate hung up on her. A newer sign, one she'd never seen before, had been erected on the side of the road, bolted to a large metal stand. MO-SAIC RESORT & WELLNESS GROUP. *Rediscover yourself.* That was new, she thought, wondering when some company had arrived to turn their sleepy little town into more of a tourist destination. The camp-ground was one thing, but this was another. This was real development. She studied the map etched on the bottom of the sign, trying to figure out which farm was sold to make space for the building. Would her parents be the next to give up their property for some fancy resort wanting to capitalize on the peace and quiet of country living, appealing to the wealthy and elite as a getaway from their busy lives?

By the time she reached the gas station, she could see the rest of their tiny Main Street. Kate could easily do laps of the place and its mom-and-pop shops: there was Sunnyside Diner, painted in bright coral colors with windows dressed in yellow sunflowers; the Pint Pub, aptly named by Old Joe, who had tended that bar since before Kate was born; a single hardware store, carrying a strange collection of camping gear, tools and house-wares; one used clothing shop and a small art gallery supplied by local talent.

Although there was something reassuring about the fact that this street hadn't changed much in her absence, Kate had spent part of her life wondering how anyone could survive an entire lifetime here.

She certainly never thought she could.

Kate cut across the parking lot of the gas station. A bell dinged as she threw the door open and passed a rack of chips and candy bars on her way to the back corner of the building where the small post office was housed. A woman with graying hair pulled into a tight bun stood at the counter, sorting mail.

"Hi, there, honey. What can I do for you?"

Kate walked up and pulled out her ID. "Picking up for Katherine Cardiff."

The woman glanced at her ID, then disappeared into a back room for a second before returning with a stack of mail. She pulled the top envelope free and passed it across the counter. "We would have delivered these."

"It's okay," Kate said, smiling as she slid her finger along a tear in the corner of the envelope. "I needed the walk."

She turned away, scanning all the lab results. She didn't expect any of the levels to be critical, but she was interested in getting a baseline for the horses. Nothing she saw came as a surprise, just the expected changes that came from getting older. Like humans, animal needs changed as they aged. Kate's first thought was that she'd keep an eye on the levels for the next several years, watch as they progressed and treat them accordingly. Then she remembered that she wasn't the usual vet for these animals. Nor did she know where the ranch would be in a few years.

Kate lifted her hand in farewell to the gas attendant and the woman at the mail counter. And as she stepped back onto the road outside, the clouds collided in a menacing gray mass, hanging just overhead. *Great*, she thought as the first raindrops started to fall. She picked up her pace, wishing she wasn't about to admit that maybe Nathan had been right about the rain.

Chapter Seven

By the time Kate returned to the ranch, the clouds were starting to gather, hanging low and heavy over the house. She jogged the last mile, determined not to be outside when the storm finally let go. A low thrum of thunder had chased her all the way from town, a few sprinkles of rain teasing her with something worse.

As she neared the ranch, she could see that the horses had been brought back inside. She hurried across the field and up the porch steps to the front door, slamming into it when the door didn't immediately give way. She frowned, trying the doorknob slowly only to meet the same resistance.

Definitely locked, she confirmed.

Kate turned and glanced around the front yard, then wandered down the porch steps to check the side of the house. Her mom's truck was missing. The house was locked. She took out her phone and called her mom. It had hardly been an hour since they last talked. Her mom knew very well that Kate was going out. But now she felt like an idiot for not taking her keys. She could envision them sitting there on her bedside table. Leaving them was more of a habit than anything. Her parents had never locked the door when she was growing up, though the ranch used to be more lively, with people coming and going constantly: her father and the ranch hands in and out of the office, her mom supplying coffee and lemonade and baked goods to a revolving door of people. Kate had simply come and gone as she pleased.

Of course, that was fifteen years ago. Now they apparently had hooligans sneaking around the ranch for Instagram-worthy pictures.

Her mom's phone went directly to voice mail, so Kate assumed she was still driving. A clap of thunder startled her from the silent curse she was muttering, and she looked around as Nathan drove up, hanging out the window of his own truck as large raindrops started to ricochet off the windshield. *Perfect*, she thought, climbing the porch steps until she was back under the safety of the porch roof.

"Horses are secured in their stalls. I'm heading out for a bit. I'll let them out again after the storm passes."

Kate nodded, wondering where he was headed. Then she spied his camera on the passenger seat. This was probably exactly the kind of weather Nathan and his friends had traveled out here to photograph.

"Did my mom say where she was going?" Kate asked.

"To the hospital. She forgot she wanted to be there when the physiotherapist came around to talk about cardiac rehab. She said something about your dad being a poor historian and not liking to exercise."

That sounded exactly like her dad. Oh, he was no slouch with hard work. He'd spend all day in the stables mucking out stalls, but ask him to eat healthy or exercise and he'd wave you off with a gruff sound and shake of his head. Trying to explain the benefits of cardio to that man went in one ear and tumbling out the other.

Luckily for her dad, her mom would take detailed notes.

That meant she would be gone for the next few hours at least.

Great.

For a second, Kate wondered why her mom didn't try to call or text before heading to the hospital. Why her first instinct was to leave a message with Nathan. But the longer she considered it, the more it made sense. Her mom had gotten used to not having Kate around.

Kate was off living her own life, just checking in from afar on occasion.

She hadn't meant to lose this part of her life when she'd left Hatchet Lake. She'd only been desperate to see what existed beyond it. How could she possibly be happy with fields and horses and the same small town of people for her entire life?

But then she'd become a vet, taking care of livestock for a living, and now she spent most of her time in other people's small towns. On other people's farms and ranches and fields.

"Are you locked out?" Nathan asked as it finally dawned on him.

"Looks like it," Kate muttered. She glanced back at the door, contemplating breaking into the house or scaling the side of the porch the way she used to do as a teenager. She decided against it, feeling far more breakable than she did when she was fifteen.

Birthing calves and running around after livestock was hard on the joints.

Her mom would also probably frown on Kate breaking a window because of her own stupidity, so she stopped eyeing the perfectly palm-sized rock in the garden bed.

Another crash of thunder and Kate shivered. She wasn't cold. Not really. But the idea of sitting here on the porch for the next three or four hours sounded unpleasant. She supposed she should head back to the stables. She had waited out her fair share of summer storms there before. At least the horses would be good company.

The sky darkened overhead. At this rate, she'd be soaked even if she ran to the stables.

"Do you want the key to the guest house?" Nathan asked.

"No, thanks," Kate said. Sitting in the guest house, knowing that it was his space right now, would feel strange. There was a level of intimacy, of *friendship*, that came with being welcomed into someone's space, and seeing as they were definitely *not* friends, taking Nathan up on that offer was the opposite of what she wanted to do.

"You can't just sit out here." Nathan watched a gust of wind drag raindrops up the porch and over Kate's shoes. "Your mom could be gone for hours."

"Oh, I don't doubt it," Kate said. "I'll just sit in the stables with the horses."

"Or," Nathan said as a grin tugged at the corner of his

mouth. "Consider this. You get in the truck and come with me."

"I'll take my chances in the stables."

"Oh, come on. The damp, musty stables, where you'll inevitably start doing chores to pass the time. Or a warm, pine-fresh vehicle." He flicked the tree-shaped air freshener hanging from his mirror. "Seems like an easy choice to me. And you get to spend quality time with one of your dearest friends."

"Not friends," Kate said, making that clear.

"Would someone who's not your friend offer to save you from the rain?"

"I don't need saving."

Nathan rolled his eyes at her, deliberately, making sure she saw. "You are the most stubborn woman I have ever met."

"Thank you. I take after my father."

"Of that I have no doubt." He inclined his head in a come-hither motion, and Kate planted her feet. "Just get in the truck and don't make me beg. You might even have a good time if you stop fighting me for five seconds."

"Doubtful."

He sighed, drumming his hands along the wheel. He didn't look at her. "Kate, get in the truck."

"No."

"Do you really expect me to tell your mother that I left you out here by yourself in the middle of a thunderstorm?"

"I'm a big girl. Pretty sure I'll survive."

"Kate," he sighed, taking his camera and placing it on the back seat. "Just remember that I'm doing this as a friend."

Before she could utter the words "Doing what?"

Nathan was out of his truck. He grabbed her from the porch, scooping her off her feet in a smooth motion and throwing her over his shoulder like she was nothing more than a bundle of straw. Kate yelped, startled, grappling for a handhold as her world spun. She awkwardly managed to take hold of the belt loop of his pants, steadying herself. She watched his boots sink into the mud as he carried her to the passenger side of the truck.

"Put me down!" she demanded, hoping that he could hear the threat that oozed out between her clenched teeth.

"Sure thing, Princess." He set her down, grabbing her shoulders to steady her as she got her bearings.

"Are you crazy?" she stammered.

Nathan just swung the door of the truck open, looking at her sternly, his dark brows meeting in the middle. "Get in."

Kate did but only because she was too dizzy to march away. She slumped into the seat, waiting for her head to stop spinning.

Nathan was back in the truck and adjusting the controls on the dashboard in an instant. "Now we're both soaked. Are you happy?"

"I'm pretty sure that's your fault."

"For dealing with your stubbornness? Yes, that's all on me."

Kate huffed, crossing her arms as a warm blast of air poured out of the vent. She didn't say thank you because if she had learned anything, it was that Nathan had a bad habit of trying to save her from things she did not need saving from. But as the heat enveloped her, she found that she was glad not to be waiting out the storm huddled on the porch.

Though she'd never tell him that.

Maybe she was taking her obstinacy to the extreme, but it was a trait that had carried her through life. There was no point giving it up now.

"Where are we going?" Kate finally asked as Nathan took a left down the road instead of a right toward town.

"On an adventure."

"An adventure?"

"Yeah, ever heard of it? I think you could use a little fun. I don't know if you get a lot of that."

"For someone who apparently wants to be my friend, you're walking a fine line."

"Hey, real friends are the ones who tell you how it is. And you, Kate Cardiff, are far too stubborn for your own good. It's time for you to see the world through my eyes."

And with that, he raced down the road, music blaring, taking them into the heart of the storm. After a while the rain grew heavier, and Nathan turned on his windshield wipers just as another boom of thunder rumbled through the truck.

He drummed excitedly on the steering wheel. "We're getting close!"

"How close do we have to get?" Kate wondered, turning down the music to hear him better.

"As close as it takes to get the best photo."

"And how close is that?"

"We go with our gut. It's what separates us from the amateurs."

Kate shook her head, unable to help the smile that curved the corners of her mouth. She was no beginner at driving in the rain. Usually, she wasn't that bothered by it. But her first instinct would probably not be to drive straight into a massive storm cell.

"Hey, was that a smile? Look who's already having fun."

"It's a smile of disbelief."

Nathan pressed on the gas. "You haven't seen anything yet." He sped down the country road, fields of wheat and tall grass pressing in on either side. The grass eventually gave way to cornfields, and a spark of lightning snapped in the distance.

The rain fell heavier as they approached the mass of clouds opening like a dark mouth to swallow them whole. Nathan flicked the windshield wipers up to max.

Kate's blood hummed beneath her skin, her heart rate kicking up. There was something thrilling about the chase. Something terrifying as well, racing toward the twisted lightning strikes.

Another boom of thunder sounded and she grabbed the edge of her seat, feeling the vibration through the truck.

The thunder and lightning worsened as the storm passed over them, the cloud system stretching its gnarled, broken fingers over the green fields that bordered the stretch of quiet highway.

"Heart racing yet?" Nathan asked as they drove through a sheet of rain.

A roar ripped through the air, the road beneath them trembling again, but this time it wasn't the storm. It was a large, olive green Volkswagen van that came racing down the road behind them.

"What the—"

"Don't worry," Nathan said. "That's just Rusty and Tara."

"Your photographer buddies?"

He nodded as the van swerved around them into the

oncoming traffic lane to pass. They blared the horn just because they could, and Kate watched as a man and a woman waved at them from the other vehicle.

Nathan tapped his horn in greeting, then the van pulled ahead, tearing off down the road.

Just as the butterflies started racing up her throat again, the rain eased, the storm pulling away from them and gathering over the field. They drove another minute, and the rain stopped altogether.

"There," Nathan said, pointing ahead to a spot on the shoulder where the van was already parked.

He pulled over behind the van and they piled out, shoes sinking into the rain-soaked gravel on the side of the road.

"Took you guys long enough," Rusty called, pushing back a mop of fiery red hair as he hopped out of the van and straight into a puddle. He was lanky and freckle-faced, sporting a flaming red sunburn across his nose.

The woman, Tara, was petite, with long, dark, pin-straight hair and an impressive pair of biceps. She pulled open the sliding door on the side of the van to join them. Inside were modified living quarters with a small bed, seating area and kitchen, but it was the sheer amount of technology hooked up to the dashboard and strung across the van that caught Kate's attention. Green weather graphs and storm-tracking apps lit up the space and, for the first time, Kate realized just how serious this whole photography business was.

"This is Kate," Nathan said as they approached. He held his camera in one hand, his other at the small of her back like he was afraid she might bolt. "Rusty," he said, nodding to his friend. "And Tara."

"Ah, the rancher's daughter," Rusty said, reaching

out to shake her hand. "Nice to finally put a face to the name."

Kate shook his hand, wondering what exactly Nathan had been saying about her. Probably complaining about how stubborn and difficult she was. It was basically what she'd been doing with Sarah in regard to him, so she supposed that was fair.

"He finally dragged you out here, did he?" Tara said, something of a smirk on her face.

"Entirely against my will," Kate agreed, glaring at Nathan. "Practically kidnapped me."

"Hey, I was just being nice. Otherwise you'd be soggy and sitting on the front porch."

"Do we even want to know?" Tara asked.

"The princess here forgot her keys," Nathan explained.

"Oh, so we're back to that?" Kate said, crossing her arms at the word *princess*.

"We never left."

"Looks like we're getting a little break," Rusty said, glancing in the opposite direction. A band of streaky white clouds interspersed with blue daylight passed overhead, but behind them came another band of the storm. It was like a ripple in a calm pond, moving across the sky.

"This is perfect," Nathan said, looking at the cloud formations piling up in the field. "Tara?"

"Already on it," she said, fitting a different lens to the front of her camera. She lifted it up, focused through the viewfinder and started snapping. She took a rapid succession of shots. As she did, the sky lit up across the field, lightning spiraling in the distance.

"I got that!" Tara shrieked, looking down at her camera to confirm. She reviewed the photo. "I freaking got that!"

"Yeah, you did!" Rusty cheered. He climbed back into the van and music spilled out as he cranked the radio.

The second band of the storm rolled overhead and the rain started again, dropping sporadically at first. Kate tilted her head back, watching the clouds speed over her. Before the clouds could let go, she took shelter in the van.

Nathan grabbed a rain jacket with a comically large hood and something to cover his camera, then he dashed out into the field with Tara. His smile was as electric as the storm, his laugh contagious. Tara perched on a rock way out in the field, wearing cutoff overalls and combat boots, the wind catching her long, dark hair. With her camera, she looked like some sort of explorer set to embark into the wilds of an unknown land.

"So," Rusty said over the din of the music. "How's your first storm chasing experience? It is your first, right?"

"To take pictures? Definitely." Kate lifted a shoulder. "It's better than I expected, but if you tell Nathan I said that, I'll have to kill you."

Rusty made an exaggerated show of crossing his heart. "I'll take it to the grave."

The rain grew heavier, and Tara gave a little shriek, running back to the van. She snapped a picture of Kate and Rusty as she approached and then ducked inside to stash her camera. Nathan raced back as well, skidding to a stop and diving into the van beside Kate. He knocked his hood back and grinned at her. For the first time, Kate noticed the way his hair curled when it was damp, the freckle beneath his left eye, and the way his eyelashes fluttered when he was laughing. For a moment she was breathless. Completely and utterly. It was as if she'd been caught in some sort of spell.

But it was also the most alive she'd felt in months. Since Cal had cheated and they broke it off. Maybe even before that. It was like the blood pounding beneath her skin, and in her pulse points, and in her ears, finally meant something again.

Lightning struck hard in the distance, flashing across the van. Nathan turned away, the spell between them shattered, but Kate's heart continued to thunder in her chest as she looked at him, the beat stronger than any thunder that rolled across the sky.

Chapter Eight

Hospitals smelled like rusty metal.

Kate had always thought so.

And despite the fancy finishes in the room and the clean linens on her dad's bed, this hospital was no different. Hidden beneath the aroma of his half-eaten breakfast—plastic-looking eggs and cranberry juice—Kate could smell it.

The rust.

She hated it.

"Hey, Dad," she said as he looked up from his meal tray. Kate dumped her things onto the chair in the corner of his room. Her mom had gotten sidetracked at the nurses' station as she so often did. Apparently it was easier to get the truth out of them when her dad wasn't cutting in and denying everything they said.

"Morning, baby," her dad said, holding one arm out for her.

Kate flitted to the edge of the bed, folding into his side. No matter how old he got, how much gray leaked into his hair or how many wrinkles appeared beside his eyes, the strength of his hugs never seemed to waver.

"I see they snagged you a paper," Kate said, glancing at the headlines.

"I have an understanding with the porters."

She chuckled. Only her dad would be more concerned about sorting out his morning paper situation than the reason he was actually in the hospital. "I hope the understanding doesn't include supplying you with a bunch of junk food, because that definitely does not abide by your new diet and I will have to tell Mom."

Her dad gaped in mock offense. "I would never."

"Mmm-hmm," Kate said, smiling at their teasing. She pressed her nose against his shoulder, feeling the smile fall from her face. "But how are you really feeling?"

"A little slow today. A little run-down. But I'm blaming this hospital bed. It threw my back and both hips out of whack."

"Sure that has nothing to do with the heart attack?"

Her father grumbled and flipped to the next page of his paper. "You're starting to take after your mother more and more."

"Funny. She says I'm exactly like you." Kate rested her head on his shoulder, surprised when she felt his head lean against hers. Her dad wasn't an emotionless sort of man, but it was rare to find him so unguarded. For a moment Kate just basked in the simplicity of it.

Of the knowledge that her dad was alive, here with her another day. She had a chance to not take that for granted. It was funny how easy it was to lose track of the people you loved when you never expected to be without them.

When she was younger, she used to think of her dad as immortal, like the gods of Olympus. This hulking, weathered, tough-as-nails man. The kind of man that would leap into the pen of a spooked horse, facing the bucking hooves with a steady voice and a calm hand. He was the kind of man that illness and disease would never touch.

That fantasy was shattered now. She knew better.

And though he was no Hercules, her dad still thought of himself as such, and he could be highly dismissive of his own health. So, if Kate had to act like her mother to get him to take it a little more seriously, then that was something she was willing to do.

"Are you okay?" her father asked.

She nodded.

"I don't mean just with this," he said, gesturing to the beige-patterned walls of his room. "I mean with everything. Your mother tells me you're still pining over that boy."

"Pining? Dad, Cal's been out of the picture for months now. He's not even given an inch of space inside my head." That wasn't exactly true. Cal was still there. A memory. Or a shadow. Looming over her life at inconvenient times, like this one. In a space where he should take up no room at all, he found a way to weasel himself in.

"I never liked that boy," her father said.

"You met him once," Kate reminded him, her lips pursed. It would be sweet, her dad defending her like this, if only she weren't mortified by the fact that she'd brought Cal around the ranch to meet her parents in the first place. It should have been obvious to her then that they would never work. It was during her only visit in the last five years, and Cal had hated every moment of it. He'd barely come out of the guest house. It was so awkward they'd ended up leaving early.

"And that was one time too many," her dad muttered.

"You could have told me then, instead of letting me waste my time."

"When do you ever listen to anything I say?"

"All the time."

Her dad laughed boldly. "It would only have made you cling to him harder."

She had been clinging pretty tight, Kate admitted to herself. She'd been holding on to him when she should have been reading the signs well enough to let him go. It felt like there was just so much pressure to make it work. To finally say she was in a serious relationship, the way people expected of her at her age. Marriage. Kids. The rest of the white-picket-fence dream.

She huffed, annoyed that society still seemed to be able to foist these pressures on her when most young people couldn't even afford the house attached to that white-picket-fence life. The world was different now. If only she could convince herself of that enough to let Cal go for good. To cut her losses and start over with someone who actually wanted to be with her.

Her dad coughed, clearing his throat of a tickle. "How are the horses?"

"Beautiful," she said. She steered the conversation away from her checkups of the horses and Doc's comments about missing annual visits. She didn't want to burden her dad with those kinds of questions.

Not here. Not now.

Maybe when he was stronger.

When he was home.

"I forgot how much I missed them. And the ranch. And you and Mom." Kate rubbed a gentle circle into the back of his hand. "I'm sorry I wasn't around to help. Before all this happened."

"Don't apologize," her dad said. "I just want you to be happy. Wherever that takes you." A quiet beat ebbed between them. "Are you?" her dad asked after a moment.

Kate had to hand it to him. He'd always been the one that was able to get right to the heart of her feelings. To pick up a thread of thought and follow it right to the weight of her troubles.

"I thought so," she said, more to herself than him. Truth was, she'd been happier since she'd been back home. Despite the circumstances that brought her here, she was more at ease on the ranch. More herself than anywhere else she'd ever been.

Her dad squeezed her fingers gently. "Sometimes the heart calls us home."

"Or sometimes Mom does," she quipped.

Her dad chuckled. "All right, I'll give you that one."

Kate stood up, letting her dad finish the newspaper as she wandered to the doorway. Down the hall, her mom stood with a woman who Kate suspected was the coordinator she'd been hearing about—the one arranging all the cardiac rehab that her dad would need once he left the hospital.

It was a serious conversation. Kate could tell because her mom was taking notes. She felt like a kid again, standing in the doorway, and a spark of mischief ignited in her bones.

"Is your mother conspiring with the nurses to suck all the fun out of life?" her dad idly inquired.

"Probably trying to," Kate said. He'd need a new diet. An exercise routine. All very important things for his recovery.

"Oh, goody," her dad said. "Well, that physio woman should be here momentarily to take me for my daily walk. As if I can't walk myself up and down the hallway. She follows me around with a wheelchair."

"That's in case you get tired."

Her dad harrumphed.

"How about a jailbreak instead of waiting around for your physio session?" Kate offered, her smile hardly containing the glee. There wasn't a lot she could offer him when he was locked up here, but maybe a loop of the cafeteria or something would put him in a better mood. He could do his physio after.

A sly smile crossed his face. "I knew you were my favorite daughter."

"Dad, I'm your only daughter."

"I'll get my coat," he said, reaching over for the hospital grade housecoat tossed over the back of one of the chairs. "You keep watch."

Kate did for a moment, before realizing that her dad was having some trouble getting his arms into the housecoat. She abandoned her view of the hallway and her mother to help him navigate the armholes instead.

"There," she said, tying a bow in the front to keep it closed. She looked up at him. "Now we need wheels."

"Check the closet," her dad said while stuffing his feet into slippers that looked like they came from home.

Kate swung the closet door open to reveal a wheelchair. She drove it up beside him and put the brakes on. "I promise to keep my driving under control. And before you say anything, yes, Mom complained about you grumbling about her driving while she was transporting you to the hospital to save your life."

"When else would I have had time to complain if I had croaked upon getting here?"

"Don't even joke," Kate whispered, taking off the brakes and rolling the chair up to the doorway slowly. She leaned forward to spy down the hall, realizing her dad was doing the same thing. They probably looked utterly ridiculous, and Kate liked to think that the three nurses who just glanced up and then away were politely pretending to be oblivious because they had more important things to worry about than this very modest jailbreak.

Kate was never really worried about the nurses anyway. Her mom and the coordinator woman, however, might have argued, so she was pleased to find that they were still engaged in a hearty conversation. Kate tightened her grip on the handles of the wheelchair, then booked it down the hall toward the elevator.

"Kate!" her mom called after her. Exasperated. "Katherine Anne!"

"Oh!" Kate said as they turned the corner sharply. "She middle-named me."

In the reflection of the stainless steel on the elevator, her dad was grinning so widely that every wrinkle was showing. After that, Kate couldn't bring herself to care about the lecture she was probably going to receive from her mom about wasting the physiotherapist's time. They would be back in ten minutes tops.

"I'm going to blame this on you," she said as the door to the elevator opened and they rolled in. "Say you were the mastermind. She's not going to lecture you right now."

"I'll just pretend to fall asleep while she's talking."

Kate hung a right as soon as they got off the elevator at a sign that read MEMORIAL GARDEN. Her only other option was taking her dad down to the street outside the hospital and she knew for a fact that her mother would kill her if she did that.

She followed the engraved signs all the way down the hall and to a pair of frosted double doors. The doors slid open, and Kate pushed the wheelchair through, scanning the yard. It was a slightly sloped square of neatly placed flagstone, raised garden beds and trickling fountains decorated with bright wildflowers. Seashells and pretty baubles lined the garden beds that spilled over with hearty growth and tall, climbing greenery. Giant trellis ladders looped from one garden bed to the next, letting ivy climb to its content. At the back of the garden sat a pair of benches painted in hues of sky blue.

It was the kind of peace that she imagined people always meant to look for.

She pulled up to the bench, and her father climbed out of the wheelchair and sat down, holding his arm out for her, appreciating the change of scenery. She tucked herself beside him like she was five and not thirty.

"Your mother tells me you've met our new ranch hand."

"Nathan? Yeah, he's something," she said sarcastically, though perhaps she didn't quite mean it the same way she would have a week ago.

Oddly enough, he'd become sort of a fixture in her day-to-day life. An integral part of it, really, if she was telling the truth. He was there in the mornings, drinking coffee at her parents' place more often than not. He was in the stables mucking stalls, or in the fields with the horses. Somehow, he became a little more ingrained in her world every single day. And now she'd been pulled into his, whether by his intentions or a force of weather. She'd met his friends, watched with fascination as he stood out before the majesty of a thunderstorm, doing the one thing he loved most in the world. Surprisingly, she didn't hate every minute of it. In fact, she sort of loved it. And at night he was on the porch of the guest house, enjoying the sounds of the ranch as it slipped into darkness—crickets and croaking frogs and wind chimes with the soft bray of horses—the same way she had most of her life.

Nathan was just suddenly everywhere, as if he'd always been there.

As if he was always meant to be.

"I know he doesn't have the most experience," her dad said thoughtfully, "but he was willing to learn. He kept up with everything I asked of him. And there's something to be said about that kind of work ethic in a person."

"He's not terrible," Kate finally relented.

Her dad chuckled, patting her knee, nodding in that way he did when he knew he was exactly right.

Chapter Nine

Thunder rumbled somewhere far away, and despite the fact that she was barely awake, Kate's first thought was of taking pictures in the rain. Morning had dawned dull and gray, and as she reached the bottom of the stairs in search of breakfast, Kate found her mom puttering around the kitchen. The scent of blueberry muffins filled the entire room, and a thousand things were happening on every available inch of counter space. Warm muffins cooled on silver trays. Dirty bowls piled high in the sink, bubbly water threatening to overflow. Her mom whirled between everything with a hand mixer that dripped gooey batter and a bowl on her hip. The oven timer sang, signaling another batch was done. And beyond the patio door, birds squawked a wary song.

"Want some help?" Kate said just as her mom opened her mouth to beg, "Can you grab those?"

Kate took the oven mitts from the counter and pulled the muffins out, shutting off the timer. She placed them on a rack to cool just as her mom dropped another batch of scooped muffin tins in front of her to put back in the oven.

"How long?" Kate asked as she closed the oven door and adjusted the timer.

"Twenty minutes." Her mom shut the water off to the sink with her elbow before it overflowed. She smiled at Kate. "Good timing. Everything sort of got away from me for a second there."

Kate chuckled. "Looks like it. What's all this for anyway?"

"I thought I'd take them up to the hospital later when I visit your father. The staff all work so hard taking care of him and goodness knows your father is as stubborn as they come."

Kate climbed onto a stool, and her mom pushed coffee and a hot, buttery muffin in front of her. It was a small piece of perfection this early in the morning.

"Sounds like a storm is passing," her mom said.

Kate looked up from her breakfast, wondering about the darkening clouds on the horizon. There was a coffee mug and a plate full of crumbs beside her.

Nathan's.

He must have come and gone before she was up, talking business with her mom.

Another boom of thunder echoed. It still sounded distant. Maybe so far it might not even sweep this way. But if Kate knew anything about the unpredictable summer weather, it was that one storm always gave way to another. "I should go make sure the horses are okay. See if Nathan needs help with anything."

Her mom's eyebrows shot up.

"What?"

"Nothing. It's just nice to see you offering to help."

"And when have I ever not been a nice person?"

Her mother walked around the counter and wrapped her arms around Kate, squeezing her head so hard Kate almost slopped her coffee everywhere.

Her mom didn't say anything, just hugged her and then busied herself with Nathan's dishes. She got like that sometimes, quiet and emotional, where no words seemed right. It had been a lot lately for her mom to handle, and Kate was amazed every day at how strong and sturdy she was through it all. For a second, Kate wanted to inquire about the finances, wanted to ask if she could help alleviate some of that burden from her mother's shoulders.

But it wasn't the right time.

Maybe it never would be.

"Thanks for breakfast," she said quietly before slipping on her shoes and heading out the door for the stables.

The air was heavy and humid as she took that first breath. She inhaled deeply, each subsequent breath getting stuck in her lungs. It was the kind of weather that bred thunder and lightning.

She made her way to the stables. It was quiet inside, and Kate walked straight through to the other side of the building, leading to the pasture. Shade was there among the other horses, grazing contentedly. She looked around for Nathan and found him refilling one of the water troughs with a hose.

"Morning," he said as she approached.

Kate stopped beside him, leaning against a fence post. "Mom thinks it's going to rain."

"She's a smart lady."

"Do you think we should bring the horses in?" she said. A little rain wouldn't hurt them. It was warm out. They had plenty of grass to eat. And it wasn't like they couldn't access a pasture shelter if they wanted—though thunder and lightning posed more of a problem.

He looked up and off into the distance for a minute, considering something. "I don't think it's going to swing this way. All the weather radars show the storm passing on the outskirts of Hatchet Lake."

"Oh," she said. "That's good."

"Speaking of passing storms," he added. "How would you feel about going out again? And before you bite my head off, Princess, Rusty and Tara extended the invitation."

Kate felt her lips twitch. She suspected he was lying. His cheeks pinked beneath the scruff on his face as she stared at him. A small part of her was tempted to call him out.

"You could just say no," he finally mumbled.

She pursed her lips and crossed her arms against her chest. "Maybe I don't want to say no."

"Well, I'm sure Rusty and Tara will be pleased."

"I'm sure they will."

He nodded. "Good."

"Great."

He passed her the hose, then gestured to the stables. "I'm gonna go finish mucking out the stalls."

Kate watched his reflection ripple across the top of the water in the trough.

It faded eventually, but the pulse beneath her skin only intensified.

* * *

It was almost an hour before that olive green van came trundling down the dirt road next to the ranch.

Tara jumped out, studying the property with an artist's eye. "Nice place," she said.

Kate grinned, walking out of the stables to meet them. In the distance, one of the horses whinnied. Tara turned her head to follow the sound with an intrigued look.

Nathan walked up behind Kate, dusting his hands off on his jeans. "I know you're usually the lie-down-in-the-wild-for-hours type," he said to Tara, "but if you want to get in some wildlife practice, the horses make good studies."

"Would you mind sometime?" Tara asked Kate.

"Feel free to stop by whenever," Kate told her.

Rusty rolled the side door open, revealing a sort of organized chaos as he strung an extension cord around his arm. He gave Nathan a pointed full-body look. "What happened to you?"

"Excuse me, I work for a living."

Rusty snorted. "Smells like it."

"Watch yourself, pal," Nathan threatened but there was hardly any bite to it.

Rusty swiped a pile of junk from two converted seats that doubled as the mini dining area and collapsed a small table against the wall. He pulled the straps of a seat belt free for her. "M'lady," he said, gesturing from Kate to the newly revealed space.

"Don't start that," Tara said to him, though she inclined her head to Kate. "Please hurry, before he launches into a full Shakespearian monologue."

Kate climbed in and sat down. There were more cords than last time, each of them emerging from a laptop sitting on the modified kitchen counter. A spiraling green storm system crawled across the screen on repeat.

Rusty slid through to the front of the van and plopped himself down in the driver's seat. "I'm just being friendly."

"Kate doesn't understand what that means," Nathan teased.

"Just because I don't want to be *your* friend," she said.

Nathan gave her a look, hanging onto the roof of the van as he leaned inside. Beads of sweat gathered at his brow. Kate watched one fall along the tantalizing curve of his jaw.

Tantalizing?

It slipped down his neck and beneath his shirt.

Oh my god.

Heat flamed beneath both her cheeks, and she just barely resisted the urge to melt into a puddle of embarrassment.

Nathan glanced up at the sky as a gust of wind kicked up and ruffled his dark hair. He tapped the roof twice. "All right, then. Buckle up. Adventure awaits."

Tara climbed into the passenger seat next to Rusty.

"So," Kate asked Tara. "Where are we headed?"

"Here." Tara tossed her a tablet. It landed in her lap. The giant green storm system crawled across the screen. Nathan climbed in and sat in the empty chair across from Kate, leaning forward to examine the tablet.

"This looks…"

"Wicked," Rusty supplied.

"Big?"

"It's blowing a little far past us," Tara explained. "But we're gonna try to catch the very edge of it."

"I think we already are," Rusty said, kicking up the windshield wipers one notch. And just like that, they were off, racing down the dirt roads.

A clap of thunder sounded. For a moment Kate could've sworn they were right under the storm, only the black clouds were still swirling in the distance.

Nathan whistled. "She's a strong one!"

Rusty glanced at them through the rearview mirror. "We'll get so close you'll be able to feel the thunder in your bones!"

They drove toward a looming patch of darkness. Daylight seemed to shrink all around them like it was suddenly the middle of the night. Kate leaned forward, watching the clouds pile higher and higher as she stared out the windshield. "I still don't know if you three are brave for driving into this or completely reckless."

"It's the price of our art." Tara shot Kate a grin over her shoulder, lifting her camera and giving it a little kiss. "And in the grand scheme of things, we've been in way worse situations for a shot."

"Don't even ask about Australia," Nathan said and now all Kate wanted to do was hear that story.

"Yeah, this is nothing compared to that. Totally safe," Rusty agreed, leaning over the wheel to get a good look at the sky. "It's hardly talking."

As if in answer, a roll of thunder trembled overhead.

"Someone just posted a wicked-looking storm swell on Twitter," Tara said.

"How far?" Nathan asked, scrolling his own phone for info.

"Like twelve miles from here." Tara gestured to a signpost. "Cut over to Highway 4."

Rusty made a sharp turn onto an uneven farmer's road, and for a second, Kate could swear the van was about to break into a dozen pieces.

Then an alarm started to ding.

"What is that?" Tara said, setting her camera aside to peer over Rusty's shoulder. "Are you serious?"

"What?" Nathan asked.

"He's running on fumes."

"Man, seriously?"

"You didn't fill up before we left?"

"No, Tara, I was sort of busy organizing your menagerie of storm tracking equipment."

Tara opened her mouth and made a face but nothing came out.

"There's a gas station like two miles from here," Kate said. "Just before the junction."

"I forgot we had a local in the van," Rusty joked. "Who knew you'd come in so handy?"

"Don't get too excited," Kate said. "If it's a horse trail, I can find it. Anything too far out of town and I'll be absolutely no help."

"I've never understood horses," Rusty said. "They freak me out."

Kate laughed. "Why?"

"I don't know. They're freakishly tall. And then people ride them around. I don't get it."

"Some people just aren't horse people," she agreed.

"He just dislikes all farm animals because when he was six a goose got a hold of him and chased him around his uncle's farm," Tara said in a conspiratorial whisper.

Rusty gasped. "I told you that in confidence!"

Kate and Nathan dissolved in a fit of laughter that didn't end until they were both wiping tears from their eyes.

"Please tell me you have pictures," Nathan said.

"A home video," Rusty remarked. "My own parents didn't even save me. Just filmed while I raced around the property screaming bloody murder."

Kate's sides hurt from laughing.

"Just wait," Rusty said, glaring at Nathan. "One day you'll try to climb your ass on a horse and I will be there, waiting, camera ready."

Kate sobered after that. Had Nathan never ridden a horse? The man that mucked their stalls and fed them and rounded them up at the end of the night. A strange look must have come over her face because he glanced at her and said, "What?"

"Nothing," she answered.

When they reached the gas station, there was a line of cars parked off to the side in a gravel lot. Kate watched some of them unpack expensive-looking camera equipment from their trunks.

"Looks like you're not the only ones here chasing storms," Kate said.

Rusty and Tara lifted their hands in greeting as they passed a few familiar faces.

"It's sort of an annual thing," Nathan said. "The area attracts a lot of photographers in the summer."

"It's a good place for amateurs to start," Tara said. "No stakes. No competition. And you can pretty much bet on the next storm. Not a lot of sitting around and waiting."

"Yeah," Nathan agreed. "We've all had our fair share of sitting in bushes waiting for something to happen."

"Pro tip," Rusty said. "Bring snacks."

"Speaking of snacks," Tara said, holding out her hand.

"Do I look like a bank?" Rusty complained, though he doled out some cash from a drawer in the van. Tara pecked him on the cheek.

"C'mon," Nathan said, nudging Kate toward the door.

They followed Tara out of the van and across the lot.

A wave of frigid air-conditioning enveloped Kate as she pushed inside the cramped convenience store. The aisles were sparse in places, bare in others, already picked over by the amassing photographers.

Kate stared at an almost-empty rack of chocolate bars. The coconut delights weren't exactly calling her name.

"Cheese Poms or Onion Sticks?" Nathan asked.

Kate looked up. He was standing on the other side of the aisle, tall enough that she could make out his head and shoulders and the two bags of chips he held up.

"Aren't they at least supposed to be Cheese Puffs?"

"We've been robbed of the good stuff. Just questionable knockoffs for us."

"Oh, then definitely the Onion Sticks."

"Good call," he said.

Kate toed a box at the bottom of the shelf. "How do you feel about coconut?"

He made a face that matched how she felt on the inside. "Guess it's just these onion things," he said, looking down at the bag again. "My treat."

He wandered away to pay. Kate looked down the

aisle to where Tara was stocking up on soft drinks with Rusty's money.

Nathan waited for her by the door and the two of them headed back outside, into the heat, and she immediately started sweating.

"Got anything good?" Rusty called as they approached. He was just twisting the gas cap back on.

Tara ran up behind them and shoved a plastic bag into his arms.

"This looks expensive," he said.

Tara gave him a wicked grin. "It was."

They piled back into the van and pulled onto the road, following the distant sounds of thunder to their unknown destination.

"You guys have a pretty good setup here," Kate said, enjoying a handful of knockoff onion-flavored chips.

"Ha!" Rusty said, looking at Nathan. "And you said it was unnecessary. He refused to bunk in the van with us because, and I quote, 'I'm not cuddling up with a laptop.'"

"Where is there room for me to sleep in here?" Nathan threw a chip at him. "And I didn't say it was unnecessary. I said it took some of the fun out of it."

"Just because we prefer to have elite topographical knowledge does not mean it's not fun."

"I don't think Google Maps is elite, but okay."

"And now we have a professional storm tracker," Rusty said, clapping Tara on the shoulder.

"That I am," she agreed. "If there's an app, I have it."

"See?" Rusty said to Nathan. "Technology is your friend."

Nathan grumbled something about doing things the

old-fashioned way, but because he was also shoving a handful of chips into his mouth, no one else heard.

"Are you going to sell any of these photos?" Kate asked as Nathan offered her the chip bag again.

He shrugged. "Maybe."

Rusty made a humming noise. "It's not really about the money. More like the challenge of getting that perfect picture, you know?"

Kate had no idea.

"But it's also about the money," Tara said, and they all laughed.

A swell of black clouds began to build, lightning fracturing in the distance. Kate had hardly noticed the storm gathering again, but now she could almost feel the rumble of thunder beneath her seat.

"We should probably look for a place to pull over," Tara said. "I think we should be able to get some good shots from here without the storm raining us out."

Rusty found a pull-off on the side of the road, one overlooking a wheat field.

The sky above them was still gray, but the worst of the storm raged so far in the distance that until the thunder boomed and the lightning struck the sky, it was simply a silent shadow.

A dry heat with a strong breeze greeted them as Tara rolled open the van door. Kate jumped out, watching a wicked spark of lightning split the sky.

Tara quickly swapped the lenses on her camera, an excited smile lighting up her face. As she ran out into the field, Nathan strung his camera around his neck, framing up a shot.

Rusty reached into the back of the van and produced

a lawn chair. He set it up right in the middle of the gravel.

Music flowed from inside the van, and there was something nice about it. Kind of like when you sit in a coffee shop surrounded by dozens of other people, all simultaneously working, together but alone.

It was comforting.

"Hey, Princess." Kate looked up to find that Nathan had relocated to the roof of the van, his legs dangling over the edge. "You coming up? Best view's up here."

"Oh, how many times has that line worked!" Rusty crowed, settling down with his own camera.

Nathan threw a handful of chips at him this time. Rusty plucked one off his shirt and stuck it in his mouth.

Kate grinned, stepping up on the edge of the van and taking Nathan's offered hand. He heaved and she jumped. Before she had a second to consider what would happen if she didn't stick this landing, she plopped down on her knees. Kate turned around and scooted away from the edge to make sure she wouldn't slip off. The only thing more embarrassing than not being able to get on top of the van would be landing flat on her face by falling off it.

"Guaranteed you've never watched a storm like this before," Nathan said.

"I mean, maybe a drive-in movie. Never a drive-in thunderstorm."

He offered her the bag of chips. "Admit it. This is so much better."

"Definitely unique." Kate took a handful of chips, shoving half in her mouth.

Rusty cracked a can of soda below them and took an

exaggerated slurp, throwing his long legs out in front of him.

A flash of lightning sparked in the distance and Rusty, Nathan and Tara all simultaneously cheered. It continued like that for a while.

"How long have you known Rusty?" Kate asked Nathan, sneaking another handful of chips.

"Since he was small enough to look like a real-life Chucky doll."

Kate laughed.

"My mom has the pictures to prove it. He was terrifying."

"Guess he grew into his looks."

"Or out of them," Nathan said, quirking a brow.

"My looks have only gotten better and you know it!" Rusty called without looking back at them.

Kate lowered her voice. "What's the deal there?" she asked, throwing a chip up and catching it in her mouth. Her eyes tracked from Rusty to Tara where she stood out in the field.

"Oh, that," Nathan said. "No deal. Rusty leaves a string of brokenhearted ex-boyfriends everywhere we go and Tara's here to keep us both in line the way she did in college. This is a strictly platonic business-friendship thing we have going on, though we do spend a ridiculous amount of time together."

"Doing what you love," Kate said.

"Doing what we love," Nathan agreed. He watched the storm clouds for the right moment before snapping his next photo.

The sky flashed and the clouds swirled into a billowing mass, so tall Kate had to crane her neck to see the top of the formation. Tara was perched on a rock way out in the field now, crouched down like she meant not to startle the storm.

"So, how long have you been doing this?"

"What?"

"Chasing thunderstorms."

"It's not just the thunderstorm. It's about chasing the next shot. And pretty much my whole life," Nathan said thoughtfully. "I never really pictured myself settling in one place forever, which worked out well for the kind of photography I've done throughout my career, but lately I think I've started looking."

"For a place to settle?"

"Yeah. A place to come back to. A person to come home to. Something a little more permanent."

"Like a home base?" Kate said.

He nodded. "There's something freeing about picking up and leaving everything behind. Starting fresh in a new state. A new country. Somewhere with a new culture to understand. But sometimes I'd like to be able to go out, complete my contract and go home."

Kate could understand that. "Do you have any family you could settle close to?"

"I mean, if it felt right, though I don't think so," he said. "Don't get me wrong, I love my family, but I was the youngest of three boys. And the youngest by a fair bit, so when my siblings grew up and moved out, I was kind of left to my own devices."

Kate frowned.

"This isn't a sob story," Nathan laughed. "I honed my photography skills by keeping myself busy in the summers while my brothers worked part-time jobs and got girlfriends. They're both married with a couple kids each now. I visit on holidays and birthdays, but we all live pretty independent lives. Besides, I like forging out on my own and creating my own path." He grinned. "Might be some of that youngest sibling rivalry thing. You know, having to prove myself to my big brothers."

That, Kate was less familiar with. "You're talking to an only child here."

"Even an only child has something to prove. So, what is it? What are you chasing?"

"I'm not chasing anything," she said.

"We're all chasing something."

Kate simply shook her head. If anything, she'd spent her life running away. Away from this place. Away from her parents. Away from anything that resembled small-town life. When she was growing up all anyone could talk about was getting away from here, and Kate had felt like she would be left behind if she didn't get out.

So she had, escaping to Michigan State University for both undergrad and veterinary college.

When she met Cal, they'd settled in Grand Rapids for a while, and Kate had tried to fit in among the hustle and bustle of a bigger city. But it was hard to be a large animal vet in the city, and she'd found herself missing the very thing she'd tried to run away from—this small-town life. Maybe that was why she and Cal never really had a chance. Maybe they were just too different.

There was a click. Kate looked over as Nathan lowered his camera. He was looking at her hard. Like he was trying to spy inside her head. "You had a very contemplative look on your face."

"Like I was thinking too hard?" she said, making the joke for him.

He tilted his head but didn't take the bait. He didn't tease her. Instead, he studied her, and it almost made her breathless. "It's like you were drifting, somewhere far away."

"I guess I just always thought that when I finally got out of here and settled in a bigger city, everything would fall into place."

"No horses in the city," Nathan said.

She smiled wryly. "But there are bedazzled Pomeranians and high-maintenance Chihuahuas."

He laughed. "And yet here you are."

"Here I am." Maybe Nathan was right, and she had been chasing something. A fantasy that wasn't really about wanting a big-city life but simply craving this image of what she expected her life to be at thirty. Marriage. Family. Maybe a kid. Kate thought she'd find Mr. Right if she got out of Hatchet Lake, but it had only been one miserable relationship after another. She'd also thought she'd set up a practice taking care of people's small pets, but her heart was never in it. She would never really feel settled in a city no matter how successful her practice became.

"Guess you couldn't leave the smell of manure behind?"

"Don't make me hurt you." She glanced at the ground. "It's a long way down."

"Not long enough."

"It'd still hurt."

"Now, what kind of friend would you be then?"

"We're not friends yet."

"You sure? Not even like acquaintances?" He held his fingers out, measuring. "Just a little bit."

She rolled her eyes. It was sort of hard to deny that anything existed between them when she was sitting on top of a van with him, eating chips and having in-depth conversations about life.

"Acquaintances," she conceded. "Barely."

Nathan punched the air slowly in celebration. "Now we're talking."

Chapter Ten

Morning dawned sunny and clear. Kate peeked through a hole in the blanket that was wrapped around her head, squinting at the uncovered window. Nothing but cloudless, blue sky peeked back at her, dotted by the odd swooping crow and barn finch. She lay there long enough that she even saw what she thought was a hawk pursuing its next meal.

She sat up slowly, blinking herself to life, feeling the last bits of sleep fleetingly fall away. Her hair stuck up in something that once resembled a bun but was now just a tight knot of terror. She could feel the tacky, weird shape held together with the remains of an elastic band, and she was already dreading the moment she had to unravel it.

First order of the day seemed like a shower. She ran her tongue over her teeth, coated in a fine layer of film. Yeah, the bathroom was definitely priority number one.

Kate threw her legs over the side of the bed, recoiling for a moment before she realized it was only her clothes from yesterday, bunched up in a pile. She must have stripped and dumped them there last night. Truthfully, she hardly remembered coming up to bed. At some point Rusty had rolled up outside the ranch and dumped her and Nathan off, then they'd marched straight to the stables to finish evening chores and let the horses in. Kate had spent extra time brushing down Shade and the other horses while Nathan sorted out an order of straw bales that had been delivered.

She'd been so exhausted by the time the day drew to a close that she'd gone straight to bed without even touching the dinner her mom had wrapped and left in the fridge for her.

Kate padded to the bathroom and stepped beneath a hot stream of water, letting it absorb her groan. No matter how many calves she helped deliver, there was something different about the work it took to muck stalls and chase horses around with more than just a medical bag. She'd forgotten about this part.

Kate stretched beneath the water, wanting to sink into the heat forever. As she did, her mind wandered, inevitably landing on Nathan. The fact that he had somehow crept into her life and wedged himself somewhere closer to friendship than she'd ever meant to let happen was concerning. At the rate things were changing, she was going to lose this stupid bet and have to admit to her parents that he was the best ranch hand they'd ever hired.

Was that the truth?

From what she'd deduced yesterday, the man had

never even ridden a horse. But he was kind and hard-working and treated the animals well.

Animals could tell a good person from a bad one, and she trusted that more than anything.

So, while he certainly wasn't the most knowledgeable ranch hand her parents could have found, he was dedicated, and that was what this place needed right now.

Kate thought about Nathan while she scrubbed the tangles from her hair.

The dimple in his cheek.

The way he looked, perched up there on top of the van, capturing moments with his camera.

The way his hand felt in hers as he pulled her up to sit beside him.

The way her pulse jumped when he called her *Princess*.

Kate groaned, rubbing the soap from her eyes. These were not the thoughts friends were supposed to have. And despite the fact that Sarah would tell her to go for it, Kate didn't think she could handle another relationship that would inevitably end up like the one with Cal.

Nathan was a photographer. At some point he would be offered a contract that was too good to pass up and he would be gone, gallivanting off to whatever far corner of the globe called to him.

And Kate would be tied to whatever small town she found work in. Small towns and globetrotting adventures didn't really mix.

She wasn't even going to entertain the thought any longer. She wouldn't open her heart up to that kind of hurt.

The best they could be was friends.

Maybe.

Kate lathered up the rest of her body. She rinsed and shut the water off in an impressive ninety seconds before stepping out of the shower and wrapping herself in not one but two fluffy towels.

It felt like a fluffy towel sort of morning.

She walked back to her room and spied the blinking blue light on her phone. When she turned it on, there were a few notifications on her home screen. One of which was a text message with half a dozen pictures attached. They were all from yesterday's storm, and they looked amazing.

Someone had also captured her and Nathan sitting on top of the van. There was a genuine smile on her face in the photo.

Kate realized she'd had fun yesterday.

She was happy.

Something stirred in her gut. It felt as if it had been forever since she'd been able to say that.

There was a message attached to the photos that must be from Rusty, because the contact was saved in Kate's phone as Most Gorgeous Redhead You Know. The text read, Glad you came out with us yesterday, with about twenty emojis of a thundercloud.

Kate grinned stupidly at her phone for at least thirty seconds before a chill finally set in and she marched about the room, shimmying into an old pair of jeans and a plain tee.

Her phone started to buzz, and from across the room, she could see Sarah's face lighting up the screen.

"Good morning," Sarah sang when Kate answered. Parker imitated her in the background.

"Morning," Kate said, putting the phone on speaker before returning to the bathroom to squeeze the water from her hair. She took a brush to it, wincing as she pulled through the knots.

"How is everything?"

"I am exhausted. I forgot how much work it was lugging things around the stables and now I appreciate Nathan and his muscles all the more."

She hadn't meant anything by it, not really, but Sarah squealed on the other end of the phone, making Parker shriek with glee, and Kate had to turn the volume down a couple notches.

"Something happened!" Sarah said immediately, like a bloodhound picking up a trail.

"What are you freaking out about?"

"There was a distinct lack of disdain when you said his name. And the offhanded mention of muscles. What happened? Give me all the details. A steamy kiss in the barn? A roll in the hay?"

Kate burst out laughing. "You and your damn romance novels. I meant muscles in the more practical sense, you know, like a body that could drag straw bales around that wasn't necessarily mine."

A flash of an image filled her mind: Nathan sweeping her off the porch the other day and throwing her over his shoulder to carry her to the truck. If she told Sarah that, the woman would probably have a stroke, and Kate would have to fly out to pick up Parker.

"Hmm," Sarah hummed. "All right, keep your secrets, Kate Cardiff, I'll find out soon enough."

"There's nothing to find out."

"That's what people say when there is something they're trying to hide."

"Parker, tell your mommy she is crazy."

"Crazy!" Parker shrieked.

"Thanks. That's all I need him to be screaming the next time we go grocery shopping."

Kate chuckled at that image, then bit her lip. She considered telling Sarah about the thunderstorms. About chasing the rain down dirt roads to take photos with Nathan and his friends. She also thought about telling her how it made her heart race. But she was afraid Sarah would read far too much into it. And after Cal, she was afraid to get too involved in anything if it wasn't exactly right. So, for now, she stayed quiet because she wanted these moments just for herself. It was easier to separate it that way. Easier to put up a wall between her head and other pesky little things like her heart. She came back to the conversation as Sarah veered onto the topic of work.

"I haven't re-signed my contract yet. I think Parker and I are ready for a move."

"Move. Move. Move!" Parker chanted in the background.

There was a crash and Kate envisioned his toys being catapulted across the room. "A move where?"

"Not sure yet. I'd sort of like to try something new, but emergency medicine does allow for the most movement. They're always short-staffed in that area."

"Maybe something hot and tropical," Kate suggested.

Sarah sighed dreamily. "Wouldn't that be nice."

Kate threw her hair in a ponytail, taking her phone with her. She let Sarah and Parker babble for another few minutes while she tidied up her room and threw the comforter over her bed.

"Well, I better get this monkey to the sitter," Sarah said.

"Okay, I'll talk to you later."

"You bet you will. And you better have more details by then."

Kate snorted, saying her goodbyes before hanging up the phone. She tiptoed her way downstairs. The house was oddly quiet, and Kate wondered if her mom had gone out. She found her keys and wallet on the counter, so that answered that question.

"You're up!" her mom said suddenly, walking in through the back door. She shed a pair of gardening gloves and an oversize, floppy sun hat. "Breakfast?"

"Sure," Kate said, letting her mom place a giant blueberry muffin and coffee in front of her.

"The hospital called."

"Hmm?" Kate inquired around a mouthful of muffin.

"They said your dad's doing well and he can probably look at coming home by the end of the week."

"That's good news!"

"It'll be nice to have him here," her mom agreed. "As long as I can keep him in his rehab program."

Kate smirked. "If anyone can, it's you."

"I do have many long years of practice forcing your father to do things he doesn't like for the good of his health."

"Exactly," Kate said. "This'll be a walk in the park."

It was easy to joke with her now that they knew he was coming home. There'd been this sense of uncertainty surrounding everything since the heart attack. He'd spent days in the hospital, recovering, and they hadn't wanted to say anything for fear of jinxing it. But now it was like they both let out this metaphorical breath they'd been holding.

Now things would get back to normal.

Whatever that looked like.

"Plus, I'll be here," Kate added. "I can just guilt-trip him if it comes down to it."

Her mom laughed but squeezed her hand. "Your father does hate to disappoint you."

Kate gulped the rest of her coffee and left her dishes to soak in the soapy water in the sink. Then she headed out to the stables to meet Nathan. By the time she arrived, he was already finishing up the morning chores.

"Good morning, sleepyhead," he said.

She watched the muscles bulge in his arms as he hauled a bale of straw out of the walkway. Now she sort of felt bad for not elaborating on her muscles comment earlier, at least for Sarah's sake. Despite everything else she thought, Nathan was probably perfectly suited to Sarah's spicy romance fantasies.

Kate promptly stopped thinking about that before the blush she felt could spread down her face. "So," she said, "it has come to my attention that you have never been on a horse."

"Where did you get that information?"

Kate shrugged. "Just something Rusty said."

"Well, that information is false."

"Oh, really?"

"I rode a horse as a boy. It promptly left the group we were with and took an unmarked side trail through the trees. Did not respond at all to my commands. And then proceeded to drag me through a bunch of brush like a rag doll. Not my fondest memory."

Kate chuckled. "I can see how that would scar someone."

"Your laughter is giving me a very unsympathetic vibe."

"I'm laughing with you, not at you."

"Who said I'm laughing? This was a very serious incident from my childhood. I'm still processing it."

"Right," Kate said, biting the inside of her cheek to keep from smiling.

"I'm not afraid of them, if that's what you're thinking. Just not really in a hurry to get back on one."

"Maybe you just didn't have the right teacher," Kate said.

"And you think that's you?"

"C'mon, ranch hand." She pulled an adult helmet from the rack on the wall. "Let's give it another try."

"Fine, but if I get dragged away into the woods by another horse, I don't think this friendship is gonna make it."

"Acquaintance-ship," Kate said, pushing him down the stables toward Samson's stall. He was the youngest of the horses the family owned, but also the biggest, making him the best option to support all of Nathan's muscles. *Wouldn't Sarah just get a kick out of that.*

Kate opened the door of the stall and Nathan walked in behind her, helmet tucked under his arm, looking like a scared toddler. It was almost adorable.

"What do I do?"

"First we saddle," Kate said. "It's easier out here." She inclined her head and Nathan led Samson into the main aisle while Kate retrieved Shade. "Hey, girl," she said, leading Shade out of her stall. She brayed excitedly, probably eager to be out on the trails. Kate had no idea how long it had been.

She pulled the gear off a post, handing a saddle to Nathan before grabbing one for Shade. She went through the motions and Nathan copied exactly what she did.

Kate saddled Shade like it had been mere hours since their last ride and not years.

Satisfied with the fit, she checked Samson, tightening things where they needed to be tightened and straightening them where they needed to be straightened.

"Are you gonna need a step up?" she asked, turning around. "I think we have a stool around here."

Nathan looked down at her, closer than she anticipated he'd be. She could smell his bodywash and the mint on his breath. He smirked, and her heart skipped a beat. Then she handed him the reins and stepped out of the way so he could haul himself onto the horse. It took him a second to get his bearings but eventually Samson settled under his weight and Nathan grinned at her. How he went from a smoldering hunk to a giddy five-year-old in the span of a minute she didn't understand.

Kate turned around and pulled herself up on Shade, leading the horse from the stables. Once they were outside, Kate turned Shade around, facing Nathan and Samson. "You've probably figured it out by now, but you bump your heels gently against his sides to ask Samson to move forward. 'Whoa' and a little pullback on the reins will get him to stop." Kate demonstrated everything on Shade. "This is to get him to move left. And this is right."

"When do we get to run?" Nathan asked.

Kate chuckled. "Let's just get out on the trail and see how you do." She led them both to the edge of the fence line and hopped down long enough to let them both clear the gate before locking it up again. The last thing she wanted to do was go chasing down horses. It wouldn't be the first time it'd happened, but she didn't really want to do that today.

Samson went prancing past her, and Nathan made a horrified face.

"He's just excited," Kate laughed.

"He probably wants to run off some of this energy."

"Maybe we'll work our way up to a trot."

"On a scale of zero to ten, how fast are we talking?"

"You've got four gaits. Walk, trot, canter and gallop."

"We're only getting up to speed two? Are you kidding me?"

"I'm being a responsible teacher." Kate put one foot in the stirrup, grabbed the pommel and hoisted herself back into the saddle. She picked up the reins and clicked her tongue. Shade set off in an easy walk as the sun crested the tree line.

As the sunlight split between the trees, it painted the pasture with shadows of golden fire. Kate had missed this sight. Dust jumped beneath the horses, cast up by their hooves as the trail turned from packed earth to the rich mud of the forest. They followed the trail through the woods for a time and then the trees broke away to an open field.

"You want to try a trot?" she asked, clicking her heels to tell Shade to pick up the pace.

Nathan did the same and grinned as Samson responded. "Should we race?"

Kate grinned, digging her heels in hard. "C'mon, girl," she yelled, urging Shade on. It was addictive, the feeling of the horse flying beneath her. She couldn't believe she had gone this long without it.

"Cheater!" Nathan called from behind her. "I thought we were both going to trot." He clicked his tongue, holding tight to the reins, keeping Samson in check. It was clear the horse wanted to run, and Kate was impressed with the amount of control Nathan had over him. Maybe he was more of a natural than he thought.

"Are you sure you haven't done this as an adult?"

"Why?" Nathan teased. "Are you impressed?"

"Don't let it go to your head."

"Too late."

They trotted through the field to where the trail picked up again, sloping gently up a hill. Kate pulled ahead, keeping Samson in line in case he got excited. As they crested the hill, Hatchet Lake unfolded below them, and Kate remembered this exact view. The same cabins. The same campground. The same sunrise pouring over the water like liquid fire.

"I wish I'd brought my camera," Nathan breathed.

"This is one of my favorite places," Kate said, climbing out of the saddle. When she said it, she realized that she'd forgotten about it, and something tightened in her chest. She gave Shade's nose a rub, looping the reins over her palm.

Nathan climbed down beside her, holding tight to Samson's reins. "Tara and Rusty would love this."

"We should bring them sometime." *Bring them while we can*, she wanted to say.

"Why do you sound sad?" he asked.

She lifted a shoulder. "I guess sometimes you take things for granted, expecting that they'll always be there."

"You think your parents are going to sell?"

"I don't know," Kate said. "I haven't pushed the topic while my dad's been in the hospital. But now he's coming home, and I don't know what that means." She fiddled with Shade's noseband, smoothing it down.

They walked together for a time, leading the horses along the trail, both of them just enjoying the view until Kate couldn't help but ask, "How long do you think you'll stay?"

Nathan shrugged. "I probably won't start looking for a new contract until the end of summer. Once the weather starts to turn."

"No more thunderstorms to chase," Kate said.

"Exactly. But I won't just up and leave your parents in the lurch," he said. "If that's what you're worried about."

Surprisingly—or selfishly—that was not what she'd been thinking about. She'd actually been wondering how much more time she would have with him. How many more mornings they might be able to sneak away to the peak overlooking Hatchet Lake. It was different, having someone to share it with.

Everything was a little different with Nathan, and maybe there was a part of her that was a little unnerved by that. But mostly she was just sad to think that this strange thing that was developing between them would end eventually.

He would go back to his real life, and she would go back to hers, and it would be like these moments never existed. Maybe that was why he liked capturing moments so much with his camera. "You should bring your camera next time," she agreed, going back to the comment he'd made earlier.

He nodded. She didn't expect him to continue, but silence did funny things to people. Sometimes it was just easier to fill.

"So," he said. "You brought me out to your secret

hilltop. This must mean you like me enough to call us friends."

"I wouldn't go that far." She smiled at how easily he shifted the conversation. At how comfortable she could be around him. "I tolerate you."

"For my dashing good looks?"

"More for your ability to muck a stall in under ten minutes. And for your friends. Rusty saved himself in my phone as 'Most Gorgeous Redhead You Know.'"

"Rusty makes the contact list before I do?"

"What can I say," Kate said. "When you know, you know."

"I see how easily I was replaced." Nathan shook his head in mock defeat. "But just so you know, Rusty won't step foot in a barn or any other place that might involve the word manure. And we've already established he doesn't like horses. So you might want to choose your friends more wisely."

"You know, my mom's said the same thing to me. Not about friends, but about other people."

"You mean like significant others?"

"Yeah."

"Am I about to get a tell-all into Kate Cardiff's dating history?"

"Not much to tell," she said. "Everything just sort of…ends."

"So your mom thinks you're a bad judge of character?"

Kate's jaw dropped. "She does not think that. She just thinks I sabotage myself by getting into relationships with people that aren't right for me."

"And that would be like who?"

"People that are just genuinely uninterested in a long-

term relationship," Kate quipped. "Or any kind of mo-
nogamy, apparently."

Nathan howled with laughter and Kate was taken
aback. Sarah had called her an idiot for entertaining
the relationship with Cal for as long as she did, but she
had never outright laughed at her.

"You *are* a terrible judge of character. I'm siding
with your mom on this one."

"You hardly know me!"

Nathan sobered at that. "Look, Kate, if someone was
stupid enough to cheat on you, then they were completely the wrong person from the start."

Kate felt the breath in her lungs stall. She didn't
know what to say. She was pretty sure that was a compliment. Nathan licked his lips and she was drawn to
the sight.

They stopped walking, the horses boxing them in
from either side, and just stared at each other for a long
moment.

"As your almost-not-quite-a-friend-yet, I'm going to
have to ask you to have higher standards for yourself."

"That's funny," Kate said. "My best friend Sarah
thinks I just have to get back on the horse."

Nathan snorted at the expression, but his words
were quiet, almost whispered. "Can't it be both? Just
rip off the Band-Aid but maybe with the right person
this time."

Kate's heart was racing, her pulse fluttering in her
wrists and at her neck and in the center of her chest. She
felt like she might explode. "Sounds nice," she agreed
just as quietly, and for a second, they were drifting toward each other. Kate looked at Nathan, from his lips
to the gray eyes that were blown wide. Wild and dark.

And then Shade moved, jostling Kate, and the spell broke. She snapped out of it, and turned around to climb back into the saddle. "We should get going," she said.

Nathan nodded, and she wondered if she was projecting when she thought he looked puzzled as he climbed back onto Samson.

Kate clicked her tongue, setting out at an easy trot, and smiled to herself when Nathan kept pace on Samson, looking comfortable in his seat. Whatever *almost* just happened between them, they left it behind, and by the time they reached the stables again, everything felt normal. So normal that they let the horses out to roam the pasture and even went to town together to retrieve an order supply.

And there was nothing like hauling supplies out of the truck for the better part of an hour and sweating through her shirt to remind her of just what exactly they were both doing there.

When they finished up, they settled the horses for the night. "You want something to drink?" Kate asked. It was the least she could do. Her mother would probably be proud of her hospitality.

"Sure," Nathan said immediately.

Kate gestured to the house. "Mom's always got decaf on at this time. But there's probably something stronger if you'd prefer that."

"I'll take whatever you're having."

Nathan followed her up the porch steps, holding the door open as she slipped by him, brushing close enough for her skin to flush.

Inside, the warmth quickly dissipated when she spied her mom clutching her phone and racing frantically about the kitchen.

"Mom?" Kate said, her heart immediately in her stomach. "What's going on?"

"The hospital just called," she said. "Where are my keys?"

"What did they say?" Kate asked, following her mom around the kitchen island. "Did something happen? Another heart attack?"

"They don't think so." Her mom didn't even look at her, just blindly gathered her things from the counter, throwing her wallet into her purse, moving in a way that told Kate she wasn't even registering what was happening right now.

"What does that mean?"

"I just… I don't have all the answers right now, Kate!" For the first time her mom looked genuinely scared.

Kate's heart beat painfully beneath her skin. "Okay," she said, somehow quiet and calm. Mustering a clear head, she picked up her mom's keys from the counter. "I'll drive."

Chapter Eleven

Complications.

Kate hated that word.

In every sense.

Relationships could be complicated. Family could be complicated. Handsome photographers that lived and worked on your family's ranch could be complicated. Health…that could be complicated, too.

Kate had reached her limit.

She rubbed her hands over her face, then glared at the buttons on the coffee machine again. This shouldn't be that difficult, and yet she couldn't for the life of her figure out how it worked beyond eating her money. Kate was about ready to give up, get in the car and drive to the nearest McDonald's when a familiar voice called her name.

"What are you doing here?" she asked, looking over

to find Nathan coming down the abandoned hallway. It was late. Past eleven already. Only family members with sick relatives were left now to pace the halls, waiting for news that never seemed to come.

Kate never wanted to step foot in another hospital as long as she lived, especially this old addition that they were currently in which didn't seem to think a cafeteria was necessary.

"I wanted to make sure you were okay," he said when he reached her. "See if you or your mom need anything."

Kate swallowed the bulge in her throat because for some stupid reason she now wanted to cry. Wanted to sink down to the floor in front of this stupid machine and cry until there were no tears left.

She knocked her fist against the coffee machine instead. "We're good," she said.

"Really?"

"Really."

"Because you look like you're about to throw down with this coffee machine."

Kate gave him a warning look.

"Here," he said gently, shifting her to the side. He fiddled with the buttons, and a steaming stream of black coffee emerged from the machine.

Kate wanted to kiss him.

"When you spend enough time in strange airports waiting on connections, you become adept at navigating all these strange coffee machines that haven't been updated since the eighties."

"Thank you," she said when the paper cup was full. He didn't say anything about the way her hand trembled, but they both saw it, so she didn't even bother fighting him when he steered her toward an alcove with those hard-backed chairs.

It was vacant but for some lone magazines that probably hadn't been read since last year.

"What happened?" Nathan asked.

"Pulmonary embolism." Kate sat down with her coffee, finding that the words stuck between her teeth.

"And that is?" Nathan began. "You're going to have to say it in nonmedical terms for me."

"It's rare, that's what it is," Kate said, and it sounded like she was complaining. To whom, she wasn't sure. But of all the complications that could have happened, not only was a pulmonary embolism supposed to be rare, but it was also extremely dangerous. The kind of thing her dad very well could have died from. And wouldn't that just be the kicker? If the man survived a heart attack, but it was the recovery period that actually took him out?

Kate shook her head, playing with the edge of the paper cup in her hands. She realized she was squeezing the cup when Nathan touched her hand gently. Immediately, she loosened her grip before she could spill coffee everywhere.

"It's basically a blood clot," she said. "One that traveled to his lungs and blocked blood flow."

"Was it caused by the heart attack?" Nathan asked, his brows meeting neatly in the center of his forehead as he tried to put the pieces together. "Or the stent placement?"

"It's hard to know," Kate admitted. "These clots usually form in deep veins like in the legs. Then they break free and travel to the lungs, which makes it difficult for the heart to pump blood to the rest of the body. Then your blood pressure drops, which delivers less oxygen to the rest of your body and—"

"It's okay," Nathan said as she cut off abruptly. "You don't have to explain how it works anymore. I get it."

Kate nodded. "It's possible that this is a complication, or maybe just a terrible coincidence." She didn't know which was worse. "Another day. A few more hours. He might have been home when this happened and there wouldn't have been anything we could have done but try to race him back to the hospital." *And the ranch is so far away*, she thought helplessly. "He probably would have died."

"That's terrifying," Nathan said. He didn't try to make it better with platitudes and she appreciated that.

It really was terrifying. She imagined it now. Imagined her dad being at home with her mother when the symptoms started. Shortness of breath, chest pain, loss of consciousness. They would have assumed it was another heart attack. And her mom would have lost him when mere hours ago he was well enough to be discharged.

Kate would have lost him.

"Can they treat it?" Nathan asked quietly.

"They caught it early, which is a good thing," Kate explained. "They'll run more tests, see what they can do about it. They might find he needs medication to help treat this once he leaves the hospital. More of a long-term thing." She rubbed her eyes with her hand, massaging away the tears that threatened to fall.

Nathan did something unexpected then. He took the coffee from her hand, put the cup on the small table beside them, then he wrapped her in a hug.

For a moment, Kate didn't know what to do. She

just froze. But then his warmth seeped into her, his steady calm ebbing with the beat of his heart, and she sank into the embrace. His shirt was soft against her face and sweet-smelling. She rubbed her nose along his shoulder, letting his scent overwhelm her, letting his arms support her.

It was a strange feeling, the ease with which he'd ingrained himself into her life. Even when she was with Cal, it was never really like this. They just existed in the same space most of the time, but not *for* each other. Nathan was different. He filled up her space until she felt like she could finally stop falling. Like he was somewhere safe to land.

But this wasn't that. This was just a hug. A friendly, supportive hug. He could tell she needed something to ground her. To pull her from the tumbling thoughts inside her own head and bring her back to the moment.

She pulled away slowly.

"You okay?" he asked.

She lifted her shoulder. "Don't say it."

"What? Make an untimely remark about us being friends now?"

"Yeah, that."

"Okay, I won't."

She swiped at her eyes, and he pulled her back in for another hug, his chin resting on the top of her head. She'd never realized just how tall he was, even with them sitting down.

"Now what happens?" he asked.

"Now we wait to see if the treatments work."

"How do they—"

"Anticoagulants," she said, sensing his question. "Possibly surgery if he doesn't respond to that." Kate had sat with her dad for a while, watching the medication bag hang from the intravenous pole above his head. Watching the clear solution drip into his veins. Watching the nurses flit in and out of the room, charting notes, checking vitals. Watching the residents pop in and out of the room, double- and triple-checking their orders.

It had all made her too anxious to stay. Her mother was a resolute statue, perched in a chair by her father's side, her hand held tight to his. But Kate had felt like she was climbing the walls. She had to take a breather. Get some coffee. *Do* something.

"I don't know how long we'll be here," Kate said. "Mom won't leave his side and I don't blame her."

"Neither do I," Nathan agreed.

Kate knew they would have to drag her mother out to get her to leave now. She wondered briefly if there had ever been anyone that Nathan had loved that much.

"C'mon," he said.

"C'mon where?"

"You're gonna be here for a while, right? Might as well be more comfortable and these chairs are not it."

He stood, offering her his hand. Kate took it, letting him pull her to her feet. She wasn't sure what he had in mind, but she let him lead her. Let him take control, if only for a few minutes, because it was so nice to just shut her brain off. To stop making decisions that didn't seem to matter one way or the other.

When they exited the hospital, Nathan led her across the clear glass bridge to the parking garage. They took the elevator to the top. To the exposed roof where his truck was parked.

He stopped by the back door and pulled out a bundle of blankets before tossing them into the bed of the truck. Then he climbed into the bed and held his hand out for her. Kate took it, pushing her foot off the wheel well. One moment she was suspended in the air. The next she was standing so close to him that she could feel the heat of his skin.

Together they spread out the blankets on the bed of the truck and lay down side by side. It was a warm, clear night, and all Kate could see from here were the stars.

"This has to be better than those chairs."

"It is," she assured him, getting lost in the constellations. She traced them with her eyes. The North Star to Ursa Minor. Ursa Minor to Ursa Major. Orion and his belt.

It had been a long time since she stargazed. She couldn't remember exactly when, but she'd probably been a girl, sneaking out to sit in one of the fields with her dad long after her mother had told her to go to bed. Kate had loved those moments. Moments with just the two of them and the endless world stretched out like some kind of fantastical puzzle she was meant to solve. She didn't remember when she'd stopped stargazing or why. It seemed likely that she thought she'd outgrown it. Like so many other things that you simply stopped doing once you left those childhood years behind. It seemed ridiculous now that she ever thought that, and she wondered how many nights of stargazing she had missed out on with her dad.

Kate glanced over at Nathan, finding him looking up at the stars too, arms pillowed behind his head. "Did you stargaze as a child?" she asked.

He shook his head. "I grew up in New York. Just smog and dust and city lights there blocking out the sky. But when I moved away to chase photography contracts, that's when I started looking at the stars. I've probably lain out under the stars in every corner of the world."

He talked about those moments reverently, like they were something he held close to his heart.

"It was comforting in a way." He spoke in the quiet that stretched between them. "No matter how far I went in this world, the stars were constant, and it always felt like coming home, even when I didn't necessarily have one to come back to."

She remembered what he'd said that day in the rain, sitting on top of the van, about wanting that one place he could return to over and over. A home base he could come back to once his camera roll was filled and his contracts were finished.

"I used to sit out and watch the stars with my dad," she said. "He would sneak me out of the house after my mom already thought I was in bed. It always felt like our secret, but now I'm pretty sure she was in on it."

Kate had never considered how fortunate she was to have those moments. How lucky she was to grow up on the ranch, always having a place to call home. Even leaving as a young adult and trying to make her way in the world, Kate always knew the ranch was there. Always considered that home. She hoped Nathan would find that one day.

"Your mom definitely knew you were sneaking out," Nathan laughed. "That woman knows everything."

"It's one of her many talents," Kate agreed. Somehow it felt like the world was a completely different place out here with Nathan. Like if she closed her eyes, she could pretend for a second that none of this was real. That her dad was fine. Home. Curled up on the sofa with her mom where they were supposed to be.

"I think there must be a sixth sense parents develop when it comes to their kids."

"Must be," she said. Then, a little while later, she asked, "How did you know to come?"

How did he know she would need him? That everything could be made better by his presence?

Nathan shrugged beside her. She didn't see it. She wasn't looking at him directly, still captivated by the sky. But she felt it in the way the blankets moved around her. The shift. The gentle push and pull near her shoulder. "I just didn't want you to be alone," he said, like it was the simplest thing in the world.

She didn't say anything to that. She couldn't find the right words. Instead, her heart pounded straight against her rib cage so intensely she wondered if he could hear the strange staccato thumping.

Kate turned to her side, enough to see his profile against the dark shadows of the night. He was starlit, the dip of his brow and arch of his nose and gentle curve of his chin visible. She watched his lips part and waited for the words that sat on the tip of his tongue. Before the words, his tongue darted out, moistening his lips. Kate studied the rise and fall of their gentle peaks. She studied him so intensely she could trace him to paper from memory.

She caught her breath, caught her tumbling thoughts, lost in him somehow.

"What?" Nathan asked, turning his head slowly in her direction. "You're staring."

"No, I'm not," Kate lied ardently, even as she continued to stare.

"You are."

"Prove it."

He grinned, a flash of white teeth illuminating his face. They lay like that for a long time. Kate kept her cell phone on, waiting for news. None came, making her hopeful, and slowly the sun started to rise, turning the horizon pink with the faintest hints of lilac.

"There's something ridiculously beautiful about a sunrise, isn't there?" Nathan said, lifting his hand to trace the bands of cream and gold and seafoam blue.

"Almost makes me wonder why you guys waste all your time chasing thunderstorms instead of sunrises."

"I guess we like the challenge," he joked. "Or the unpredictability of it. Sunrises are beautiful, as are sunsets, but there's something different about a storm. About the way the rain can be gentle and caressing or heavy and violent."

Kate rolled back onto her side, pillowing her head on her hand, staring at him instead of the sky. "Why do you really like photographing in the rain so much? I've never understood that part."

"Rain washes away everything," Nathan said. "The past. Mistakes. It's beautiful when you capture it in just the right way. And everything is better for it afterward."

"And the thunder and lightning?"

"Every good moment needs a little drama. It keeps things interesting." He looked at her then, in a way that tangled her insides into tight, unreachable knots. They twisted and twisted inside her, building to a pressure she hadn't felt in a long time. That tantalizing feeling of *wanting* and *being wanted*.

Nathan watched her, gaze flickering down to her lips and back up, like maybe he wanted to take her face into his hands and kiss her.

Kate thought he did.

And maybe she wanted that, too. But just then, her phone buzzed in her pocket and Kate snatched it up, her hand suddenly trembling so badly she struggled to get her password right.

"It's my mom," she said when she finally got the text open, and it felt like she could breathe again. "It just says Dad's awake, so I guess that's positive." She sat up quickly. "I should go see him."

"That's great news," Nathan said, immediately climbing to his feet. Sunlight spilled across the parking deck. He hopped down from the truck and offered her his hand, his lips curving into a smile. "C'mon, I hear hospital coffee tastes especially delicious after an all-nighter."

Chapter Twelve

"I think we're finally caught up. Let's get out of here for a while," Nathan suggested from across the stables as morning faded into afternoon. He wandered over nonchalantly, hands in his pockets, giving her a little shrug. He acted as if the idea had been spontaneous, but Kate knew he'd been watching her all morning, silently hovering. Silently worrying.

"Nathan, I can't." She put down the body brush that she'd been using to comb through Shade's coat and gave the horse a pat. "There's too much to do here." As Kate glanced around her, everything appeared to be in order, but the stress thrumming through her told her something must be amiss.

"What?" he said, looking around.

"The water pails—"

"You know full well I've already dragged the hose through here and filled the water pails."

"Then the horse feed could be inventoried."

He pulled the gate of Shade's stall open, beckoning her out with a flick of his head. "Oh, you mean the feed that you inventoried and ordered more of two days ago?"

Kate rolled her eyes and picked the body brush back up on her way out of the stall, but Nathan threw his arm out, catching her around the waist as she attempted to get to Tully.

"If you brush the horses anymore they're going to end up hairless," he said with a twisted smile. She looked up at him, so close she could see every neatly trimmed hair along his jaw. Shade made a chuffing sound and Nathan lifted his hand as if to say, *Thank you.*

"That's not funny."

"It's a little funny." He plucked the brush from her hand and hung it back on the hook where she'd taken it from. "You've been working nonstop since we got back from the hospital the other day. Your mom talked to the doctor this morning. Things are looking good. Running yourself ragged here isn't going to help your dad. Or your mom," he added.

Kate squinted at him. "Did she put you up to this?"

"I'm not at liberty to discuss," he said, flashing her a grin that revealed exactly what he wasn't saying.

Kate pushed his shoulder, knocking him out of her way, but he caught her arm, his hand sliding down to hers. It sent electricity humming beneath her skin.

"C'mon," he said. "Take an hour."

She waited for him to tack on something else, like this was what friends did for each other, but he didn't; he just continued to look at her with that hopeful grin. When she sighed, he squeezed her hand, and there it was again—the comfort she so desperately craved. Much like the other night in the hospital, she could feel that Nathan was quickly becoming someone she wanted to trust.

That idea terrified and exhilarated her in equal measure.

"Fine. One hour," she said. "That's all you get. But I get to pick the place."

"Can Rusty and Tara come to said place?"

"Yes," Kate said quickly. After what had almost happened in the hospital parking lot, perhaps it was better not to leave them alone completely.

Nathan tucked an arm around her shoulders, leading her from the stables toward his truck. "Good, just making sure you weren't luring me off to the woods to bury me or anything."

On the outskirts of town, far past the campground and the lake, was this little ice cream parlor. It had been there since before Kate was born. A blink-and-you'll-miss-it kind of place. But the ice cream was superior to anything she'd ever tried, and because it wasn't within walking distance of Main Street, it didn't get bogged down with tourists the way everything else did in the summer months.

"So this place we're going to—it's a local secret?" Nathan confirmed again.

"Most definitely," Kate said. "So if you tell anyone, you know, I'll have to kill you."

"I thought we just established there would be no burying bodies in the woods?"

"We can't just let those kinds of secrets leave here. It would ruin Hatchet Lake."

"Guess I'll take it to my grave."

Kate snorted at the look on his face, then grabbed the door handle as Nathan zipped through town. His truck dipped into a pothole, spraying the puddle of water into the ditch, and Kate gasped.

"Oh, come on! That wasn't even that fast."

"Um, I'm pretty sure we almost spun out."

Nathan barked a laugh, something that filled the entire truck with glee. "I have stellar driving skills. *Star Wars*–level reaction time."

"Okay, Yoda, just keep your eyes on the road."

"Who needs eyes on the road when you have the Force?"

Kate reached across the truck and shoved him.

"I'm kidding!" he laughed again. "Just kidding. Look. I'm being so good." They rolled to a stop at a crossroad, and she barely noticed when the truck actually stopped moving.

Nathan continued that way until they weaved their way through the crowded camping area filled with people on vacation and families meandering down to the lake.

As they reached the quiet stretch of highway, Nathan jammed his foot into the gas pedal. "Don't say anything," he said. "This is literally the speed limit."

"I wasn't going to say anything."

"Sure, you weren't. Over there screaming like Chewbacca." Nathan reached across the truck and needled her side. Kate squirmed away.

A loud *honnnnnk* sounded. In the side mirror, Kate spied Rusty's van following them down the road. It was only about ten more minutes before she spotted the ice cream place. "That's it, right there."

Nathan slowed down to turn into the parking lot. The entire lot was filled with a line of snaking cars all leading up to one drive-thru window. A similar line of people flowed out the front door.

"I thought you said this place was a best-kept secret?"

"It is!" Kate complained. "Or it was! I haven't been here since I was a teenager."

Nathan pulled ahead and joined the drive-thru line for ice cream.

Kate rolled her window down, letting the breeze blow through the truck. "Never underestimate the power of children on vacation and their parents' desire for peace."

"You're saying they're bartering this ice cream for silence?"

"Yes. Why do you think I've brought you here?"

It took Nathan a moment, then his mouth opened. He scoffed. "Oh, I see how it is, Kate Cardiff."

"Mmm-hmm," she hummed as Rusty pulled right up to Nathan's bumper. Kate could hear the beat of the music rolling from the van. Behind them the line continued to grow, now stretching out to the highway.

In the field that bordered the lot, other people had parked, climbing out to lean against their cars to eat their ice cream. Above them, swirling gray clouds streaked across the sky, turning the day from blue to bleak.

They waited what felt like another half hour and in that time they'd only moved a few car lengths. Nathan put the truck in Park.

Behind them Rusty screamed, "Why are you taking so long to order? We've already been in line for eighty-four years! You should know what you want when you get to the window!"

"Calm down," Tara shouted back at him.

"They're taking forever!"

Nathan and Kate burst into a fit of giggles that only ended when they both had tears in their eyes.

"This is what happens when I don't feed him," Nathan said.

"Is he about to start throwing things?"

"Probably."

Kate looked out the back window to see Tara point a long finger at Rusty. He rolled his eyes in response. As they waited, raindrops started to fall against the windshield.

"Feels like the closer we get, the slower it moves," Nathan said. "Like some sort of time paradox."

Suddenly the sky opened up. People scrambled back into their cars, ducking out of the summer storm. "Where'd this come from?" Nathan muttered, turning on the windshield wipers so they could watch the rain. There was no thunder or lightning yet. The clouds moved with speed, streaking across the sky so quickly the rain started to ease off only a minute later.

A honk issued from behind them, and Nathan stuck his head out the window.

"Are you seeing this?" Rusty screeched.

"What's going on?" Kate asked.

Nathan pulled his head back inside the truck, glancing back and forth. Then they both saw it. The clouds had blown across the sun, the rain easing off to a light, barely there sprinkle, and a pair of dazzling rainbows had appeared.

"We have to go," Nathan said, revving the engine. He reached across the truck and yanked on Kate's seat belt to tighten it. "Hang on!"

Before she could ask why, Nathan yanked the wheel

hard to the right and jumped the curb, getting out of the drive-thru line. He cheered as the truck bounced up and over the curb, coming down hard on the other side of the small hill of grass. The truck spun out in the gravel lot as Rusty and his van came barreling over the curb toward them. Kate shouted as Nathan and Rusty braked hard, their vehicles coming face-to-face.

Kate could feel her face frozen in utter terror, but Rusty and Nathan broke into matching maniacal laughter, then Nathan threw his truck into gear and went spinning past Rusty, heading for the exit. The van turned hard and came chasing after them.

Nathan stuck his phone up on the dashboard, video-calling Tara. She answered, connecting the two vehicles.

"Where are we heading?" he asked her.

"The end of the rainbow's not on a map, genius. Just drive."

The corners of Nathan's mouth turned up. "I like the sound of that."

Kate grabbed hold of the door again as Nathan and Rusty went racing down the highway, music blaring, chasing the rainbows to their ends.

"Stop swerving," Tara shouted over the call at Rusty, meaning that she must be trying to snap photos of the rainbows while he was driving.

"You're a professional," Rusty yelled back. "Adjust!"

"I can't adjust for your terrible driving!"

Nathan glanced at Kate. "See, I could be so much worse. They're like *The Fast and the Furious* back there."

Kate grinned. She had to admit the thrill of the chase was exhilarating, and the pulse beneath her skin began to race.

She expected the rainbows to disappear suddenly, but they didn't, stretching for what looked like forever. People had pulled over on the side of the road to snap pictures on their phones.

"Amazing," Nathan said, leaning over the wheel for a better look.

"I know a place we could stop." Kate pointed to a turn in the road. Nathan didn't hesitate, just made a right. They kept driving, following the direction the rainbows dropped, and soon they'd reached a lookout point that stared out over the lake. They both stepped out of the truck, careful to avoid Tara, who jumped out of the van before Rusty even stopped rolling, snapping photos with a speed that impressed Kate.

Rusty got out and drummed on the side of the van. "Look at how perfect that shot is. Is this the best thing we've photographed since we got here, ladies and gentlemen? I think it might be."

Tara looked down at the display on her camera, grinning. "These look incredible."

Rusty hovered over her shoulder, then kissed the side of her head in excitement. "You are a brilliant, camera-wielding genius." He crowed into the wind, his voice sailing right over the bluff and out across the water. Tara joined in, their voices as tangled as the storms they chased, stretching toward the horizon.

"Better than ice cream?" Nathan asked, his voice a whisper among the mingled laughter and cheers.

"Better than ice cream," Kate agreed.

After the rainbow chase, they all headed to the ranch. Tara and Nathan spent time photographing the horses before calling them in for the night.

Rusty regarded it all with a hand over his nose.

"It's not that bad," Tara complained, tugging his hand away. "Where did you disappear to?"

"Kate's mom is a baking goddess. We made brownies, then watched *Reno Disasters*."

Kate laughed. "She probably adores you now."

"Who doesn't?"

When they finished in the stables, they congregated on the porch of the guest house.

The sun hadn't quite sunk into sunset mode yet, but it still painted everything in pale tangerine, casting a long shadow along the side of the house.

"There's this one trail you have to see. Kate and I rode up there the other day—" Nathan's voice trailed off as he and Tara headed inside to get drinks. Then it was just Kate and Rusty on the porch.

She sank down onto the step as her phone began to buzz. Pulling it out, she saw Sarah's face grinning back at her.

"Hello?" she answered.

"Hey, just calling to check up on you. Your dad. You know, the usual welfare check on my favorite people other than my son."

"You know, before Parker was born, I was your *only* favorite person."

"And before you met Rancher Hotstuff, I was yours."

Kate rolled her eyes, but Rusty looked over, immediately intrigued, and she realized he could hear the conversation. "You know, now's not a great time for that kind of talk."

"You're with him right now!" Sarah gasped. "I'll see myself out but you owe me one very long conversation. With detail, Kate Cardiff. I want explicit details. Do you understand me? Rated *M* for mature."

"I'm hanging up on you now," Kate said, sighing

inwardly. All Sarah did in return was cackle until the call cut out.

"Oh, I like her," Rusty said, moving closer. "I think your friend and I could stir up some trouble together."

"I don't doubt it."

Rusty sank down on the step next to her, and his smile faded. "How's your dad really doing? Nathan said it got a bit scary there for a second."

"He's on the mend. Hopefully for good this time."

"Poor man probably just wants out of that hospital. I was a sick kid for a while," Rusty explained. "In and out of Emerge all the time. The smell of the hospital used to physically make me ill. Still can't stand them."

"He'd much rather be at home," Kate agreed. "Fingers crossed that in another week or so he'll be discharged."

"And then you can update him on your life with Rancher Hotstuff."

Kate's eyes grew wide as Rusty grinned conspiratorially. "Don't you dare," she said.

"Oh, your secret is safe with me."

"You're just as bad as Sarah. You two really would be perfect for each other."

"I'll have to meet her one day."

Kate shook her head. "I used to cringe at the idea of her wanting to meet Nathan and now I think if she got ahold of you it would be ten times worse. The chaos you two would cause."

"Sort of feels like destiny."

"Not if I can help it," Kate muttered.

"What feels like destiny?" Nathan asked, walking across the porch, mugs in either hand. He sat down on the step next to Kate that Rusty had vacated, passing her a mug.

"Wouldn't you like to know." Rusty gave him a once-over before waltzing away to the van.

Nathan, for his part, wasn't that much bothered by his friend's strange behavior. "Is Rusty making your life complicated?"

"I have Sarah to do that for me."

Nathan tilted his head in question.

"She's like my very own version of Rusty. But also my very best friend. It's almost scary how similar they are at times."

"You mean like she could take over the world if she decided to use her powers for evil?"

"Oh, definitely," Kate laughed.

"Guess we all need a Rusty in our lives."

"Keeps things interesting," Kate agreed. She glanced at Nathan without realizing how close he really was and a tumble of butterflies erupted in her stomach. She caught his eye, those smoky gray eyes that faded to black as the sun set.

For the first time since they met, she remembered just how ridiculous attraction and feelings could make a person. Everything was just butterflies, butterflies, butterflies all the time.

She glanced away, feeling her cheeks heat.

She hadn't been looking for anything when she came home.

Definitely not Nathan.

But he was here now, and the way he edged toward her until their shoulders bumped... Well, she couldn't exactly say she didn't like it.

But it was wrong.

This would be *so* wrong between them.

Complicated.

Kate had experienced enough complications for one lifetime. The only thing to do was put some distance between them. So she did. A little scoot. An inch of space. "I didn't say thank you for the other day."

"For what?"

"For coming up to the hospital," she said, reminding him why they were both here. Putting things into perspective before any sort of pesky feelings could get in the way. "You didn't have to do that. But I'm glad you did."

"Of course," he said, studying the mug in his hands.

Silence grew between them, and though she tried to tamp it down, there was something else.

Longing.

It grew there, too.

Chapter Thirteen

Her dad was discharged the following week.

Kate played chauffeur, and they arrived home by early evening, stocked with a walker, new medications and several sheets of handy discharge notes that her mother had pored over for the better part of the drive.

If that woman didn't already have everything committed to memory, Kate would be surprised.

The sun sat low on the horizon, the horses already tucked away for the night. A peach sunset peeked out between the evergreens that stood proud on the west side of the ranch. Kate watched a figure cross in front of the stables and jog toward them. Nathan, dressed in jeans and a dark plaid jacket, blended in perfectly with the shadows that eclipsed the front of the house.

"I didn't know you'd be back so quickly," he said.

"Surprise," her mother answered. "My daughter and

my husband share a penchant for speeding on the free-way."

Nathan mock-gasped at Kate. "And you have the gall to complain about my driving."

"I was going like ten over," she argued to both her mother and Nathan.

"If that," her dad said, to which Kate grinned. "I've been on faster Thoroughbreds."

"Like father, like daughter," her mother muttered, climbing the porch to unlock the front door and turn on the lights.

"Well, you didn't burn the place down," her dad said to Nathan by way of greeting as he opened the door to help him out of the truck.

"It's not for lack of trying, sir."

Her dad laughed, thumping him on the shoulder, and Kate considered the easy comradery there, developed before Kate had ever received that terrible phone call from her mother. It was almost weird seeing that relationship. Like peering in through a window to witness something she was never invited to see.

Kate made her way around the truck to act as her dad's crutch. He'd emphatically told them for most of the drive that he did not require the walker.

In a few weeks, that might be true. Right now, Kate wished he was a little less stubborn. They reached the porch steps, and her dad grasped Kate's hand with a strength she wouldn't have imagined him possessing. Nathan supported his other side. Together they made their way up the stairs and into the house.

Her dad was short of breath easily, and doing the stairs exhausted him. Part of Kate was glad that Nathan was around tonight. It wasn't that she didn't trust her mother, but having an extra set of hands that weren't also pushing sixty was comforting. The last thing her dad needed was to slip on the stairs and be dealing with a fractured hip.

"Couch?" Kate asked. Her dad nodded wordlessly, shuffling in that direction. He was miles better than he'd looked in the hospital, but even so, an unfamiliar weariness clung to him.

It would take time for him to recover. Weeks and months of rehab and medications and a proper diet and exercise.

Kate was glad to have him back, but she'd be even happier to see more glimpses of his old self.

"Thanks, son," her dad said as Nathan helped lower him into the corner of the couch. Her dad shifted around, getting comfy, finding his slippers in the same spot they always were—butted up against the leg of the coffee table.

The corner of Kate's mouth turned up, happy to see that some things never changed.

"You okay?" Kate asked him. "Need anything? A drink? The remote?"

"Get my books for me?" her dad requested.

"Dad, I think the ranch will survive the night."

"Let me pretend to do something productive," he said, slipping on his reading glasses.

"All right," Kate said. He'd spent enough time cooped up in the hospital, and now he'd spend the rest of his recovery sitting here, having her mother dote on him to within an inch of his life. She supposed it was the least she could do.

When she turned around, her mom gave her a look from the kitchen where she'd started to prepare dinner, but Kate lifted her hands in defeat. She knew her mother would much prefer that her dad just turn the television on, but Kate was not about to argue with the newly discharged patient.

Instead, she headed down the hall to his office. Nathan followed, maybe for something to do other than awkwardly stare at her parents, though there was very little about him that was awkward. Maybe it was the photographer in him. He blended. Adapted. Just found himself sinking into the middle of a situation like he was always supposed to be there. So maybe it was curiosity that sent him after her.

"What are the books?" he asked.

The books captured everything: finances, orders, new client information, lessons, bookings. Each year her father started a new one and each year it was the Holy Grail to maintaining the ranch. "Pretty much the key to running this entire place," she explained.

Perhaps she should have read the most recent one if she truly wanted to pick up where her dad left off while he was in the hospital, but Nathan had seemed to have enough information to keep things moving for the time being, and there was something oddly final about thinking about reading it. Something almost intrusive. Her dad hadn't died, but going through his book would have made Kate feel like she was waiting for the inevitable. It had been weird enough hunting for the vet records without him there. Her dad would never begrudge her any of this information, he just wanted to be the one to provide it.

He was proud of it.

Proud of this place.

And Kate respected that.

She always had, probably because she had a little of it in her, too. It was the same reason Nathan had rubbed her the wrong way during their first meeting. When he pulled her out of Shade's stall, thinking he was protecting her, she'd been miffed that he'd seemingly walked all over her territory with no regard for her work.

He hadn't known, of course, that she was a livestock vet at that point. But it still had irked Kate, as it would anyone whose worth and work were disregarded.

She understood that. So the last thing she wanted to do was try to step into her father's role while he still might be capable of doing it. It was also why she was hesitant to bring up the finances in front of him. Why she hesitated to ask if there was something she could do to help.

Her dad would have to be the one to ask.

She knew he never would, not until he was desperate, and by that point it might be too late. Too late to save this place and the livelihood her parents had worked so hard for. The thought made her sad, so she pulled her dad's most recent book from the office and turned off the light before she dredged up any more unpleasant thoughts.

Nathan waited in the hall, staring at a myriad of family photos.

"Is this you?" he asked.

"Who else would it be?"

"Your hair is different." His fingertip traced a photo of four-year-old Kate crouching in a puddle with giant rubber boots on and a smile that took up half her face.

"It was really blond when I was little. I think I used to spend every hour of the day out in the sun."

"And this one," he said.

It was a picture of Kate with Shadow, Shade's mother. Kate was wearing a ridiculous outfit. She figured she was about twelve. "We'd just come back from a competition. I had a short-lived love of show jumping."

"That thing where you jump over hurdles and stuff like in the Olympics?"

"Exactly that."

"What happened?"

"Jumping for competition is way more pressure and way less fun than riding around the ranch. I didn't want to hate my time spent with the horses, so I decided to stop."

"That's a very mature decision."

"I was a very mature preteen."

"Guess it worked out for you, since you did the whole veterinarian thing."

"Guess so."

Nathan continued down the wall of memories. He reached her school photos, watching Kate grow almost in real time from the chubby-cheeked four-year-old to the awkward teenager and beyond.

"Is there a collage of your face stuck to the wall in someone's house?"

"My grandmother's, for sure," Nathan said, "but I have to share the wall space with my brothers and all their kids now."

"That's the problem with being an only child. Your parents tend to plaster pictures of your face on every vertical surface." At least, in Kate's case they had.

"How could they not, when you're this adorable?" He stood in front of her ninth grade photo, when she had braces and had discovered heavy winged eyeliner for one brief semester. The corners of his mouth twitched.

"Ha ha. Yes, you're so funny." Kate shoved him down the hall.

Nathan stopped, fighting against her when she tried to push him past her graduation photos. First high school, then undergrad and eventually veterinary college. She hadn't changed that much from the last photo.

"At least the braces came off by graduation."

"Small miracles," Kate said.

"You look kind of angry here," he remarked.

"Because the photographer told me to smile without my teeth. Do you know how hard I had worked for that smile?"

"Whoa," Nathan said. "Photo taking 101, do not piss off your client."

"I'm pretty sure I was contemplating strangling him here."

"I can see that." Nathan leaned closer to inspect the photo. "I've been on the receiving end of that look myself. A thing of nightmares."

"And don't you forget it," Kate quipped. She touched the photo gently. "Good thing you can't see my fists in this picture."

"Tell me you left a one-star review?"

"No, my mother ordered multiples of every shot and sent them out to every single person she'd ever met in her entire life."

Nathan leaned against the wall, watching her, his bottom lip caught between his teeth. "Well, that's cute."

"Says you." The dimly lit hallway made her feel like they were entirely alone in the house. Her skin crawled in that delicious, enticing way it did when you were anticipating something wonderful happening.

Nathan leaned toward her. It was so slow that at first

Kate thought she was imagining it, but then she could suddenly see the way his pupils dilated and the way his lips parted, and every fine hair on his unshaven jaw.

"Kate," her mom called, breaking the spell of attraction. That was the only thing it could be at this point, and the realization winded her. "Katie?"

"Katie," Nathan repeated in a singsong voice.

"Don't," Kate warned him, following the sound of her mother's voice back to the kitchen. She dropped the book off with her dad before glancing over at her mom.

"Set the table for me?"

"We're eating in the dining room?" The dining room was strictly reserved for Thanksgiving, Christmas and Easter. Sometimes a special guest or an old friend her parents hadn't seen in a while made the cut, but even those moments were few and far between. Kate had never seen the dining room set with anything other than her mom's good china, and that meant it was a special occasion.

"It's your father's first night home," her mother said, muttering the words as if that would stop her dad from hearing. "I'd like it to feel special."

She gave Kate such a hopeful look that all she could do was nod and say, "Sure."

"And you'll stay for dinner, Nathan?"

"I wouldn't miss it," he said, not even hesitating for a moment.

Kate watched her mom's pleased expression as she bustled around the kitchen.

"Hey, family dinner," Nathan said, elbowing her. "Guess I'm moving up in the world. Maybe even to the level of friendship."

"Maybe with my mom," she quipped.

"C'mon, Katie," Nathan said, looping an arm over her shoulders and pulling her along to the dining room. "I'll help you set the table."

"I am not above bodily harm," she muttered under her breath. She jabbed him in the side with her knuckle for emphasis.

"Kate, don't stab the company," her dad warned from his place on the sofa as they walked by. "Your mother doesn't like blood on the rug."

Nathan squeezed her shoulder, leaning close to her ear to whisper, "Why does it sound like he's speaking from experience?"

"There might have been an incident," she said. "Once."

Nathan quirked a brow in question. "I think this is a story I would like to hear."

"It's not really a story," she said but the turn of his lips said differently. "You know how parents always tell you not to run with scissors?"

"Yeah?" Nathan said hesitantly, wincing in anticipation.

"Well, they really should tell you that about knives, too."

"That part should be obvious, shouldn't it?"

"I was six," Kate defended.

"And a murderer," Nathan stage-whispered under his breath.

"Nobody died. There was barely any blood."

"You really should lead with that then, Katie. A person could think all kinds of thoughts."

Kate rolled her eyes. "Call me Katie one more time and I might make the murderer thing a reality."

"Your mother doesn't keep sharp knives in here, does she?"

Kate pulled open a drawer on the china hutch and grinned. "The sharpest." She closed it again after pulling out the cutlery. "But I'd probably just use a scalpel."

"And you just happen to have one of those lying around?"

She nodded. "I have a few. In my vet bag. Good for lancing abscesses."

Nathan wrinkled his nose. "Right, the animals. So, what's the plan? Chop me up and feed me to the horses?"

"You'd be wasted on the horses. What we really need are some pigs." A curious look crossed his face before Kate elaborated. "They'll eat anything."

Nathan pretended to shiver. "You terrify me, woman."

"And don't you forget it." She looked at him from across the table, where he was expertly laying a place setting. Plate. Fork. Knife. Spoon. Something warmed in her gut, a feeling of familiarity, although she'd never quite been in this situation before with Nathan. Maybe it was some more of that *wanting* that she'd felt at the hospital with him.

Kate tried to put it out of her mind when her mother called, "Don't forget the wine!"

"*I* didn't," Nathan said, already holding a pair of wineglasses from the china hutch.

Kate resisted the urge to roll her eyes at him again as she started down the long, narrow staircase, deep into the chilled concrete cellar she'd been terrified of as a child. Now tomato sauce and pickled vegetables stared back at her from one of the shelves. Another shelf of homemade wine sat to her right. At the back of the room, around an ominous corner, was a door, this one leading to a menagerie of junk that had accumulated in the house over the years. It was, perhaps, an even more terrifying room as far as eight-year-old Kate had been concerned. All shadows and aged things covered in layers of dust. Boogeymen of all sorts frequented the room beyond the cellar.

As an adult, she could see it now as just where her dad hoarded the things he didn't want her mom to find: old suitcases, VHS home movies and the living room set that was supposed to move to Kate's first college apartment with her.

Kate trailed her hand over the wine shelf, debating between a bottle of red and a bottle of white. Would Nathan care? Did he even drink wine? He didn't really strike her as a wine person. Then again, what did a wine person look like? Besides, all Nathan ever really did was surprise her. So, what did she know? Perhaps he was a connoisseur of fine wines from all his traveling. Kate snorted, quite sure that if he was in fact a regular wine drinker, he'd really appreciate a bottle of Dale Cardiff's finest. For some reason, the idea of Nathan choking down some of her dad's wine filled her with glee. Mostly because she knew he'd try to do it with a smile on his face. Nathan seemed to be able to do no wrong as far as her parents were concerned, and Kate was certain that the wine might be his undoing.

Then again, maybe Nathan was a cheap wine kind of guy, straight out of a box, and this would be right up his alley.

Before she pulled a bottle from the shelf, a shadow crossed the wall in front of her and she turned sharply, swallowing the gasp that almost spilled from her lips.

It was only Nathan, with a perfectly innocent little grin on his face. She hadn't even heard him on the stairs, never mind sneaking up behind her.

"You scared the crap out of me!" she said, heart hammering.

"Sorry," he replied, though she knew he was not sorry at all. "Your mother clarified. She would like red wine, please."

Kate let her heartbeat slow before she reached for a bottle of red.

"Nice place you got down here," Nathan said, casting a look around at the cellar. "I can see why you're so creeped out."

"It was worse when I was a kid," Kate promised. "I'd only venture down here under duress."

"And what did that look like?"

"For eight-year-old Kate? The threat of no dessert. You've never seen a kid run up the stairs so fast. Trust me."

"Dessert seems like a worthy cause. And now?"

"Now, I'd prefer if you didn't jump out of the shadows at me."

"I did no such thing."

"My heart rate would beg to differ. How'd you avoid the squeaky step?"

"You're talking to the youngest of three brothers here, remember? Everyday survival required absolute stealth." Nathan demonstrated as he moved across the cellar, taking very wide, exaggerated steps before returning to her side.

She handed him the wine, and he followed her back upstairs. The table had accumulated a salad bowl and slices of buttered bread in her absence. Kate could smell the meatloaf. That meant it was almost done. She handed Nathan the corkscrew from the china hutch and he went to work opening the wine.

Kate retrieved her dad from the living room, bracing herself as she pulled him up from the couch. He was more lively, and Kate wondered if it was from the promise of home cooking and not whatever mass-manufactured goop he was getting at the hospital. It was probably very healthy goop. But food-shaped goop nonetheless. Kate settled him in at one end of the table. Her mom was already plating meatloaf for everyone.

Nathan filled the wineglasses without missing a beat.

When her dad reached for the saltshaker, her mom snatched it away before he could grab it. She sat at the opposite end of the table, leaving Nathan and Kate each on their respective sides of the square.

They avoided looking at each other for the first five minutes of the meal, as her dad grumbled and her mother held the saltshaker hostage. It only lasted that long, then Kate snorted into her wineglass. Nathan shook with silent laughter.

"It's just a bit of salt," her dad said exasperatedly.

"Tell that to your arteries!"

"The doctor said *low* sodium. He didn't say *no* sodium."

"Do you know what has sodium in it?" her mother demanded. "Everything. Besides, why do you need the salt? Is my meatloaf not good enough by itself?"

Years of being married must have triggered something in her dad because he picked up a forkful of meatloaf and shoved it in his mouth. "It's wonderful, dear."

Her mother preened in her chair. "That's what I thought."

After that, dinner moved on to less combative topics, which wasn't necessarily better. The one thing her parents did seem to agree on right now was regaling Nathan with all of Kate's most embarrassing childhood memories; so, as she had to relive all of that, she downed her glass of wine and then another.

"Okay, we do not need to talk about that," Kate said, just barely managing to interrupt a story about an alpaca farm and a first kiss and *holy shit*, she was going to melt into a mortified puddle of slime and sink under the table. She sort of wished her parents were still fighting about the salt.

If she'd learned anything tonight, it was that she was not a very stealthy teenager. Apparently she'd just willingly told her parents all of these things. Another one of those only-child problems.

By the time dinner came to an end, Kate was trying to decide if she wanted to get another bottle of wine from the cellar. It might be the only way to survive whatever after-dinner coffee nonsense was about to happen. However, the rest of the evening was pretty mellow. Her parents settled down in the living room with their coffee and the one biscuit her mother allowed her dad to have. Nathan and Kate cleaned up from dinner. She found she didn't mind doing the dishes as much when he was the one drying. In fact, he had made this entire night much easier than it could have been. Grateful didn't even begin to cover it.

Dealing with a sick parent was scary, but doing it alone, that was so much worse.

But Nathan had been here the whole time.

"You just gonna keep soaking your hands in there?" he said, gesturing to the soap that had bubbled up around her wrists in the sink. "Or are you gonna get to the washing part anytime soon?"

"Shut up and dry," Kate said, handing him a sopping wet plate.

"Or what?"

"Or I'll make you wash *and* dry while I drink wine."

Nathan mimed zipping his lips.

The television played in the background, the low hum of the news filling the silence as they worked. The weather forecaster came on the screen and murmured about rain in the coming days. Kate imagined Nathan out there with his camera and his dimpled smile.

She handed him another plate. He stacked everything in neat piles destined for the china hutch again.

"You should get your parents a dishwasher for Christmas."

"Mom will say she doesn't need it and when you ask why, she'll say it's because she gave birth to a dishwasher."

Nathan laughed. "She's got it all figured out."

Kate inclined her head in a way that said even now her mother was probably listening to them, making her own assumptions and filing away details to be used later. And just to confirm her suspicions, Kate could see her mother's face turned in their direction in the reflection of the window.

She passed Nathan the last plate before dunking the wineglasses. She washed and rinsed them and put them in the dish drainer.

"Take leftovers if you want," her mom called over to Nathan.

"I think I will, thanks," he said.

Kate dried her hands on the same towel Nathan held,

and then went to the island to spoon out a few portions of dinner into a large dish. It took her a moment to find the matching lid to cover it, but rule number one about her mother's kitchen was that they didn't mention the Tupperware cupboard.

"I better get this home," Nathan said when Kate passed him the container.

"I'll walk you," she offered. "Make sure you get home safe and all that."

"Your concern for my safety would earn you a five-star rating."

"It's the full host package deal. We cook, then force you to clean up and take leftovers whether you wanted them or not. Then we drop you off on your doorstep to make sure you go right to sleep so you can get up at the ungodly hour of dawn to start work."

"When you say it like that, it sounds ten times more wonderful," Nathan snarked.

"Only the best when representing my mother."

Nathan turned to her parents as he followed Kate to the front door. "Thank you again for dinner. It was lovely."

"Anytime," her mom said, and Kate knew she meant it.

"See you in the morning," her dad called.

"You are not getting up at dawn," her mom began to say as Kate and Nathan exited the house, avoiding what was sure to be another grumbling argument.

"They love each other," Kate said. "I swear. You wouldn't be able to tell from that, but they do."

"She's just worried about him," Nathan said. "It's sweet."

"It's going to drive my father crazy. But she's normally right."

They made their way down the path and past the stables. Kate heard the gentle whinny of the horses in the dark.

She walked Nathan all the way home.

Or to the guest house, which should be hers, but seeing as her parents offered it up to him before she got there, it was technically *his* home.

For now.

Nathan slowed as they reached the porch, like he was trying to make the moments last. Eventually they reached the door. "I'd invite you in," he said, "but you sort of seem like the type to judge a place and I haven't folded my laundry yet."

"I am definitely going to judge you," she assured him.

"I could tell." He tilted his head a bit, like he was trying to see her better. Then he leaned toward her in the dark, his voice drawing nearer. Near enough that she could smell the wine on his breath. "It's very Princess-y of you."

"Haven't called me that in a while."

"Guess I'm slacking."

"Guess you are."

"I'll have to make up for it."

"I'd expect nothing less."

And then he kissed her.

Her surprise turned into a gasp as their lips connected, the breath of air exhaled in a rush of adrenaline and excitement and a thousand giddy butterflies racing up from her gut. Kate leaned in, deepening the kiss, her arms slipping around his neck to hold him closer. Nathan's hand sank into her hair, the pressure of his lips gentle but constant. Willing and ready and comforting.

Genuine connection.

God, she *wanted* this.

Not just the kiss, but this exact feeling, with him.

He pulled back a measure, just enough to separate their lips. Kate licked her own, searching for his eyes in the dark. She was glad it was dark. It was easier this way. Easier not to think about the lines of his face and the dimples in his cheeks. She didn't have to think, she could just feel.

Kate let her fingers dance over his shoulder and around the back of his neck, playing in the soft hair at the base of his skull. She pulled then, pulled him closer, and their lips connected once more. With a sigh, Kate relaxed into the utter bliss of the moment.

When his tongue nudged for entrance, she gave it, groaning at the feeling of him exploring the back of her lips and the silk of her own tongue. Kate suddenly wanted his tongue everywhere. On every shuddering part of her.

His arm wrapped around her, holding her close, his fingers pressed against her soft curves, touching and feeling and exploring where her skin peeked out just beneath her shirt.

"How am I doing?" he whispered in between the ebb and flow of the kiss.

"With what?" she rasped, the fog hardly clearing from her mind as her body ignited everywhere his hands roamed.

"With this friendship thing."

He pressed her against the wall. She felt all of him, and *oh*, she wanted him. Wanted to wrap her legs around him and bask in the heat of his kisses upon her skin. "I think we skipped a few stages on the scale," she managed to say before his mouth was on hers again, swallowing the gasp she let loose as his hand slid up her side to squeeze her breast.

She should be embarrassed by the sounds she was making, by the way her legs turned to liquid beneath her, but Kate couldn't think of anything except how good his hands felt.

How easily his lips glided against hers.

How right this was.

How right this felt. How right…

How *wrong*.

An errant thought struggled to life in Kate's mind, pushing past the brain fog and the wine and the thoughts of Nathan and family dinners. Of them tangled up together. It almost made her ill the way it all staggered to a halt inside her, the feelings crashing up against a brick wall of regret.

They weren't anything.

Not really.

Strangers who'd barely grazed the surface of friendship. She'd hated him only weeks ago, and now she was simply trying not to fall head over heels for him.

It was bad news.

Complicated.

And she hated complications.

Her hand landed on his chest, pushing gently. Nathan pulled away, his heated breath against her cheek, a question in his fiery gaze.

"I shouldn't have," Kate said, tearing her eyes from his. Somehow the dark made it harder now. Harder to pull away when all she could do was feel. Harder to say *no* when her entire being was screaming to say *yes*. "I should have known better. It could…" She swallowed hard. "It'll get messy."

"There's nothing messy about this," he said, his voice hot against her cheek. "Not yet, at least."

"Please, I... I'm sorry." She panicked. Hard. This was too close and she knew that. She knew *better* than to let herself get swept away in feelings. After everything that happened with Cal, Kate thought she would be better at this. Better at maintaining the distance when she knew it wasn't right. When it couldn't possibly work out.

Nathan wasn't the sweet ranch hand from down the road, destined to work and live and love in the same little town he was born in. Nathan traveled extensively. He chased thunderstorms for fun. He was here like a ship passing in the night.

And soon he would pass right out of her sight.

What the hell was she doing to herself?

Nathan took a step back. Kate immediately missed the warmth of him. The fire he kindled inside her. "You don't have to be sorry," he said.

"I am."

The smile on his face was sad as he stroked her cheek once, twice. Then he pulled his hand away. "I'm not in any kind of rush, Kate Cardiff. You know where to find me when you're ready."

And then he disappeared inside, leaving Kate alone on the porch.

Just like she'd wanted.

Chapter Fourteen

Kate woke up with a headache throbbing behind her eyes.

She would blame it on the wine, though she hadn't drunk nearly enough of that last night. No, this wasn't a hangover.

This was a headache of regret. And though she tried not to think about who and what exactly she regretted this morning, it all filtered back to her in fragments and snapshots and heated images that sent tingles down her spine.

She groaned into her pillow, replaying the scene with Nathan on the front porch of the guest house over and over. They'd completely skipped over the platonic friends part, and he'd gone straight to being someone that Kate wanted to see naked in her bed. More than once.

But Kate wasn't good at doing the naked thing without feelings.

She never had been.

And for that reason, she knew she couldn't let him in any more than she already had.

Her head throbbed again, as if in warning, telling her to stop thinking about Nathan. To stop thinking about that kiss or the way her skin ignited beneath his touch. She needed to get up, have a shower, maybe pop a couple of Tylenol.

Routine would save her.

Or at the very least, it would give her something to do other than wallow in regret.

Her phone buzzed from somewhere beneath the comforter and Kate went digging for it, twisting in the mess of sheets and blankets until she found it wedged under one of the pillows.

It was Sarah.

She answered immediately.

"Are you alive?"

"Yes?" Kate grumbled, confusion coloring her voice for half a second.

Sarah chuckled on the other end of the phone. "Are you still drunk?"

"I was never drunk."

"Kate, you do know you were drunk texting me at like two in the morning, right?"

Kate squinted at her phone, flopping back on her pillow as she scrolled through her text messages, trying to recall the moments between when Nathan stopped kissing her and when she ended up in her bed. It was mostly a haze of fog that she was trying to block out. Did she look like an idiot traipsing away from the guest house with her swollen lips and mussed hair? Probably.

Did she feel like an idiot, standing outside his door,

wishing he would throw it open again and just drag her inside? Most definitely.

Was she going to flame in embarrassment when she had to see him today? Absolutely.

The only saving grace last night had been that her parents had miraculously gone to bed before she got back to the house, so Kate did not have to pretend to avoid her mother's questioning gaze. The last thing she needed was her mom getting involved.

With all those wonderfully terrible thoughts going through her head, Kate didn't actually remember texting anyone last night. But then she found them.

"Hate to break it to you," Kate finally said, rubbing her hand over her face, "but these are very sober text messages."

"You're sure?"

"Very sure."

"Well, now I'm concerned," Sarah said.

"As you should be. My life is ending." Kate rolled over, phone caught between her shoulder and her ear, hugging the pillow to herself. The day was bleak and gray. As gray as she felt inside. From her spot on the bed, she could just make out the fine film of clouds hanging ominously over the ranch. They teased her with a streak of blue sky for a moment, but even that was eventually swallowed up.

"Do you want to explain," Sarah asked, "or am I going to have to threaten you? And don't think I won't. I'm becoming very adept at it. I think my mom skills are leveling up."

Kate pressed her hand to her head, squeezing her eyes shut. "I did a bad thing."

"I need more than that to go off of. Or I'll just assume the worst."

"What's the worst?" Kate wondered.

"Probably murder, but I'm open to suggestions. Maybe something more creative. But if it's going to land you in jail, I know a lawyer you could probably call."

Kate hesitated for a second, then muttered, "I kissed him."

As if her brief but steamy entanglement with Nathan could really be summed up simply by the word *kiss*. If it had gone on any longer, Kate would have been stripping on the porch. Her face flushed at the image she pictured in her head.

"Rancher Hotstuff?" Sarah clarified, carefully keeping the glee from completely overtaking her voice.

"Sarah," Kate complained loudly.

"So what?" Sarah said, chuckling under her breath. "You kissed him. I don't get what the big deal is."

"The big deal is that I never should have done it. I never should have kissed him. I never should have let him kiss me," Kate said, almost breathless. She was surprised by the longing in her own voice. "It was wrong. He works for my parents. He's an employee at the ranch. I can't just... I can't just ruin that."

"Did I miss a part of the story? Are there actually feelings there?"

"I was practically ready to scale the man, Sarah. And you know me, I don't do that without feelings."

"Oh," Sarah said softly. It took her a moment to respond. "I didn't think you were really that interested in him."

"I don't know," Kate said. "I don't want to be. I didn't mean to be, if I am. Trust me, this is the last thing I thought I'd be doing in the middle of my dad coming home from the hospital and trying to get the ranch back in order."

Kate climbed to her feet, pacing across the floor until she was as dizzy as the thoughts she couldn't seem to untangle. She slowed next to the window.

It started to rain. Just a drizzle at first, then something heavier. Kate watched it *plink, plink, plink* against the roof.

She pressed her head against the glass. The cold felt good, dulling the headache.

And then it didn't.

Kate pulled back suddenly, watching Nathan's truck drive past the house, most likely with his camera on the passenger seat, destined for a chase with Tara and Rusty speeding along beside him. Perhaps she imagined it, but for a second he slowed outside the house, not quite stopping but lingering.

She wondered if he was looking for her.

If his own thoughts were as tangled as hers.

Maybe she had not even crossed his mind this morning. Maybe he was simply lingering to share a few words about the ranch with her dad, who'd no doubt been up since dawn much to her mother's dismay.

"I know you don't believe me," Sarah said, "but I'm going to try to talk some sense into you. This doesn't have to mean anything, Kate. Not if you don't want it to. Not if you're not ready for it to mean more."

She hummed in response, not really agreeing because maybe that was the problem. She was tired of feeling like it didn't mean anything. Like her life didn't mean anything but a continuous cycle of work and sleep.

Like her relationships didn't mean anything but an inevitable ending for one reason or another.

She was running because she couldn't have this *not* mean something. It couldn't all be for nothing. She couldn't do it again and again and again.

Each time broke a little something from her.

Soon she wouldn't have anything left to give.

So she couldn't let Nathan have any more of her. She'd probably given away too much as it was.

Kate watched him drive off the ranch and down the road. Until last night, she might have been going with him.

"You are allowed to have a little fun. If that's with Nathan, then great. If that's with the next guy who comes along, that's fine, too."

She wanted it to be more than fun, though. Maybe all these twisting, turning, spiraling feelings in her gut were telling her that it already did mean more. That she'd already slipped up and let herself fall too far into this.

She knew she had.

She knew because she was already certain that she didn't want there to be a next guy.

But she couldn't say that. She couldn't set those feelings free.

The whole idea about loving something and setting it free was bullshit. There was no closure in that.

It just hurt.

So Kate vowed to keep her messy, complicated feelings right where they belonged. Buried, with the rest of her failed relationships. In the past.

This thing with Nathan was behind her.

She could ignore it.

She would have to.

Sarah's voice cut through her silent musings. "Kate, are you crying?"

"No," she said. What was there to cry over? That would be stupid.

"Oh, honey."

"Let's talk about something else," Kate said, dabbing at the unshed tears in her eyes. "I've had enough of men."

"Wish I could say the same thing," Sarah muttered. "They're honestly more trouble than they're worth most of the time."

Kate choked on a sad laugh. "The men are giving you trouble? Queen of two-Tinder-dates-in-one-afternoon?"

"I was wild, wasn't I," Sarah mused fondly. "Those were the good old days. The pre-Parker days when I didn't have mom things to worry about."

Hearing his name, Parker must have come bounding right at Sarah because she grunted and said, "You're going to break Mommy's old lady knees."

"Old lady knees!" Parker roared, then he must have run off because Kate couldn't hear him anymore.

"Honestly, I think you got the good end of the deal with Parker."

"Me, too. He's about the only man I can handle right now."

"I need a Parker so I can stop thinking about Nathan."

"I can express-post him to you. Should be there within seventy-two hours."

"Make sure you put tracking on him. Wouldn't want him running around the country without a chaperone."

"The chaos," Sarah said. "Did you know people actually put their children in the mail back in the day?"

Kate laughed at the ridiculousness of it.

"I'm serious. The History channel told me in between Parker's *CoComelon* marathon."

"Children watch weird things."

"*CoComelon* keeps the toddler quiet and me sane. Trust me, it's worth it. I would be an absolute nightmare at work if it weren't for that show."

"I believe you. How is work, by the way?"

"My last shift at this hospital is next week."

"You didn't end up re-signing your contract?"

"No," Sarah said. "Honestly, I'm just bored here. It's been almost a year."

"You did say you and Parker were ready for a move."

"I think so. Maybe I'll take some time off and think about it."

"A vacation sounds nice," Kate agreed.

"Somewhere warm," Sarah said at once. "We'll go somewhere we can lie out on a beach all day with those tiny little umbrella drinks and a bunch of gorgeous, muscled distractions."

Kate laughed, her spirits lifted somewhat. Maybe that was all she needed. Sarah and some distractions. "I miss you."

"I know." She could tell Sarah was grinning into the phone. "I am the best."

"The very best," Kate agreed, feeling those same, unshed tears spark to life behind her eyes.

"Kate Cardiff, are you crying again?"

"No," Kate lied.

Chapter Fifteen

Kate had done a lot of stupid things in her life.

Well, maybe not a lot, but a fair few.

Kissing Nathan Prescott on the porch of the guest house was definitely one of them.

But if Kate prided herself on anything, it was learning from her mistakes. And that was one mistake she'd resolved not to make again. The best way she knew how was to go out of her way to avoid the man. A solid plan that was easier said than done considering they lived and worked on the same property. But after a few days of it, Kate had pretty much figured it out.

That was until her mother's endless hospitality got the best of Kate.

As she came down the stairs that morning, she immediately backpedaled, slipping on her socked feet as she spied Nathan sitting at the island, nursing a coffee.

He would've usually had his breakfast by now, so she had no idea what he was doing there.

Wincing, Kate moved carefully. Maybe no one had noticed her yet. She'd been quiet on the stairs. Hopefully, she could just turn around, slink her way back up them and bury herself beneath the covers for another twenty minutes. Then he'd most likely be gone.

Good plan.

Best she'd ever had.

"Kate?" her mom called just as Kate was preparing to sprint back up the stairs.

Kate swore under her breath. She'd been spotted. "Yeah?" she called, coming into the kitchen like she hadn't just meant to retreat and hide.

"Good morning," her mom said.

"Morning," Kate tossed out. She didn't stop, just kept moving straight through the kitchen like she was on a mission that could not be interrupted for anything. There was no mission and she had nowhere else to be other than here, but she'd committed to the farce now and she'd have to see it through or else risk looking like an idiot.

She stuffed her feet into her shoes, barely giving her mom time to register the front door opening.

"Where are you running off to?" her mom asked. She looked around for the clock that hung on the wall above the sink.

"I have to pop by the post office. It's a work thing."

It was a complete and utter lie, and Kate felt sort of bad about it. Her mom believed her, though, because of course she assumed there were vet things Kate had to look after. There was absolutely no reason she needed to go to the post office for work, but it was the first excuse that had sprung into her mind. When she'd picked up and came home because of her dad, Kate's roster of clients had been absorbed by the other vets at the practice. If they really needed to touch base with her, they would have just called.

But it worked. It was her escape from a potentially awkward breakfast situation that she was not ready to face. She was not ready to sit beside Nathan and make small talk.

Not yet.

Maybe not ever.

"Can I borrow the truck?" she added quickly. She was absolutely not in the mood to make the hike into town on foot, though she could probably use the time to clear her head.

"Of course." Her mom tossed her the keys.

"Thanks."

"I feel like I haven't seen you in days," her mother complained.

Kate frowned at that. Had she been avoiding her parents as much as she'd been avoiding Nathan? She didn't think so, but now she wasn't sure.

Nathan glanced over his shoulder at her. Kate looked anywhere but at him.

"I'll be home in an hour," she said. "If that."

"Do you want breakfast before you go?"

"Thanks, but I'll grab something when I get back." She left them with a fleeting smile before she ducked out the door.

"Oh, Kate! Wait," her mom shouted before the door closed.

Kate paused on the porch step as her mother ran after her.

"Can you stop by the diner for me? Diane made up a couple of her strawberry rhubarb pies. They're your father's favorite."

"Sure," Kate said, half glad for something to do that did not involve lies or secrets or fake missions to the post office.

Her mom caught Kate's chin in her hand before she could pull away. "You okay?"

"Yeah," Kate said, shrugging her off.

"I've been your mother for thirty years, Kate." It was her way of saying that she absolutely did not believe that Kate was okay.

"I'm fine. Just tired."

Her mother let her go, but the concerned tilt of her brow and the worry lines around her mouth remained firmly in place.

"I'll be back soon," Kate promised. "With Diane's famous pies." And hopefully Nathan would no longer be sitting in their kitchen.

The corner of her mom's mouth flickered. "Thank you."

Kate climbed into the truck then, before any more questions could be asked. She drove off without looking back.

She reached town as the radio host was droning on about a series of intense summer storms that were going to be passing through the area in the coming weeks. Storms only made her think of Nathan now, so she clicked the radio off in a hurry.

Kate did stop at the post office, parking in front of the gas station, because if she knew anything about small towns it was that her comings and goings would inevitably get back to her mother. That was how places like this worked. If Kate came all the way to town and didn't go to the post office, her mother would hear about it and know something was wrong.

That was the blessing and the curse of knowing all of your neighbors.

Kate wandered around the gas station for a minute before buying a postcard from the rack on the counter. It had an aerial photo of Hatchet Lake as the picture and looked as if it had been there since the nineties. She took the pen offered by the cashier and scribbled Sarah's address into the corner but addressed it to Parker. She signed it, *Love, Auntie Kate.*

Then she bought a stamp from the woman behind the post office counter and mailed it off. Well, that should serve to keep her lie intact.

Kate exited the gas station and drove the truck over to the brick building at the corner of Main Street and Hatchet Lake Road to retrieve the pies she'd promised her mother. She parked along the sidewalk, wedged in between early-morning brunch seekers.

Couples filled the windows of Sunnyside Diner, no doubt gorging on Diane's famous blueberry pancakes and staring longingly at each other. At least, that was the way it looked to Kate. Was the universe taunting her now? Literally throwing it in her face? Everywhere she looked, another nauseatingly perfect couple seemed to appear. She groaned, leaning her head against the steering wheel. No matter how hard she tried to push Nathan from her thoughts, the feelings festered and spread like an illness.

Lovesick.

Was that what this was? Kate took a deep, steadying breath. No. That was ridiculous. She was a more rational person than that, and she wouldn't let these feelings eat away at her. This was it, she resolved. No more running away every time they crossed paths. She was an adult. She could do this. Kate lifted her head, ready to try again, only to find a couple lip-locked on the steps of the diner.

Fed up with it all, Kate threw her head back and swore loud enough to make her mother blush.

Things did not improve over the next couple of weeks. Kate's resolution to face her feelings head-on promptly dissolved upon returning to the ranch, and she went out of her way to avoid Nathan whenever possible. She threw herself into shadowing her dad, learning the intricacies of running the ranch, while also spearheading his cardiac rehab.

Kate spent so much time chauffeuring her dad around to appointments that there was hardly time to dedicate to her complicated thoughts.

Only when it rained did she let the thoughts loose.

Only when it rained did she wonder what Nathan was doing or thinking or viewing through the lens of his camera.

Only when it rained did she think maybe she loved him.

But that was ridiculous, and as the sun returned and the rain dried up, so did her feelings.

At least that was what she told herself.

When Kate eventually ran into Nathan in the stables, it was almost unavoidable. This was his domain now, but also her solace. She'd always found comfort in the animals she cared for.

"Hey," he said, a smile in his eyes. He leaned on his pitchfork as she carried a saddle into Shade's stall.

"Hi." She didn't take her eyes off the saddle as she threw it over Shade's back and adjusted the straps.

Nathan walked up, patting Shade's back, running his hands over the midnight hair, making him impossible to ignore. "You've been riding a lot lately," he said.

What was she supposed to say to that?

To get away from you.

To stop this sickness that's eating away at my heart.

"Kate," he said. Just her name. It was a question and a statement all wrapped into one.

She glanced at him. Her eyes lingered on his lips, drawn there by some unknowable force that did nothing but fuel the reckless desire inside her.

Kate tore her eyes away. She didn't have an answer right now. She didn't know how to just be his friend.

She never really was.

She climbed into the saddle and kicked off hard, ignoring the hurt she could see crossing Nathan's face. Kate begged Shade to take her away, and she did, running straight out the door and propelling them onto the trodden trail that led to the woods.

Kate held her breath until they were swallowed by the long reach of tree limbs and the shallow darkness of the forest. Her hair whipped loose around her face, sandy locks flying free as Shade raced up the trail, each muscle working in time with the clip-clop of her hooves.

The forest felt like freedom.

But when Shade exploded into the field, lime-green grass dotted with the yellows and blues of the wild flowers, it felt like a sanctuary.

Like her heart could finally be still.

Shade slowed, picking eagerly at the fresh grass and the occasional dandelion. She meandered across the field and Kate let her, in no rush to head back to the ranch.

She didn't need another run-in with Nathan today.

There were times when it was painful to see him, like just now in the stables, his smile open, his gaze eager. She missed him. The fun, considerate, kind man she might have eventually called a friend. But other times being near him felt almost dangerous.

It could happen in an instant—the quirk of a brow, the tilt of a head—and suddenly these seemingly unromantic feelings heated until boiling, and Kate wanted to reach for him.

She almost had, the other day, when they were passing on the trail outside the pasture fence. Her dad had asked Nathan to reinforce the gate where the hinges were starting to come loose. Kate had been on her way to take Shade out for a ride.

He'd looked at her, pushing his hair back with one hand, his eyes intense as they caught hers.

She'd stopped by the fence, waiting for Shade. He'd stopped to watch the horses, leaning against the fence next to her. Deliberately close.

Beside her, she could feel the heat of him through her clothes and it settled somewhere deep. She'd been itching to touch him. Itching to have his hands roaming the way they did that night on the porch.

When he asked her what she was thinking, she'd almost said as much.

She'd almost slipped.

These past weeks had been filled with too many *almosts* to count.

It was as if Nathan was the cat and she was the mouse, dodging each other at every step, but he always managed to catch her in the end. The risk of it thrilled her. The idea of crossing that line.

But some small stitch in her chest reminded her how much it would hurt when it all went sideways, so Kate continued to push him away and hoist the walls up around her heart.

Kate reached the ridge overlooking the lake. It was dull today, almost a green-gray from up here. In the distance, Kate could see a few lone campers along the shore, though they seemed to be retreating from the water, not making their way toward it. It was just after noon but a mountain of black clouds converged over the lake, casting a cool shadow.

Shade snorted, pawing at the ground.

"Okay," Kate agreed. "Let's go." With light pressure from her heel, she turned Shade around and they began their descent. The last thing they needed was to be caught in a storm.

Shade made quick work of the trail, galloping down the last bit before pulling up short outside the fence.

By the time they reached the stables, the sky was filled with billowing gray clouds, not a strip of blue peeking through between them.

Kate dismounted and led Shade by the reins. There was no point in letting her go in the pasture. Whatever was brewing in the sky was bound to be nasty. Kate pressed a kiss to Shade's snout in thanks. The horse nickered in response.

Nathan was just getting Tully and Samson tucked

away when she entered with Shade. He had his camera hanging on a strap around his back, probably anticipating the thunder and lightning that seemed to be brewing in the clouds overhead.

Kate walked past him, leading Shade to her stall before she started to pull at the girth that secured the saddle to her back.

Nathan appeared at the gate of Shade's stall. "Can we talk for a minute?"

"I can't right now, Nathan. I'm busy." It was a bold-faced lie, and they both knew it. She was not too busy to talk to him; she just couldn't let it happen. She knew that if she did, she wouldn't be able to stop him from coaxing the heat beneath her skin to life. She'd beg him to do it. Beg him to touch her. To hold her.

It would all be over.

She would have ruined everything.

"We can talk here," he said.

Kate removed the saddle and the bridle, running her hands over Shade to check for any sores. She heaved the saddle onto the gate. "What is it?"

"Did I do something wrong?"

"No," she said immediately, because this wasn't on him. This was her. Everything wrong with this moment was because of her.

"Then why won't you talk to me?"

"What do you call this?" she said as she passed by him to retrieve a fresh bucket of water. She returned and Shade lowered her head to drink.

"You know that's not what I mean. You've been avoiding me or ignoring me for weeks. We kissed. It happened. And maybe I was reading everything wrong.

Maybe you didn't feel the way I felt in the end. But I thought we were friends at least."

This was exactly why she hadn't wanted that. The *friends* thing. Now even that was ruined. She could barely look at him because she didn't want to be his friend. She wanted to be more.

But more just ended up trampling over her heart.

And she regretted it every time.

She didn't want to end up regretting him.

"Kate," he said.

"Stop," she begged quietly. Her jaw tensed, trying not to tremble. "Please."

"Why are you fighting this so hard?"

"I can't keep doing this to myself." She closed the gate to Shade's stall and turned away, but he caught her arm. Caught her and didn't let go.

"You're so stubborn, Kate Cardiff."

"This isn't me being stubborn," she said. "This is me…protecting myself."

"From what?"

"From you!"

"You think you have to protect yourself from me?"

"I do."

He took a step closer, his gaze intense. "You think I'd hurt you?"

Her shoulders lifted in that inevitable way. "Maybe you wouldn't mean to. Not at first. But that's just how things go with me. They don't work out, and I can't do it again."

"You're pushing me away now so you don't have to do it later?"

She waited there, emotionless, staring blankly. Not at him. She couldn't look at those gray eyes as the intensity dissolved into pain. She stared over his shoulder, at the wall, willing the tears to hold.

"Kate, this is ridiculous. Don't you get it?" He gently pulled her closer. "Don't you get that I—"

She caught him in the chest with the base of her palm. She pushed hard enough to get his attention. "Don't," she pleaded. "It never would have worked out. You work for my parents. You're their employee and I can't jeopardize that over feelings."

His face was like stone then. "These all sound like excuses to me. You can keep trying to convince yourself of all the reasons this wouldn't work even though *you* are the biggest obstacle. But what do I care? Apparently I just work here." He backed away slowly, throwing his hands up. "Keep running away, Kate. You're good at that."

Nathan turned on his heel and stalked out of the building, pulling up his hood and shielding his camera as he stepped out into a light rain.

Watching him go was painful and for a second she was reminded of Cal all over again. Only this was nothing like Cal. By the time things had ended with Cal, it was long past due. She'd been stubborn about admitting it. Especially to herself. Admitting that she'd stayed in the relationship longer than she should have because she didn't want to be alone anymore.

Watching Nathan walk away now was so much worse because he wanted to stay and she wasn't letting him. But she didn't know how to do this. How could she love someone again and risk losing them? How could she do that to herself?

Kate could hear the rev of his truck as he drove past the stables, probably off to chase storms.

Wasn't this a kindness, she wondered. Wasn't this better? If she never let herself get attached, if she never let herself want him in that way, she couldn't possibly get hurt.

Only she did want him.

And she was already hurting.

Chapter Sixteen

Kate had spent many of her worst hours in the company of horses. There was something comforting in the strong beat of their hearts. Something that helped ease her own heartache.

This one was fresh, and Shade seems to sense that, lifting her head to nudge it against Kate's. She rubbed the spot behind Shade's ear, feeling a wretched bubble of hurt and fear burst in her chest.

"It doesn't always work out," Kate whispered, not that the horse cared one bit about her relationship problems, or lack thereof, with Nathan. "I can't take that chance again."

Shade butted her nose against Kate, making a soft sound. The gentleness of it brought tears to her eyes.

In Nathan's absence, she got to work, hosing down the interior of the stables, and padding the stalls with fresh straw.

The rain had only grown heavier, a distant drum of thunder starting, so Kate doubted the horses would be let out again today.

She gave them grain and water and snuck them a few peppermints as a treat.

No sense in them *all* being miserable.

She tried not to wonder if Nathan had found what he'd been chasing this time. In fact, she tried not to think about him at all because every time she did all she could see was the disappointment on his face and hear the way he told her to run away.

She supposed she was good at that.

She'd been doing it all her life.

Lightning cracked in the distance and the lights in the stables flickered. Kate glanced up. A gathering wind cried like banshees against the walls. She walked to one of the windows, staring out into the storm. The rain wasn't that bad yet, but the wheat in the fields across the road lay almost flat under the wind.

Kate went back to work. She clicked her tongue, her voice carrying as she called out to the horses, soothing them as they began to grow restless. Shade threw her head up and down. The others paced, the storm making them uneasy. Kate figured the best thing to do was get the stables locked down.

She pulled on the large doors that led out to the pasture, dragging them against the wind as she secured the latch. "There," she said as she passed Shade's stall, reaching inside to rub a soothing circle against the horse's neck. "Are you happy now?"

Shade's answering whinny was not convincing, so Kate produced an apple and shared a few pieces between the horses. A rolling lick of thunder shook overhead. Kate gave Shade one more pat before going to check on the boarded horses to make sure they were fed and watered and had shared in the treats.

When she was convinced that the wind and the rain weren't likely to let up, Kate sighed and braved the storm, racing through muddy puddles back to the house. Her clothes were soaked by the time she reached the porch, sticking to her like an unpleasant film. Her hair was damp and dripping over her shoulders. She tied it back before wiping the water from her face.

As soon as Kate entered the house, her mother was chasing her through the living room, fingers prodding at her shoulders, directing her straight to the stairs. Kate left a damp trail in her wake.

"Go change," her mom said, leaving no room for argument. "I don't want you sitting in wet clothes."

"I wasn't planning on it." The only thing she hated more than wet clothes was wet feet, and right now she was sporting both.

Kate took the stairs two at a time, before the chill from the damp clothes could settle into her bones. Once upstairs, she stripped, dropping everything into a pile in the middle of her room. It was a delicate game of balance as she tried to peel herself out of her jeans without completely toppling over. Eventually she gave up and flopped on the bed for support.

When the clothes were off, she picked through her suitcase, changing into another pair of jeans and her patchy university sweater. The house creaked and groaned in the torrent of rain and wind and if she closed her eyes, Kate could imagine she was inside a sleeping giant. Water poured down the windowpanes, rushing off the roof of the house with so much force it spilled over the side, completely missing the eaves trough. If there was ever a storm to capture how she currently felt inside after the argument with Nathan, this was it. Cold and terrible and like she might just wash away.

Holding her arms tight against her chest, Kate felt a sense of dread settle over her. No matter how bad this storm got, no matter how much thunder and lightning and rain, it would eventually end. Kate was going to feel terrible long after that.

No blue skies and sunshine for her.

Her phone buzzed from its place on the dresser, and Kate abandoned her melancholy view to snatch it up. Opening a message, hoping beyond measure that it was from Sarah, Kate quickly realized that it was from Rusty.

Her heart skipped a beat.

There was a photo of a narrow dirt road, stretching straight between a pair of cornfields. In the sky an ominous black cloud loomed, but Rusty's face filled half the screen with an open-mouthed grin. He flashed a peace sign at the camera.

Did he know what was going on? Had Nathan told him how she'd been refusing him at every turn, how she'd stomped on both their feelings to protect her heart?

Maybe.

Probably.

Rusty and Tara were his best friends.

Why *wouldn't* he talk to them?

They'd be the ones who were still around long after Nathan and the ranch had parted ways. A part of her was glad he wasn't alone in his heartache.

Beneath the photo a text popped up.

Miss you out here, Rusty wrote.

A fleeting, flickering smile crossed Kate's face before she shoved the phone in her back pocket. She couldn't handle Rusty being nice to her right now, whether he really meant it or not. He was likely just looking out for Nathan, trying to make this impossible thing a little less difficult on his best friend. Play the mediator. But a small part of her thought he might just be reaching out for the sake of reaching out. Genuinely missing her on their grand storm chasing adventures. And if that was the case, Kate had no words, so she ignored Rusty's text completely and headed back downstairs.

As she reached the bottom landing, her mom all but pounced on her, a strong arm wrapped around her shoulders in that way mothers did when they meant to make it difficult for you to escape.

"Help me," her mom requested.

"Help you with what?" Kate asked suspiciously. As an adult child it was best never to agree to anything before knowing the full terms and conditions.

"Make some tea."

Kate hummed. Even that innocent request held a complicated kind of intent. "That sounds like a one-person job."

Her mom rolled her eyes dramatically. "Would you just let your old mother take care of you?"

"You're not that old yet. Younger than Dad, and he thinks he's twenty-five."

"Your father is an old fool."

Her dad grunted from the sofa in disagreement.

"But I love him anyway, just as I love you." Her mom

pulled her close, pressing her lips to Kate's temple. "Will you just tell me what's wrong?"

"Nothing's wrong."

"Do you want me to bake some cookies?"

Cookies and tea. That was how all of Kate's teenage crises were solved. She doubted they worked on adult-sized problems. Or heart-shaped problems.

Kate laughed it off. It was the only thing she could do under the worrying eyes of her mother. "I don't need cookies."

"I'll take some cookies," her dad piped up from behind his newspaper.

"There, make Dad some cookies. Fret over him."

"He's not allowed to have cookies."

"Everything in moderation," her dad protested.

Exasperated with them both, her mother steered Kate onto a stool at the counter. "Sit," she said. Kate did, because that was an order. A flash of lightning broke across the sky, and a booming clap of thunder followed. "You didn't go out with Nathan today? I thought you usually went to watch him photograph the storms."

"No," Kate mumbled. "Not today. I had some things to take care of."

"Things," her mom repeated. "You know I think these things have been taking up a lot of your time lately. So much time that you haven't really been yourself." She filled the kettle and plugged it in. Then she watched the storm out the window for a moment before she turned around and leaned against the counter, leveling Kate with a practiced look. "Did something happen?"

Kate delicately folded her hands under her chin, staring down her mother with the same tempered stare that had been used on her all her life. As a girl, that one look from her mother would have her confessing all her secrets. But she was older now, wise to these tricks, and she knew not to give an inch.

All her mother needed was a piece of the thread to begin unraveling it.

And Kate wasn't ready to talk about Nathan in that way with her. Not while he still worked here. Maybe never.

"Nothing happened. Nothing's going on."

"I'm worried about you." That was another one of her tactics. Guilt. She said the word *worry* and squeezed Kate's hand and suddenly Kate felt terrible for making her mother feel concerned. But it was all a great ruse, and her mother would dance with victory as soon as Kate spilled her secrets.

"Mom," Kate said. "You have nothing to worry about."

"I think I do."

Kate lowered her voice. "I think you're projecting."

"Projecting what?"

"Your worry about Dad."

"I can worry about you both at the same time. It's one of my many talents."

"Anne, stop interrogating the poor girl," her dad called from the couch. He was only half invested in their conversation, more interested in the newspaper, but at least Kate wasn't the one who had to tell her mother that she was meddling.

Pursing her lips, her mother huffed, turning around to attend to the kettle. She muttered incessantly. "...been your mother for thirty years, Katherine... I think I know when my daughter is upset... Don't you tell me not to meddle, Dale…it's my meddling that's going to keep you alive…"

It went on and on like that as her mother steeped the tea. Kate covered her mouth with her hand, holding in the laughter that threatened to burst out. One way or another, her mom had always been able to make her feel better.

Anyway, this time she needed the laughter more than she needed advice.

As her mother fiddled with the tea bags, one hand on her hip and an annoyed tilt to her chin, Kate's phone began to buzz. She pulled it from her pocket, teeth gritted in anticipation of another text from Rusty.

It was a video call this time, and Kate was relieved when a picture of Sarah holding Parker filled the screen. This was exactly the change in conversation she needed right now, and she answered the call eagerly.

"Do you know what I'm eating for lunch?" Sarah complained, launching right into the conversation just as Kate hoped she would. The camera faced the counter, and Sarah leaned into the frame, showing Kate a plastic toddler plate. "Dinosaur nuggets. Why, you ask? Oh, because my son says, 'Mommy, I want dino nuggies for lunch.' And when the dino nuggies are ready and I put them in front of him, he throws a category three tantrum because it's not a sandwich. A sandwich, Kate. And not just any sandwich. He wants a single slice of cheese between two pieces of bread. This boy is going to be the death of me." Sarah stuffed a chicken nugget in her mouth. "These are disgusting."

"Guess the terrible twos are in full swing."

"Ha!" Sarah said. "Parker's making a run for their president."

Kate laughed.

"Speaking of the men in our lives," Sarah began. "How is that whole situa—"

"And look who's here," Kate said loudly, turning the camera around to face her mother before Sarah could launch into a play-by-play of the Nathan drama. So far Kate had managed to keep the crashing and burning of this weird relationship from her parents. She did not intend to involve them now.

"Mama Cardiff," Sarah said, picking up Parker to fill the screen with his face. Sarah was good like that, going right for the one thing that would make her mother forget about everything else.

"He's getting so big," her mom gushed, coming to take the phone from Kate so she could press her nose up against it. She was just as enamored with the boy as Kate was.

"Feels like it," Sarah grunted, hoisting Parker up her hip. He grabbed for the phone excitedly. "Gentle," Sarah managed to say once before the phone went flying across the room.

Kate and her mom watched the entire thing with a kind of fondness that could only come from observing from afar. Kate was sure the in-person experience was much different.

"We're working on *gentle*," Sarah clarified as she retrieved her phone. "He's almost got it."

"Looks like it," Kate snorted.

"At least he's stopped trying to eat the phone," Sarah said. "Now if I could just get him to stop putting everything else in his mouth."

"That'll come," her mother said. "Kate would stick dirt in her mouth until she was three."

"You let me eat dirt?"

"*I* didn't let you do anything," her mom said, casting a look over at her dad. The newspaper stretched a little higher.

"No wonder you became a vet," Sarah said. "You've got the ranch in your blood. Literally."

"She also stuck half the foam from her crib mattress up her nose, so I'm not sure what that says about her."

Sarah cackled.

"I'm your only child, you know," Kate said, taking her phone back. "You might not want to insult me."

"It was said with much love."

"Mmm-hmm" was all Kate offered in response. She turned back to Sarah. "Have you made any decisions about work yet?"

"I'm considering a couple of contracts."

"Any exotic destinations?" her mom asked.

"No, everything's stateside this time."

"You don't sound thrilled about any of them," Kate commented.

Sarah sighed, plopping down on her couch. Her face was contemplative. "You know, I'm not, really. I don't know what it is. Usually something feels right and I just sort of go for it. Figure things out along the way. I'm starting to wonder if it's because Parker's getting older. If there's some subconscious part of me that's worried about moving him around constantly and messing up his routines."

"You want to settle down somewhere?"

Sarah made a face, telling Kate she found that entirely unappealing. "Honest truth—no. I like not having to get attached to a place. You know, having the freedom to leave if I don't like it. And that same freedom to go back again if it was a good experience." She wrinkled her nose. "But I guess I'm going to have to settle down soon. At least for a while. Parker will start school eventually. I won't be able to hop all over the country with him."

"You could homeschool him," her mother offered.

"Right. Just me and Parker and his homeschool nanny gallivanting around the country."

"Why a nanny? Why not a husband?"

"Mama Cardiff, we've been over this. There will be no marriages of any kind. It will be Parker and I to the bitter end. And when he eventually gets sick of me, it'll be me and a bottomless margarita on a beach somewhere."

"Priorities sound straight to me," Kate said. Her mom just walked away with a shake of her head. "What are you going to do until then?"

"Well," Sarah mused as Parker launched himself onto the couch and tried to climb her like a jungle gym, pressing his chubby hands to her cheeks. "I'm going to enjoy some quality time with my child." Parker blew a raspberry against her cheek. "When that inevitably drives me out of my mind, I'm just going to throw a dart at a map and pack our bags."

"I like that plan. Very adventurous."

"It'll be pure desperation at that point."

"Whatever works," Kate said.

A flash of lightning filled the room.

"What's going on there?" Sarah asked as thunder rumbled close enough to be heard over the phone.

"Oh, just a storm," her mother called over her shoulder.

"A wicked-looking storm," Kate clarified. "You

should see the wind." She moved, taking the phone to the living room window, but as she attempted to show Sarah, the lights flickered, the power surged and the video call cut out. She sighed. "There goes the Wi-Fi."

"Don't you have that data thing?" her mom asked.

"Yes," Kate smirked, sending Sarah off a text to explain, promising to call her later. "But Sarah will eat through that in thirty minutes."

"That girl does like to talk," her mom agreed. Her hand traced a photo of Parker on the fridge. "Tell her to send more photos."

"I will tell her the fourteen photos we have of her son on the fridge currently are not enough."

"That's all I ask," her mom replied, not taking the bait.

Kate turned back to the window again. The clouds overhead were fierce, the gray so dark it was almost black. But there was no rain right now. Just a relentless wind that screamed across the fields.

Then something plinked off the roof of the house.

Again.

And again.

Heavier and heavier.

"Is it hailing?" her mother asked.

That question got her dad off the couch.

Kate squinted, watching as tiny beads of ice gathered in the grass. The wind was strong, dragging the hail along like tiny snowballs in the dirt.

The lights in the house flickered again and her dad swore, muttering something about candles and flashlights. He disappeared down the hall into his office.

Her mother went after him, loath to let him out of her sight even for a second.

Kate's phone began to alarm in her hands and then her mother's started, ringing with a cringe-worthy scream that made Kate race toward the counter to quiet it. She frowned down at the matching red alerts that crawled across the screens.

"What is that?" her mother asked, poking her head out of the office.

"It's an alarm," Kate called. "We just got a tornado watch for the area."

Hail continued to rain down outside, and Kate's pulse raced. Her eyes clocked the side of the road again where the wheat lay flat. On the other side, trees crashed against each other. Their leaves fell, twisting violent paths across the sky.

"I think we should go down to the cellar."

Her mom returned to the kitchen and retrieved her phone to read the alert. "It's just a watch. It says that storms in the area are capable of producing large-sized hail, heavy rainfall, damaging winds and tornadoes. Doesn't mean there is one."

"That whole description right there did not make me feel better," Kate said. This wasn't the first time they'd been through this. Every summer of Kate's entire life on the ranch had been filled with menacing storms, but this felt different. When you'd been around enough of them, you could almost tell when a storm was just for show. Another crash of thunder sounded above them, shaking the house. She wondered if the tornado sirens were screaming in town.

Her dad returned to the living room with a giant flashlight and batteries. He scooped the window blinds aside with his hand. "This doesn't look good."

The clouds that trailed the sky had begun to turn a strange shade of green.

"I really think we should go downstairs," Kate said, already directing her dad toward the door to the cellar.

"Kate," her mom began to protest.

"Right now," she said, leaving no room for argument.

Abandoning their tea on the counter, her mom trailed after them, muttering about getting ahead of themselves.

Once Kate had both her parents in the cellar, she felt slightly better. Her palms were still sweaty, though, and her pulse bounded beneath her skin with uncertainty. She didn't know what she was supposed to be doing right now.

Waiting for the storm to worsen? Waiting for an update?

She slumped down on the bottom step of the staircase.

"I've been meaning to clean out this pantry," her mom said, pulling a dusty jar off the shelf. "I'm sure some of these have got to go."

Her dad took the jar, inspecting it closely. "Looks fine to me."

"Look here," her mom said, trying to show him something inside the jar. "Right here."

He squinted and she nudged his shoulder. "You don't even have your glasses on. Go sit down, Dale."

"I can help."

"You'll make more work for me, is what you'll do." Her mom pulled another jar from the shelf. Her dad settled beside Kate, grumbling under his breath.

Kate was beginning to wonder if she should have left them both upstairs to fend for themselves. Just as she was contemplating that, her phone began to scream again. The alert was different this time. "They've spotted a funnel cloud," she said. Her mom looked over with surprise before reading the alert on her own phone.

Kate jumped to her feet. She knew what to do in the event of a tornado. It was something she'd been taught since she was young. *Take shelter.* Done. But as she glanced around at her parents' preparedness, all she saw was the glass. Glass jars. Glass wine bottles.

Glass. Glass. Glass.

"Not here," she said suddenly.

Her mom frowned. "What?"

Kate took the jar from her hand, putting it back on the shelf. She tugged her mother into the other room. The dark, dank concrete box that was the equivalent of an attic underground. The one that used to terrify her.

"Dale, I told you to get rid of those suitcases," her mother said immediately.

Her dad just stared at them in confusion before plopping down on the old, musty couch Kate never took away to college.

While they argued, Kate's mind reeled. *Shelter.* Done. *Flashlight.* Done. Her phone still had enough charge that she should be able to use it if both the power and internet were down for a while. What was she missing?

It dawned on her suddenly.

"I have to go let the horses out."

"What?" both her parents said at once.

"Kate?" Her mother grabbed at her wrist, looking up from her phone. "The report says a tornado is on the ground. You're not going back outside."

"I have to."

"Kate," her dad began to argue.

"Putting the horses out to pasture will give them the chance to move out of the path of the storm."

"And leaving them out there could risk them getting hit by debris," her mom argued. "Dale?" she said, looking for backup.

"If they're locked in the stalls and the stable ends up in the path of the tornado," Kate reasoned, "it'll collapse on them. They won't stand a chance."

It was a damned-if-you-do and damned-if-you-don't sort of situation. Neither answer was the right answer. Neither answer was wrong.

But Kate knew letting them out was the better choice. It would give them the chance to fight the elements instinctively.

Her dad's jaw tightened, his teeth clenched in silent agreement. He knew she was right. It was what he would do if he wasn't in such bad shape from the heart attack.

"I'm coming with you, then," her mother said, already heading for the stairs.

"Absolutely not," Kate said. Her dad had just gotten out of the hospital; the last thing she needed was to put her mother back in it. She would be faster on her own. Kate threw her arm out, blocking the way to the stairs.

"Katherine—"

Kate lowered her voice. "Someone needs to stay here with Dad. Keep him calm. He already had one heart attack. We don't want him more stressed than he already is." She could almost see the argument occurring in her mother's head. But Kate already knew that if her mom followed her out of the cellar, so would her dad. And after everything that had happened with her dad's health, her mother wouldn't risk it.

So Kate didn't wait for her approval.

"Stay here," she said, pecking her mom quickly on the cheek before turning on her heel and racing up the stairs.

"Katherine Anne!"

"I mean it. Stay here!"

And then she was gone.

Chapter Seventeen

Kate was going to have hell to pay with her mother later. Dante's nine circles were nothing compared to the wrath that would be waiting for her.

They'd probably skip right past the yelling, and her mother would instead throttle her for making the decision to run back outside with an active tornado warning in progress.

But in that moment, there was nothing that could change her mind. Before the full scale of her own stupidity could hit her, she was already up the stairs, across the living room and out the front door.

Kate had never thought of herself as a rash person. In fact, she was usually quite good about taking her time with things. Considering all her options. Researching. Comparing. But this wasn't exactly your run-of-the-mill decision. This was the kind of decision made under pressure. And if Kate had learned anything today it was that she could be a little reckless in the face of danger.

Maybe more than a little reckless.

Her mother was likely cursing up a storm in the cellar at this point, and her dad was probably wondering if he had the strength and energy to brave the stairs again. He wasn't the kind of man to sit behind and be idle while other people did the work for him. But Lord help her father if he set even one foot on those cellar stairs.

Her mother would strangle them both.

Kate flew off the porch in a single leap, skipping the steps entirely as she raced through the storm, back to the stables. She squinted against the rush of wind, eyes casting around warily for the ominous funnel shape that now plagued her mind.

The only thing she could do was pray they weren't in the direct path if it touched down.

Warm air kissed her face, followed by a chill that sent goose bumps rippling up both her arms. A few shingles came crashing down beside her, torn from the roof of the house as easily as the maple seeds dropped from the trees in autumn.

Kate ran faster, swearing to never tell her mother about the debris she was dodging.

The world looked like something out of an Armageddon movie, the sky about three seconds from breaking open to swallow her whole. Kate tried to tamp down the uncomfortable pressure of nerves that struggled to break free in a panicked scream from her throat.

But what came out instead was a shaky, half-controlled gasp as she threw the door to the stables open. The force of the wind almost yanked her arm from its socket, and Kate grimaced in pain.

A myriad of startled cries issued from the stables, each of the horses stomping anxiously in their stalls as Kate ran to retrieve the halters. Next, she grabbed a rag and a marker from the back room where the shovels, pitchforks and feed supplies were stored with most of the horse tack. As Kate tore the rag into pieces, scribbling CARDIFF RANCH in shaky letters along with her phone number, her phone buzzed in her back pocket. She felt the buzzing go on and on, a phone call she couldn't answer with her hands full.

She hastily tied each piece of fabric to a different halter, but her phone stopped buzzing just as she fished it out of her pocket. It was a missed call from Nathan.

Disappointment filled her as wind battered the sides of the stables. She hoped he'd heard about the storm warning and that he was okay. Resolving to call him back as soon as she was done with the horses, Kate stuffed her phone in her pocket and hurried into the first horse stall. The slamming of a vehicle door caught her attention, and she ran back to the stable door, wondering if it was Nathan. In the frenzied haze of sideways rain, she spotted that familiar olive green van parked haphazardly between a stubbornly rooted tree and the house.

Climbing out of the van was Rusty, his red hair whipping wildly in the wind. He held his hands to his head, trying desperately to keep his hair out of his eyes.

Tara appeared on the other side of the van, looking windswept.

"Rusty? Tara?" Kate shouted, taking one step and then another, running out to meet them. "You guys okay?"

"Holy shit," Rusty said, grabbing her arm. He looked stunned. "Do you know what we just saw?"

"Pretty sure I can guess," Kate yelled over the roar of the wind.

"It was a tornado, Kate. A freaking tornado! Tara got it on camera." His jaw hung open. "It was just there, rolling along."

"Where?" she tried to ask him but all he could manage to do was vaguely point in a direction before stumbling against the van.

"Where's Nathan?" Tara asked.

Kate whipped around at that, registering for the first time that they were alone. Nathan was nowhere in sight. "I haven't…" she stammered. "I don't know. I thought he was with you guys?"

They looked at her blankly.

"I haven't seen him since…" A terrible ball of energy coiled at the bottom of Kate's gut as she recalled their argument. "Since before. He tried to call me once but I missed it. I didn't think—"

"He's not back yet?" Confusion drew Rusty's brows together.

Tara squinted at Kate through the rain, worry bleeding onto her face. "He was ahead of us on the road. We couldn't even keep up, he was speeding back here so fast."

Kate shook her head. "I don't know where he is."

Tara held her arm up as another shingle dislodged from the roof. "I'm sure he's fine. He's smart. Resourceful. He'll find somewhere to wait it out," she cried over the endless howl of the storm.

Wait it out? Kate sputtered in her own mind. Where the hell had he gone?

An onslaught of horrible thoughts plagued her then. Images of Nathan injured somewhere. Alone and in pain. His truck abandoned in a ditch. Maybe he needed her help, and she'd missed his call.

She immediately put her phone to her ear, willing Nathan to pick up. It went directly to a voice mail message she couldn't hear over the wind. "He's not answering!"

"Could be for a lot of reasons," Tara yelled into her ear.

Kate wanted to pitch her phone across the field, but that wouldn't solve anything. The horses still needed her help and standing here doing nothing was a perfect waste of time. The storm howled around them.

"Get inside," Kate ordered. "My parents are in the cellar. Go down there with them and don't let my mother leave, no matter what kind of bodily harm she threatens you with!" She pushed Rusty until he started to move. One leg in front of the other.

"Aren't you coming?" Tara asked.

"I'll be right there. As soon as I deal with the horses." She caught Tara's hand. "Will you try to call Nathan again for me?"

"Don't worry, we'll find him," Tara promised, and together she and Rusty staggered toward the house.

Kate fought her way back to the stables, begging for a little more time. Begging that Nathan was okay. Everything that had happened before now felt so trivial, and she couldn't bear the thought of their last communication being in anger, so she tried not to think of him at all.

It was pointless, though. Her mind screamed for him.

Shade neighed so loud at her that Kate broke from her worry for a moment. "I know," she said, throwing the door to the stall open while trying not to get trampled. "I know."

She jumped back, narrowly missing the downbeat of one of Shade's hooves. "Shh, girl. It's okay," Kate tried to soothe while slipping the halter over Shade's head. The horses were understandably anxious, knocking at the doors of their stalls with strong muscles. It was all Kate could do to keep her balance around the spooked animal.

Once the halter was on, Kate took better control of Shade, keeping a tight hold on the leather as she led Shade through the stables. She reached the halfway point before letting her go, giving Shade a quick push in the right direction. Without hesitation, Shade galloped out toward the pasture.

Kate turned around, clocking the other horses. Five more. Five more halters. Five more anxious steeds.

She mentally tried to gauge how long it would take her to turn them all loose. How many minutes were too many minutes out here? *Well*, she decided, wasting time thinking about it wasn't going to help her. Not now. But just as she was running back to get Samson and Tully, a voice cut through the wind.

"Kate!" it shouted, or at least she thought it did. It was hard to tell with the sudden onslaught of hail colliding with the roof.

She looked up just as Nathan burst through the door, drenched from head to foot, mud splattered up his front and back, each lock of dark hair twisted next to his face. He looked half-wild as he stormed across the stables. "Kate!" he said, and she could hardly hear it over the rush of blood in her ears.

Her pulse hammered as the feeling of relief exploded

inside her. She'd never thought it would feel so good to see him.

"I thought something was wrong," she said numbly. It felt like a dream. "What happened to you? Where did you go?"

"Where did *I* go?" he stammered. Racing toward her, he scooped her up in his arms, and she felt the tension bleed from each one of her muscles.

"Rusty said you were ahead of them on the road," Kate explained.

"I was."

"But you didn't come back with them?"

"My truck is parked at the side of the house. They probably didn't see it."

Oh, Kate thought.

"I ran right into the house looking for you. Your mom's frantic. It was all I could do to stop her from coming after you herself."

"She's angry at me," Kate guessed.

"What do you think?" He held her face in his hands, gazing at her intently.

Kate didn't waste another second and closed the distance between them, kissing him full on the lips. It was slick and wet, and he smelled like rain and trampled grass. Their tacky clothes clung to each other, pulling them even closer. She poured all her pent-up frustration and feelings into the kiss, letting it say everything she couldn't. Somewhere between ranching and chasing thunderstorms, he'd become so much more than she was willing to live without.

Nathan snaked his arms around her, his hands falling to her waist, holding her tighter, pulling her closer.

It was nice to be held.

To be close to him.

Then his hand moved, reaching out to grasp hers. He squeezed it once, twice, three times. Just a simple *I'm here*. Or maybe *It'll be okay*. Or maybe even *What the hell is happening right now?* Whatever it was, the gesture eased something inside her.

He broke the kiss as suddenly as she'd started it, tugging her toward the door.

"Wait," Kate cried, stopping so abruptly that she slid across the floor. "The horses."

"Kate," he said, voice cracking, "this thing is coming! We don't have the time." He didn't stop. Just kept trying to drag her toward the house.

"They won't stand a chance locked up," she begged.

"We can't stay."

"I just need a few minutes." She wasn't asking him for help. She was just asking him to let her finish the job.

He looked at her then, fire in his eyes. He growled, catching her chin between his thumb and forefinger, tilting her face. He kissed her again. It was hard and fast, and Kate's pulse faltered for a second.

"What do you need me to do?" he asked.

Kate tossed him a halter while she shook off the dizzy spell from his kiss. "Put these on the horses, and then get them into the pasture."

"Okay." Nathan turned on his heel, racing to the closest stall. Kate did the same.

Nathan slid the halter over Samson, touching the piece of cloth with Kate's hastily written info on it. "This is smart."

"At least this way if something happens and the horses get out, we might have an easier time of tracking them down." She gave Tully a firm pat, and the horse trotted out of the stables and into the torrent of rain. By the sounds of it, another band of hail was starting.

"Let's hope nothing happens," Nathan said, meeting her in the aisle with Samson. He clicked his tongue, and Samson chased after Tully. The sound of Samson's whinny was immediately swallowed by a crash of thunder.

"Well, I'd obviously prefer it if there wasn't a tornado warning right now," Kate quipped.

"And I'd prefer if you didn't run directly into the path of said tornado. But here we are. You're impossible, you know that?"

"We can fight about it later," Kate called over her shoulder, taking the last halters and hurrying toward the boarded horses. She really hoped the marker didn't rub out in the rain. The last thing she wanted to do was have to call one of their clients and explain that their horse was missing.

"Oh, you can bet on it."

Together, Kate and Nathan turned the last horses out. They disappeared into a storm so thick that Kate lost sight of them as they raced away from the stables. It was probably a good thing, she mused. The horses would be less likely to get hit by debris if they weren't standing near the building. As it was, tarry black shingles littered the mud puddles Kate had to wade through to ensure the gate to the fence was secured. It was a struggle against the wind, and Kate had to dig her feet deep into the earth.

"Here," Nathan said, coming up behind her, both of them pushing and heaving until the gate slid into place.

She hesitated a moment, looking for those dark

shapes in the field, praying that she'd given them their best chance. If she was an animal in the midst of a storm like this, she'd want her freedom, too. The chance to flee from danger.

"Kate, c'mon," Nathan shouted at her, tugging at her arm. "We're wasting time."

Finally, Kate let him drag her away.

They ran back through the stables and out the other side, the door slamming against the wall sharply. It was raining harder, if that was even possible, the water whipping across the fields so fast it felt like needles against Kate's skin.

Pausing, she held one hand up to protect her face and squinted to make out the shape of the house. All around them, the sky had darkened to an eerie shade of muddy gray-green, and the hairs on her arms stood straight up.

"We need to go," Nathan said, grabbing at her, his grip so tight it was almost painful.

Kate's hair whipped across her face, obscuring her vision until the only thing they could do—the only thing left to do—was run.

Nathan took her hand, and they ran until their lungs burned. Until Kate wanted to throw up from the stress of it.

They reached the porch at almost the same time. Rusty stood there, holding the door open for them, and Kate practically threw herself through it.

"You two okay?"

Kate nodded.

"Go," Nathan said from somewhere behind her. "Go!"

They raced for the cellar stairs. The lights had blacked out completely, but a few flickering candles had been left on the steps.

Bodies crashed into hers, Nathan and Rusty presumably, as she picked her way across the cellar, trying to keep track of her surroundings by memory and feel. Flashlight beams and phone lights blinked to life, spotlighting faces of fear and panic. The house trembled and the candlelight quivered, creating new snapshots of chaos.

Kate's chest ached from wanting to scream.

There was a sound like glass shattering and a roar so loud that she thought the sound might tear right through her.

And then she was engulfed by strong arms. Nathan's familiar scent overwhelmed her, and her knees practically gave out. She buried her face in his chest, everything inside her clawing to escape in a flurry of tears.

But it was all too much.

Too much to cry.

Too much to shout.

He just squeezed her as they sank into a pile on the floor, cramped between everyone else. Kate tugged her hands up to cover her ears as the house cried and creaked while the wind roared louder and louder.

It howled like it was grieving.

Like it was grieving, and it was never going to stop.

Chapter Eighteen

It did stop.

Not slowly, but all at once.

Everything. The wind and the rain and the hail and the storm. It just…stopped.

The lights didn't come back on, but it was over, the quiet stillness reaching across the room from corner to corner.

"Everybody okay?" came her dad's gruff voice from the darkness.

Murmurs of agreement echoed across the cellar. Cell phone lights popped on again, giving slivers of clarity to the room, and slowly they began picking their way out of the cellar.

It was organized chaos for the most part, no one pushing or pulling, just moving in a steady, bulky stream for the stairs. Nathan's hand never left her arm, his fingers wrapped around it like he was afraid he'd lose her.

Kate reached the top of the stairs first and waited as everyone else emerged into the dim living room. First Nathan, then her parents, then Tara and Rusty. Her mom wrapped her in a painfully tight hug, and all Kate could do was hug her back.

"You're lucky you're alive," her mom muttered into Kate's shoulder. "I was going to kill you for running off."

"I'm sorry," Kate whispered.

"Never again," her mom warned. "I won't survive it."

Kate nodded. She had no intentions of ever making a repeat performance of the last hour. Once in a lifetime was quite enough.

The power was still out, the only light bleeding in from outside. Glass littered the front hall from one of the windows, and her dad's slippers crunched against it as he wandered to the front door, pulling it open and stepping out onto the porch.

Kate padded through the house carefully, like she fully expected an entire wall to be missing.

"Dale, please be careful," her mother begged, and Kate could almost hear the exasperation in her voice.

Kate followed her dad. As she stepped outside, under an oddly clear sky, there was a moment where she thought everything looked okay.

And then she blinked.

The house was obviously still standing, a picturesque portrait of small-town living, minus a few shingles, the living room window, a portion of the porch railing, and the rocking chair that had once stood proudly in the corner—which Kate suspected was probably half a mile down the road.

The guest house was intact, and the stables were

still there, too, though enough siding had been ripped from the building that she could see straight through it in spots.

Entire trees had been torn from the ground, roots stretching up to the sky like gnarled fingers, and in other places, the ranch looked practically unscathed.

Kate didn't understand it.

How could a tornado rip through and completely destroy some things while leaving others untouched?

"I'm gonna go have a look around," she said. "See if there's any sign of the horses. Are you guys okay here?"

"We've got it covered," Rusty said, holding the front door open for her dad as he wandered back inside.

"I'll come with you," Nathan told her.

"Be careful," her mother begged, shaking her head in disbelief. "I mean it, Kate. Please."

It was a soft plea, the turn of her frown and the dip between her brows begging for Kate to heed her. Kate nodded—she wouldn't take her mother's words lightly. That parental worry wouldn't have fazed her before. She likely would have shrugged it off like every other adult child. Except now things were different. Now a tornado had just ripped through their town. Now her family's livelihood was scattered across the ranch under a suspiciously cheery sky.

In the cellar, Kate had spent a few terrifying minutes imagining what life would be like if she lost both her parents and Nathan and these new people she called friends. So, she looked her mother in the eye and said reassuringly, "We will."

She headed down the stairs and across the property. When she glanced back at the house, she could make out her dad's outline already fitting cardboard against the frame of the window where the glass had shattered.

"Kate?" Nathan called softly, slowing ahead.

The tinkle of wind chimes and the chirps of barn finches were familiar as she made her way up the path. She was glad for that amount of normalcy because everything else felt utterly surreal, standing on the property with Nathan by her side. She'd honestly thought that after they argued, after she pushed him away with such finality, she would only see the back of him as he returned to his old life of adventure, taking pictures on the other side of the world.

To have him here with her now felt like a dream. So much so that she didn't know if she wanted to laugh because they'd survived or cry because their fight, hours ago now, seemed like the most ridiculous thing in the world.

Nathan held his hand out to her and she took it, feeling the weight of his hand wrap around hers, loosely entwining their fingers.

As they reached the stables, he tugged on her, pulling her back from the door.

"Careful," he said, glancing up before reaching out to pull on the door. It sat slightly ajar, tugged awkwardly off its hinges.

Stepping inside, Kate could see the spots where the siding and parts of the roof had been pulled off by the wind. New spotlights of sun dwindled down to the stalls, each of them splattered with dust and dirt and straw, soaked by the rains that fell so violently such a short time ago.

"Looks sturdy enough," Nathan commented, gazing up to the rafters. "The structure has held out, at any rate."

"It needs surface work," Kate agreed. The building was meant to keep the horses out of the elements, so they'd need to get repairs started sooner rather than later. But in the meantime, the animals could be housed there once the interior was cleaned up and the stalls were bedded with fresh straw.

Kate moved through the stables to the other end of the building where she could make out the muddied pastures.

Nathan followed, his presence steady behind her. They trudged past the fallen pasture shelters and tipped water basins. Past the broken gates and tree limbs.

Kate walked among the debris, following old hoof tracks. Fence posts and railings and straw were scattered everywhere. She turned slowly, until she found Nathan again. She could see the loss reflected in his face.

"They're gone," Kate said of the horses. "The fences must have come down in the wind."

"That's a good thing, right?" Nathan said after a moment. "Means they got away from the worst of it."

"Hopefully," Kate said. "If they haven't gone far, they might return on their own. Though it's likely we'll have to go looking for them." Worry crossed her face. She could feel it in the turn of her brow and the puckering of her lips. What if the horses hadn't gotten away? What if they'd run straight into the path of the storm or been injured by flying debris? What if they lay hurt somewhere?

Kate shook that thought from her mind. Animals

were smart. Intuitive. Their best chance was setting them free. She knew this.

Together they walked back up the path, assessing the damage, marveling at the things that remained unscathed.

"Guest house porch looks a little beat up," Nathan commented.

Kate noted the eaves trough hanging by a single point on one half of the roof. Even from this distance, that much was clear.

As they drew closer, she gasped.

"It's just from the garden beds," Nathan said from behind her.

The door was splattered with mud and weeds or maybe what used to be vegetables and flowers. All her mother's hard work.

There was just so much damage. Big things. Little things. Everywhere. It was a path of destruction that Kate could trace with her eyes. Her breaths came faster and faster. How nearly this could have been Mom and Dad sitting in the path of destruction.

Kate's jaw trembled and she clamped her teeth so hard that they ached.

She wouldn't cry.

She wouldn't.

"It's okay," Nathan said, hands on both her shoulders, trying to calm her. To console her. "All of these things can be fixed. The buildings. The fences. Gardens. We'll track the horses down."

She nodded. He was right. She was being ridiculous. The most important thing was that they were all okay. That they were together. She looked up at him, remembering the moment he raced into the stables. He'd come back. And not just come back. But he'd come back for her.

"You're hurt." His hand whispered against her forehead.

"What is it?" she said, feeling the sting suddenly.

"Blood."

"A lot?" She automatically reached for her head but he pushed her hand down.

He shook his head. "Just a little. C'mon. I'm pretty sure there's a first aid kit stashed in here."

She followed him into the guest house. "Bathroom. Under the sink."

He gave her a quick once-over. "Yeah, you would know better." He took her hand, leading her down the hall. When they got to the bathroom, Nathan dug the first aid kit out and Kate sat on the counter in front of him.

"Let's get you cleaned up," he said.

Kate had the distinct impression that this was not the first time he'd had to play nurse. He rifled through the kit, finding antiseptic and gauze. He reached around her to wash his hands.

"You're not squeamish?"

"Between Rusty, Tara and me, we've had our fair share of scrapes and bruises. Someone's always tripping over something or falling over in their haste to get the perfect photo. When you're out in the field, you sort of have to MacGyver it until you can get back for some proper medical care. So, no, a little bit of blood doesn't bother me." He dabbed at her head with the alcohol-soaked gauze and she hissed. "Does it bother you?"

"No. When I was young I watched a girl fall off her

horse and break her arm in two places. That made me woozy, but I think vet school took it out of me."

"Do you know what cut you?"

"I don't even remember it happening."

"We should probably swing by the hospital later, make sure your tetanus is up to date."

Kate grinned at him.

"What?"

"I'm impressed."

"Always the tone of surprise with you." One of his hands fell to her thigh and squeezed gently. Kate wanted to fold herself against him.

"Well," she said. "I'll add it to my growing list of things to do. As far as extreme weather events go, I guess we're pretty lucky. Everyone still has all their limbs and I've had expert first aid treatment."

Nathan dabbed at her head with a dry piece of gauze now, smirking. "Only the best for you."

She knew some part of him was teasing, but it warmed her heart anyway. Then she winced as he reached a tender spot.

"Sorry. All done."

"How do I look?" she asked.

"Like you just went a couple rounds with a tornado."

"Yeah, that's about how I feel."

He stepped closer.

"Is this where you kiss it better?"

"Do you want me to?"

"Sort of."

He chuckled and picked up a box of Band-Aids from the first aid kit. He picked out one at random. It was bright green, like the grass when the noon sun hit. He peeled it open and stuck it across her forehead, near her temple.

Kate moved her hand to prod, but Nathan caught it, kissing her fingertips instead. "Don't poke at it." Then he leaned down and gently kissed the spot.

"All better?" he asked.

"Like magic."

"That's me. A regular old magician."

He was close.

So close.

Kate could see flecks of gold in his gray eyes.

"I've never worried about someone the way I worried over you," he said suddenly. "When I raced down to that cellar and your parents told me you weren't there—"

"I know," she said, interrupting him before the words could mean too much.

"It terrified me."

"I'm right here," she said. "Safe and sound."

He leaned toward her, kissing the spot on her forehead again, just a barely-there press of his lips, like the flutter of a butterfly wing. He did the same between her brows and the bridge of her nose. Finally, the corner of her mouth. Then he sank down against her lips, and Kate welcomed him eagerly.

She pulled him as close as she could as his mouth ravaged hers, tongue seeking entrance and taking every gasp and moan she freely offered.

Nathan held her, his hands splayed against her back, the heat of his skin melting the blood in her veins. It roared inside her, her pulse beating erratically in her chest. All for him.

Just for him.

"I've wanted to do this for weeks," he said.

"Then do it," Kate teased. She wrapped her legs around him, holding tighter. His hands found purchase, lifting her up. They staggered from the bathroom, clumsily knocking against the wall as he stopped to devour her with kisses.

She gasped into his mouth, tugging on the collar of his shirt.

"Bed," he rasped as he carried her into the bedroom, putting her down long enough to pull his shirt over his head.

Kate marveled at the lean muscle before her, letting her hands roam his chest. She surged forward then, pulling herself to him.

"It's just adrenaline," she said as his mouth found hers again. "A completely normal reaction. Just," she moaned, "the body's way of dealing with shock."

"This isn't just adrenaline, Kate." His eyes blazed as he pulled back far enough to see hers. "You know that."

"It's too soon," she argued, rebelling against the words he hadn't even uttered yet. "A summer isn't possibly long enough to—"

"To what?"

"To know." *She loved him.* She loved him the same way he loved her. With a fire that threatened to consume her unless she released it.

"I knew the first time I pulled you out of the stables, Kate. I've known all along." He squeezed her hip and she melted into him, feeling a hot blush creep down her cheeks and neck. Nathan followed it with kisses along her jaw, down her neck, sucking at her pulse point before pulling her sweatshirt over her head.

He stood back to regard her for a moment before he reached out, casting a gentle finger along her collarbone and down her sternum. Then he chased the blush where it disappeared into her cleavage, sucking and nipping at her skin as he went.

It was new, this thing between them, though Kate knew already that she'd miss this as soon as it was over.

How odd it was to know it in her soul, as easily as she knew her own hands, how right this was.

How could someone love a person they'd only just met? How could someone burn for them so desperately?

She pushed at her pants, sweeping them down her legs. She heard the pop of fabric as her bra fell away and then all she could think about was the cool air as it touched her breasts. Her nipples hardened in the anticipation of his touch.

Nathan slid his hand along the curve of her breast, caressing first with his thumb, the pad coarse against her sensitive flesh, and then with his tongue. Kate fell back against the bed and thought of the lean muscle that surrounded her, how deftly he held himself, how steady. She'd not known what she sought in a partner until him, someone sturdy and yet yielding. And perhaps that was what felt so right.

When she pushed against his chest, his lips slipped free from her breast and his gray eyes found hers, wide and bright and alive. She wondered how long this could last. Moments where neither what came before nor what came after mattered. Kate reveled in it. In the freedom of simple pleasure. In the feel of Nathan's hot breath on the sensitive parts of her flesh. He was so very good, so very delicate in a way that made her want to push him over and crush her lips to his. To feel the firmness of him beneath her.

He divested himself of the rest of his clothes and

Kate watched, taking in the fine lines and muscles. The dips and curves. The strength and power. When he joined her on the bed again, she swung her leg over and around his hip, feeling the length of him drag against her belly. She pushed against him gently and he rolled, falling to his back against the mattress. She straddled him now, hands pressed down against his chest, the hammer of his heart strong. It was as if she held his heart in the palm of her hand.

He had hers.

Whether he wanted it or not, he had it.

"You're beautiful," he rasped, his fingertips tracing circles in all the right places.

"You're not so bad yourself," Kate told him as she bent to kiss him.

Nathan chuckled against her lips, and Kate threaded her fingers into his hair as he left a dizzying flurry of kisses behind her ear and down her neck. "How am I doing so far?" he whispered into her skin.

"You tell me," she groaned.

"I mean, I'd give myself a gold star."

Kate laughed through the haze of pleasure that was quickly infiltrating her brain. She tugged on his hair, just so. Gently. And yet with enough pressure to get his eyes to trail up to hers. When they connected, something inside her melted.

"I love you, Kate Cardiff." He surged up and kissed her then and it felt like it was the first time she'd ever been kissed. She wanted to dive into that feeling and just sink. Sink until the need for air forced her to the surface. When they broke apart, she gasped.

The air between them felt like electricity.

Nathan's hands began to roam again, and every part

of her tingled. He rolled them over, and Kate arched her back for him.

The pads of his fingers were roughened from days spent on the ranch. These were hands that had known a hard day's work. And as much as they did, they also knew how to be gentle enough to drive her wild.

Kate didn't know why it felt so right.

She knew why it felt good, obviously, because Nathan was built like an athlete, with his dark looks and sinewy muscles stretched across his body. But feeling right and feeling good were two different things.

And she got both.

Nathan's breathing grew ragged and she could feel the length of him pulsing against her. "Is this okay?" he asked before going any further.

She nodded, kissing him again before reaching down to help guide him where she wanted him most. As he slid inside, Kate saw stars, her eyes practically rolling to the back of her head. Her hips moved of their own accord, seeking friction as they both chased the mounting release that built between them.

"You're kind of good at this," Nathan teased as they found a rhythm that drove them both a little wild.

He was thorough with his ministrations and everywhere his hands roamed, Kate burned, a fire roaring to life in her belly. It was a tender sort of heat, delicious and warm, twisting and turning in her core.

Soon that fire became need, and Kate begged for it. The anticipation was enough to send her heart racing, and she rose to meet his thrusts.

"I might be kind of good at this, too," Nathan whispered along her jaw as his lips feathered kisses there. He drove his knees into the bed, anchoring his position, one hand wrapped tightly along the underside of her thigh, the other lifting to cup her cheek.

"Are you fishing for compliments?" Kate managed to say.

"Maybe," he murmured, leaving a slow, hot trail of kisses across her shoulder. Wet, open-mouthed kisses, with the barest graze of teeth along her skin. He soothed it with a flick of his tongue. "Give me a few more minutes before you decide."

Kate's vision grew fuzzy with desire as Nathan's breathing turned to short pants against her skin. He bucked slowly, but deep, the tension building. Kate ground herself against him unconsciously. She was needy and wanton and how had she refused herself this?

Kate choked back a cry as he thrusted harder. She wanted more.

Demanded more.

Her hands gripped the sculpted range of his shoulder blades and she dug her fingers into his skin, holding him closer, erasing whatever space was left between them. In response, Nathan pressed his head into her shoulder and groaned. When Kate's legs wrapped around his waist, forcing him deeper, his hand moved between their bodies, finding that place that sent her right over that impossible precipice.

Nathan thrust erratically against her as the tension crested and fell away. Kate cried out something sappy and unintelligible. She trembled as her walls clenched hard, wonderfully hard, sending electricity across her body like an ocean wave upon the sand. It ebbed and flowed: the feelings, the pleasure, the utter bliss of the moment.

When he stilled, Kate held him to her, certain that

everything might shatter if she let him go. Nathan didn't fight it, though, content to let them both drift back slowly from their highs. And even when she'd returned from that, Kate held him, refusing to lose even one moment.

"What are you thinking?" he asked her many moments later, letting his hand whisper over her back, tracing patterns and shapes that she'd had no luck identifying thus far.

She hummed contentedly, loath to admit that she'd been thinking of nothing in particular at all, everything in her mind a soupy sort of bliss. "I think your plan worked a little too well."

"No, this is exactly how I plotted it."

"So it was never about friendship?" She rolled toward him, pretending to be shocked. "You were just trying to get me into bed?"

"Oh, yes. Definitely. Didn't you know, the princess and the lowly ranch hand always end up together?"

"And then what?"

He dragged his fingertips across her arm. "Then there's usually some business about living happily ever after. But we can work on that part."

He pressed a kiss to her bare shoulder and then her collarbone, his lips trailing across her skin like flames upon kindling. They followed the length of her sternum between her breasts and she squirmed before he spoke again.

"I'm not in a rush, are you?"

"No," she whispered.

"Good. I'm quite happy right here."

She knew they'd eventually have to leave this bubble

and figure out all the things that made this so complicated. Soon they'd have to drag themselves out of bed to deal with the world beyond the guest house.

Right now, though, she could barely keep her thoughts straight long enough to care.

And frankly, she didn't want to.

She dragged his lips to hers once more, letting herself get lost in the taste of him.

Chapter Nineteen

As Kate's mom prepared dinner that night, there were tears in her eyes.

She looked over at Kate where she was chopping carrots for the stew that was already simmering on the barbecue. A small smile crept onto her face. One of those grateful little smiles.

And it wasn't hard to know exactly what she was thinking.

To know that it very well could have ended much worse.

If Kate knew anything after these past few months, it was that no amount of stuff equated to the loss of someone you loved.

They were lucky.

Her mom reached out, wrapping Kate in a hug. "You okay?"

"I'm good. You?"

She laughed a bit, something like disbelief. "I will be."

"Oh my," her dad said from the table where he was poring over the photos on Tara's camera. It was dim in the house still, lit by half a dozen candles, the brightest light coming from the camera screen, but that didn't seem to bother anyone. Not right now, at least.

After Kate and Nathan had returned from the guest house, Tara went out with Nathan and documented the damage on the property for the insurance company. And though insurance should eventually cover most of the damage, the ranch couldn't sit like this until then. They couldn't leave gaping holes in the stables for months while the finances were sorted out.

Kate's biggest concern now was locating the horses. They'd gone out earlier, before the sun had set, scanning the nearby roads. It was impossible to know how far the horses got. They could be hurt. Or spooked. Or hiding. Or picked up by some other local farmer. They could still be running, for all Kate knew.

It could be days before they figured out what happened.

"This is going to be expensive," her mom murmured to her dad, leaning over his shoulder to see the pictures. Kate knew she was not meant to hear it, but she did. "Where do we even start?"

"Could have been worse," her dad said just as quietly.

Her mom squeezed his shoulder.

And it was at that moment that Kate realized that her parents had no intention of selling the ranch. They wanted to stay here. Grow old together. Her heart broke for them, but again she knew it wasn't the right time for her to start pestering them about finances or for her to blurt out her offer of help. *Do you need money? Please, let me give you money.* It would only embarrass them, and they'd dealt with enough today.

Rusty walked up, carrying a couple of empty mugs destined for the sink. He leaned against the counter beside Kate, his arms crossed loosely.

"Have you had your fill of storm chasing?" she wondered.

"You know what," Rusty said. "I think I'm thoroughly chased out. Probably for a lifetime. There's just something about being chased by a funnel of doom that makes you feel like you've seen it all."

"Figured as much."

Rusty smiled. "Tara did say she got some pretty wicked photos, though."

"I'll bet you all did," Kate said. She could only imagine the things they caught on camera during their frantic drive back to the ranch.

"I was mostly screaming," he added. "A good time was had by all."

Kate chuckled even though she shouldn't. Rusty was good for that, though, finding the humor in a situation. Making everything a little less terrible. "As long as you had fun," Kate joked.

"Oh, so much fun. Almost as much as you and Nathan." He winked and lowered his voice. "I see you two have finally sorted yourselves out."

"I don't know what you're talking about," Kate said.

"Oh, please. I know bedroom eyes when I see them." Kate felt her face flush but Rusty just shrugged. "But I guess that's what's supposed to happen after a near-death disaster experience. You tell the people you care about how you really feel."

"I guess it is," she agreed.

"Well, I for one am happy I no longer have to listen to him drone on and on about you. All it took was Dorothy whipping through town."

"Dorothy?" Kate wrinkled her nose. "You named the tornado?"

"*Wizard of Oz*, duh. What else?"

"Kind of perfect," Kate said. "In an ironic, dark humor sort of way."

"That's me. Ironic and full of dark humor." Rusty pretended to flip his hair, waltzing away in a dramatic fashion. "And don't you forget it!"

Kate finished with the carrots, putting them in a pot. Behind her Nathan and Tara appeared.

"Hey, Kate," Nathan said. "Check this out."

She joined Tara and him at the island, drying her hands on a cloth.

"I've started scrolling through social media," Tara said. "They've already got a list of community resources going for anyone that needs help." She flipped her phone around to where she had Twitter open, tracking #tornadocleanup. "I can put the word out that we're looking for the horses. See if anyone has spotted them."

"This is genius," Kate said. "Thank you."

"Maybe attach one of the recent photos of the horses that you took," Nathan said.

Tara nodded, getting up to go find her camera. "Already on it."

Kate smiled at Nathan, grateful for him and his friends. Grateful that they were here during one of the worst things. It was making it all a little easier to bear.

A siren whirred in the distance, interrupting the moment. A police car from the local sheriff's department trundled up the road and onto the property, red light swooping in through the kitchen window.

"Oh no," her mom said. "What's that about?"

Kate followed her dad onto the porch. Nathan was by her side in an instant. Everyone else filtered out slowly as a young officer walked up to the house.

"Evening, Deputy," her dad said in greeting.

"Ryan Mullens," Kate said, eyes narrowed in amusement as she recognized him. Another one of these local kids that she grew up with. She thought he'd run away from here just as she had.

"Kate Cardiff," he said.

"Deputy?" she replied, surprised. What she remembered of Ryan could be summed up by the words *disturber of the peace*. Their teachers had certainly never anticipated anything more for Ryan than class clown. It was funny now to see him all grown up.

He tapped his chest. "Even have the badge to prove it."

"It's good to see you." Kate felt Nathan's hand on her hip.

"You, too. Glad everyone seems to be okay." Ryan's smile became serious. "I'm just checking in on folks. Seeing if they need anything."

"We're all good here," her dad said. "How'd the town make out?"

"It's in rough shape," Ryan said. "Some places look like all they need is a new coat of paint, others have their insides splayed out like someone took a big knife and gutted them open. A couple of storefronts are completely gone. The volunteer fire crew just put out a small blaze at the diner."

"Oh, poor Diane," her mom said.

"But so far no one was hurt beyond some bumps and bruises."

"That's a relief."

Ryan nodded. "I've still got some rounds to make. You folks have a good night."

"You too, Deputy," her dad said, waving him off.

"So," Nathan said as the others wandered inside, "how do you know the deputy?" His free hand snaked around her other hip until his arms were wrapped around her. Kate leaned into him with a soft smile.

"I had the biggest crush on him in school."

Nathan's hold tightened, igniting a fire in her belly. "Oh, really?"

She ran her hand along his arm, looking out as the last of the sun dipped beneath the horizon. "Don't worry," she said. "I grew out of it."

"That's good," Nathan murmured, his voice only for her to hear, "because I had every intention of reminding you tonight that you're mine now."

Kate's breath caught in her throat. "I wouldn't mind if you still did."

Nathan hummed, pressing a kiss to the side of her neck. "Stay with me tonight in the guest house?"

Kate twisted in his arms, leaning back to look at him. A smirk played over her lips. "Well, technically, since *boyfriends* are different than friends, you never won that bet. So the guest house is mine again, which means you're staying with me."

Nathan laughed, a booming, glorious sound. "So you'll admit that I'm your boyfriend?"

"Yes," she said.

"Right now. To Rusty and Tara and your parents?"

Kate tilted her head. "Yes."

He leaned down to kiss her. "Then I think *I* won, regardless of the bet."

Chapter Twenty

Morning came sooner than Kate expected, sunny and warm and bright, and she was already contemplating going back to sleep when she glanced at her phone to find her screen packed with notifications. Suddenly, she was wide-awake.

"What is it?" Nathan grunted.

The sound of his voice, caked in sleep, made her mouth curve in a ridiculous grin. She rolled over, basking in the warmth of him as he opened his arms to her. Kate could get used to this feeling.

She placed a kiss against his bare chest. "Someone's spotted the horses."

Nathan leaned down to nuzzle his nose against hers. "That is good news."

He held her tighter, rolling until she went with him.

Nathan tucked her hair behind her ears. "So, is this

going to be awkward with your parents when we stop in at the house for breakfast? Do they know you spent the night with me?"

"Well, Rusty saw us walk over here after dinner last night, so I'm assuming everyone else is aware. He doesn't strike me as the type to keep something like that to himself."

Nathan hummed in agreement. "I'm just wondering if Dale has a shotgun I need to be worried about now?"

Kate chuckled. "I'm pretty sure my parents loved you before I did."

Nathan brushed the hair from her forehead, studying her hard. A slow smile crept onto his face. "Love?" He bent to whisper the word against her neck, following it up with the kind of kiss that made Kate's eyes roll back. "That little thing?"

"Yes," she said as he lifted his head to look at her again. "That pesky, little thing."

She hadn't been able to say it until now. Not out loud, at least. But Nathan had been patient. And though it was no big romantic declaration, he didn't seem to mind.

He grinned as Kate's phone began to buzz. She answered a video call from Tara, making sure to strategically angle the phone so everything and everyone was covered. Her hair was in some kind of monstrosity after last night, though by the time she realized, the call was already connected and it was far too late to fix.

"Are you alive?" Tara asked, answering the call with her eyes covered. "I've been texting you for an hour already."

"Yes," Kate said. "I just woke up."

"Are you decent?"

Kate laughed. "Yes," she assured her before Tara even considered taking her hand away from her face.

"Is Nathan? I've already seen more of him than I ever wanted to because he and Rusty have a bad habit of taking their clothes off when they get drunk."

Kate gaped in glee at the screen, then looked over at Nathan, who was conveniently pretending to sleep again. "I hope there are pictures to go along with this story."

"I can probably scrounge something up."

"Hey!" Rusty yelled from somewhere off screen. "You told me those photos had been deleted!"

"Always save backups," Tara stage-whispered to Kate. "For blackmail emergencies."

Nathan reached out and snagged the phone.

"Hey!" Kate protested.

"You know turnabout's fair play, right?" he said.

Tara seemed to be considering her options, and Kate grinned at the look she shared with Nathan through the phone. This friendship reminded her so much of Sarah that her heart ached to see her again. It was the kind of friendship that could outlast miles and years apart, that thrived even at a distance, but she knew she'd rather have Sarah around in person.

"Kate said someone's spotted the horses?" Nathan's brow curved in question.

Tara nodded in agreement. "The post I sent out last night got some good hits. I think adding the pictures really helped. That was a good idea."

"I have been known to have one occasionally."

Kate chuckled against his shoulder.

"A few kids think they've found them. They posted photos on their Instagram stories and I'm pretty sure it's Shade. Rusty's texting with them now. I'll send you the pictures they took, just give me a second."

A text blinked through, and Kate tapped it with her finger. Half a dozen screen captures overlaid with emojis appeared on the screen.

Her heart raced.

"That's them," she said, sitting up on her elbows. Shade and Tully and Samson for starters. Which meant the others probably weren't far.

"Where are you guys?" Nathan asked.

Tara held her phone up and Kate recognized the porch of the house. "Kate's mom is feeding Rusty an endless breakfast. Your dad got an old generator hooked up, enough to power the kitchen at the very least, and she's been cooking all morning."

"We'll meet you down there," Nathan said.

Kate rubbed the sleep from her eyes. "We can regroup and drag Rusty away from the all-you-can-eat buffet."

"Sounds like a plan," Tara said. "See you soon."

Kate hung up, setting her phone down on the side table again before turning to Nathan. He looked at her, his eyes shining with humor.

"What?" she asked.

"I like the hair this morning. It's giving Bride of Frankenstein vibes."

Kate reached up and touched the nest on her head, frowning playfully at him. "I could have slept in my own bed last night."

"Never," he said, pulling Kate so close he could probably feel the butterflies in her chest. "I like you like this. It's endearing."

Kate snorted at his comment, throwing her arms around his neck.

"Do you think they'll miss us for a few more minutes?" The words were breathed into her skin.

"I think Rusty will keep my mother occupied for a little while longer."

Nathan nuzzled his nose against hers. "Remind me to thank him."

"You and me both," Kate whispered. She kissed him for a few minutes. It was chaste by a lot of standards. Just the two of them enjoying each other's company as the morning sun crested the windows.

Then she sat up on the edge of the bed, spying her clothes from last night, wondering if there was time to shower before they set off to find Shade and the others. Touching her hair again, she figured a shower should be a priority.

"Stop looking at me like that," she said, reaching down for a sweatshirt from the floor. It looked like Nathan's, but that was his problem, not hers.

"Like what?"

"Like you're not planning to get out of bed anytime soon."

"Maybe I'm not," he said, leering at her in a way that made Kate want to lie back down.

"We don't have time for this," she said, feeling her face flush. "We need to be productive. I'm going to scrounge up some coffee and then I'm going to shower." Kate moved to pull the sweatshirt over her head.

He caught the back of the sweatshirt before she could leave the bed. "Why can't it be both?"

His hand slipped beneath the sweatshirt, pressed

against Kate's bare skin, and as desire built in her, she wasn't sure she had the ability to say no to him.

She didn't really want to.

She turned to him then, seeing the heat captured in those gray eyes, and she knew this was the sight she wanted to wake up to forever. His hand snaked up her stomach, dangerously close to her breasts.

"We'll be late," she warned.

"We'll be quick," he argued, sitting up enough that he could press his lips to the space below her ear.

Kate shivered, shifting to meet his lips. "I think we can multitask."

"Teenagers are the worst," Rusty complained as Nathan sped the ranch truck down the highway, dodging rogue branches and construction debris that had yet to be cleared up from the storm. At the rate the weather changed, it would probably be there until the next storm.

"Why?" Kate asked, looking back at Rusty.

After a hasty shower at the guest house that was less of a shower and more soaping each other up, Nathan and Kate had joined the others at the house. Nathan had impressively devoured the rest of the breakfast her mom had cooked up while Rusty and Tara had secured the directions to the horses. Soon after that, Kate had ushered them all out of the house, eager to have something to do that didn't involve avoiding her mother's very pointed gaze.

Even before her announcement yesterday, where she'd promptly told everyone that she and Nathan were together, it was quite obvious that things had shifted. A lot of the walls and blocks and barriers were gone. And it felt as if Nathan was never more than an arm's length away. Kate just hadn't wanted to talk about it over her eggs, and she made a point of getting the horse trailer hitched up to the truck in record time. Her mother would just have to wait.

Tara snorted, bringing Kate out of her thoughts. "He's just mad that they didn't think he was cool."

"That is not what I said," Rusty complained to her. "These children somehow insulted and complimented me in the same breath. And just when I thought I'd won them over, they insulted me again. Apparently," Rusty said, drawing out the word dramatically, "I don't pass the vibe check. What vibe?"

His disgruntled face made Nathan laugh. Kate caught him watching everything in the rearview mirror.

"It's because you have the hair of an eighty-year-old woman who's spent decades on cheap box dye," Tara pointed out.

"They made one comment about my hair," Rusty said. "I don't think that was it."

"That's where it started," Tara muttered. "Just went downhill after that."

Rusty frowned at her. "Traitor."

Kate turned around, leaning against the seat. "Horses are kind of like that."

"Highly judgmental?" Nathan asked.

"No," Kate laughed. "I mean, they can be, I guess. What I meant was, they can sense the vibe of a person. They probably read human emotions better than we do."

"Huh," Tara said. She patted Rusty's shoulder sympathetically. "Now you'll have the teenagers and the horses ganging up on you."

"I thought I was going to have to sell my soul for the location," Rusty said. "Our new besties conveniently didn't tag it. Though I don't know how you tag anything out here. It's just grass," he said as they passed a field. "And wheat. And more grass. Oh, wait, this one's corn."

Kate grinned in amusement. "Did you?"

"What?"

"Have to sell your soul?"

"Oh, honey, there's no soul left to sell."

Tara rolled her eyes. "We bartered. They tell us where they saw the horses. I do a small professional photo-shoot with them."

Rusty scoffed. "Sellout."

"I call it ingenuity," Tara said. "You have to talk to teenagers in a language they can understand."

"And what's that?"

Tara grinned, showing all her teeth. "Ring lights."

"Well, I don't care what you call it. Just thank you," Kate said sincerely.

"It's no problem." Tara shrugged off Kate's thanks. "I too like to insult Rusty while making it sound like a compliment, so I think I've found my people." She was quick enough to snap a picture of the shocked look on Rusty's face, laughing as he reached across the truck to jab at her.

"Children, behave," Nathan warned, but he was grinning at their antics, and Kate was starting to understand what months of fulfilling a photography contract in remote locations must be like with them. "Where'd they say they spotted them again?"

"Route four," Tara read off her phone. "Past the abandoned church."

"Sound familiar?" Nathan asked Kate.

She nodded. "We used to get drunk in that church

when I was a teenager, before they boarded it up. Figured someone would have torn it down by now."

"Well, at least the horses know how to have a good time," Rusty said, toasting them with his to-go thermos of coffee.

"There's a riding trail that starts behind the church," Kate said. "They must have started running and just followed the trail as far as it would go."

Nathan flew by another cornfield, the trailer bouncing along behind them. It wasn't big enough for all the horses, so they'd probably have to make two trips if they managed to find all the horses together.

"Are you sure this thing is safe?" Rusty asked, looking out the back window.

"Safer than storm chasing during a tornado," Kate said.

"But the photos look so good," Tara argued.

"You still haven't let me see those," Rusty complained, reaching for her camera.

Tara slapped his hand away. "You'll see them when everyone else does."

"And when is that?"

"When they grace the pages of *National Geographic*."

"Promise to never show me those," Kate said quietly to Nathan. For the adrenaline junkies in the truck, it was just another story of a close call and a good time. But Kate never wanted to know how close they might have come to losing it all.

He glanced across the truck at her, the corner of his mouth turned up in a half smile that Kate was growing quite partial to. "I promise," he said, understanding.

She nodded, putting her hand on his arm and squeezing gently.

"I think we're almost there," Tara said. She leaned up against the window. "Yeah, that looks like a busted old church to me."

"What were you drinking in there?" Rusty said as they passed. "Tetanus?"

Kate couldn't exactly say she had fond memories of the place, just the usual teenage recollections of doing exactly what her parents told her not to do. And then sometimes getting away with it.

"I think that's them up ahead," Nathan said, pulling the truck over slowly on the gravel shoulder.

Kate scanned the field. There was a shallow ditch between them and the field, but sure enough, grazing under the blue skies were the horses. Shade, Tully, Samson and even the boarded horses. "They stuck together," Kate said.

"Aw," Rusty cooed. "Like one big happy family." He threw his lanky arms over the seats, surrounding Nathan and Kate, squeezing until they were butted up against each other. "If I step in one pile of horse shit, you two will never hear the end of it."

"That, I believe," Nathan said, shaking Rusty off and climbing out of the truck. He met Kate on the other side. She grabbed a lead rope and together they leaped across the swampy shallows of the ditch and hiked up into the field. It was damp, mud seeping out around her boots.

Kate approached the team slowly, taking her dad's advice.

"Don't spook them," he had said, pulling her aside before they left the house. "Just call them nice and gentle. The last thing you want is for them to bolt again."

"I know, Dad," Kate had said, as she collected her vet bag in case any of the horses were in need of any immediate medical attention. It was hard to tell from a photo what shape they were really in.

"And pull the truck off the road a little ways down. Samson always gets spooked by the trailer. He'll make the others anxious."

"We will," she'd promised. Part of her had wanted to remind her dad that she was both a vet and his daughter. If anyone could wrangle the horses back to the ranch, it was her. Then she'd realized that the only reason her dad was hovering was because he couldn't do it himself.

So Kate had hugged him instead.

Out of the corner of her eye, Kate spied Tara. She was lined up parallel to them, camera held up to her face.

"Just pretend she's not there," Nathan said.

"Should I be worried about embarrassing photos of me appearing at some point?"

"Only if you totally botch this rescue mission and fall on your ass."

Kate rolled her eyes. "The fact that you'd let me fall instead of catching me is giving me serious red flags."

"Probably shouldn't tell you about how I throw my dirty laundry beside the laundry basket instead of in it then, huh?"

"That's a deal breaker."

Nathan threw his head back. "Ah, I knew it."

The fact that they were joking like this sent a burst of warmth through Kate's chest. It wasn't just the domesticity of it, but the concept of long-term together. Long enough for her to be annoyed by his little eccentricities. It also made her wonder what he thought about when he considered them together. What did the word *love* mean to him? Shared laundry baskets? Being able to laugh at each other? With each other?

There was a lot to unpack there.

"How do you want to do this?" Nathan asked.

"I'm gonna see if I can get Shade back to the trailer. If I do, the others might follow." Kate held the lead rope in one hand. "You should get Samson if you can. He's spooked around the trailer and if any of them are going to bolt first, it'll be him."

Nathan nodded and they both approached slowly, whistling gently. Kate watched Shade's ear twitch as she grazed. She definitely knew Kate was there. She could hear her and see her, but she made no move to run, which made Kate hopeful. A few more steps. Then Shade ambled in her direction.

"C'mon, girl," Kate called, clicking her tongue. Shade perked up at that, huffing gently. "That's it," Kate said as she drew closer, staying where Shade could see her. Kate got close enough to touch her, rubbing circles into her coat. "You had a long night, didn't you?"

Another huff. Shade pulled a wad of grass from the ground.

Gently, Kate lowered herself enough to hook the lead string to Shade's halter. As soon as she did, Shade lifted her head for Kate to pat her nose. "There you are." Kate gave her a scratch. "Did you have fun on your adventure?"

"Aw, that's my boy," Nathan said to Samson. Kate looked across Shade, smiling at the affection in his voice.

With Shade secured, Kate began to lead her across the field. She found a part of the ditch that was less steep, leading Shade down and up the other side, tying her rope off to the trailer. Just as she hoped, with Shade and Samson being led away, the others followed. It was lazy, and they got distracted by wildflowers easily, but with a few whistles of encouragement, Kate had almost gotten them all out of the field.

"This thing isn't big enough," Rusty said, starting to do the math as he looked from the trailer to the horses.

"Only for about half," Kate agreed.

"What do we do with the other three?" Rusty said.

"We'll drive them back, you babysit," Nathan said to Rusty.

"Yeah, right. How about I drive them back and you babysit?" Rusty countered.

"That might work," Kate said.

"Really?" they both said with matching looks of confusion.

"We'll put the boarded horses in the trailer. We've got a couple saddles in the back of the truck. Rusty and Tara can drive the horses back." She looked over at Nathan. "You and I can ride Shade and Samson back. We'll keep Tully on the lead rope and she'll just walk along with us."

"You trust Rusty with this thing?" Nathan said, gesturing over his shoulder with his thumb.

"You'll drive slow," Kate told Rusty. "Very slow. And watch the potholes."

Rusty crossed his heart.

"All right," Kate said. "Let's get them loaded and saddled."

Nathan corralled the boarded horses up and into the trailer while Kate kept the others from wandering onto the road. As he was closing the door, Kate grabbed a saddle from the truck and threw it over Shade's back. Nathan joined her, saddling up Samson. It felt familiar— the two of them like this. Kate thought back to the first time they'd ridden together, and taking Nathan up to the ridge overlooking the lake.

"Are we all set here?" Rusty asked.

"Just about." Kate headed to the back of the trailer once more to double-check that it was locked. As she did, a car drove by, then slowed, backing up toward them. Kate stopped what she was doing, trying to see who was behind the wheel.

When she finally got a glimpse, she realized it was Doc McGinn.

He leaned his head out the window, dark circles under his eyes. "Some storm, huh?" he called.

"What? That tornado?" Nathan joked.

"You guys make out okay at the ranch?"

"Some damage," Kate called back. "But no one was hurt. Horses went on a little bit of an adventure, though. Did some sightseeing."

"Looks like you tracked them all down," Doc said.

"Thankfully."

Doc nodded. "I've got a pile of calls after that storm. You know, if you feel like stretching those vet muscles, I'd be happy for the help. Give me a call later if it's something you think you're up for."

"I will," Kate said, genuinely considering it.

Doc tipped his hat to her and drove away.

"He looks tired," Nathan said.

"There's a lot of farms around here." Kate frowned. "They all can't have been as lucky as us. Doc's probably been out all night."

"And you're going to go help him?"

"Well," Kate said, shrugging. Of course she was.

"You're a good person, Kate Cardiff." He pecked her

on the lips before walking away. Tara came around the back of the trailer.

"I just took the best photo," she said, holding up the camera to Kate. "You wanna see?"

Kate nodded, looking at the photo she just took. It was Rusty, jaw open in terror as Samson looked his way, lips pulled back mid-neigh.

"We're definitely keeping this one."

"For what?" Kate wondered, even though there was a part of her that wanted to have the photo blown up and mounted on a wall in the house somewhere. Tara scrolled through a couple of the other photos she'd taken of the horses grazing in the field, Nathan talking to Samson, Kate reaching out for Shade, Tully leading the team toward the trailer.

"These are *really* good," Kate gushed. "I mean, seriously."

"Thanks," Tara said, stringing the camera back around her neck. "Nathan and I were talking. The ranch needs a social media presence. For that you need some high-quality, professionally shot photos."

"You were?" Kate said, oddly touched that Nathan was so eager to help out her parents.

"Nathan asked me to start taking photos of the ranch a few weeks ago, so I have some really good shots from before the storm."

Kate didn't know what to say. Tara didn't give her time to reply, just bounded away to join Rusty in the truck. Kate walked around the side of the trailer to meet Nathan. He was already perched in his saddle.

"A social media presence, huh?" she said to him. "Tara was just mentioning it."

"Oh," he said, his cheeks flushing a bit. "Yeah, I

didn't mean to overstep or anything, but I was thinking it would be good to bring the ranch into the twenty-first century. Instagram. Twitter. Basically all the socials. And a website that doesn't take eight minutes to load. I don't know who your dad hired to build that thing but we're just gonna scrap it and start again. I think we can really build this place back up. And I don't just mean the roof of the stables."

Kate bit her lip.

"What is it?"

"Nothing, you just keep surprising me. That's all." Surprising her with things that sounded serious. Things that almost sounded like he meant forever.

"If all it takes to impress you are my savvy social media skills, then I won't have to work as hard in the bedroom."

Kate blushed from head to toe. "You think Rusty is gonna be okay turning this trailer around?"

Nathan smirked at her change of subject but nodded. "The shoulder is wider down there." He walked Samson up to the window of the truck, and Kate watched him gesture as he gave Rusty directions.

Kate grabbed Shade's reins and put her foot in the stirrup, hoisting herself up and settling into the saddle. She took Tully's lead rope and the two horses started down the side of the road. She stopped them long enough to watch Rusty make a very smooth turn with the trailer.

Nathan trotted Samson back to catch up with her and after a minute, the truck appeared. "This slow enough for you?" Rusty rolled along beside them.

"Perfect," Nathan said. "Just try not to hit anything."

"No promises." Rusty sped up a little. He drove with

the four-ways on and despite his slight aversion to the horses, Kate was not even a little worried. If he was ever done with the photography thing, her parents might even find a job for him on the ranch.

"So," Nathan said, squinting into the sun as Samson eased through the long grass beneath him, nosing at dandelions.

All he needed was a cowboy hat and he'd be the quintessential rancher, Kate thought to herself. The fact that she'd once thought him to be the worst possible man for this job seemed ridiculous now. Her parents really couldn't have found anyone better.

"So," she said in return.

They smiled at each other, almost shyly. A few locks of Nathan's dark hair fell into his face as his eyes turned downward.

Kate could sense something serious coming. Nerves fluttered to life in her gut.

She'd been worried about this moment. About this discussion. About putting words to the fears she had about where they went from here.

She loved him, yes, but now what?

How did they blend these two very different lives together?

Did he even want to?

Her old uncertainties crept to life, like a vise around her chest, and for a second she found it hard to think. She was glad for Shade's even breathing beneath her, which brought her back to reality.

"I think we should talk," Nathan said. "For real this time. No more running away."

"No more running away," she agreed. Whatever was to happen now, she would face it straight on. Shade and Samson pressed closer together, bringing Nathan within arm's reach.

"You know I—"

"You'd never be happy here," Kate blurted out before he could say anything else. Now that they were going to have this conversation, she couldn't tiptoe around this one nagging worry. "Or in any small town," she amended. "Not long-term."

Even before she'd come back to stay with her parents, Kate's life had pretty much consisted of passing through one small town after another. That was where her animals were. That was where her life was. She couldn't be a livestock vet from a condo in LA or an apartment in New York. Never mind where else Nathan's work might carry him. And as adorable as they were, Kate didn't see herself with a practice in the city deworming newborn puppies.

It just wasn't her.

"What makes you say that?" Nathan asked. "Why do you think I wouldn't be happy somewhere like this?"

Kate scoffed at the point he was so obviously missing. "What would you photograph? I know you and Rusty and Tara are getting a kick out of chasing storms, but you can't do that forever. And there's only so much you can do with the wheat and the cornfields."

"Don't forget there's always pets or newborns swaddled to look like acorns."

Kate chuckled, the sound hollow in her chest. "But that's not what you really love about the profession. You want the adventure and the moments that come from disappearing halfway around the world with your two best friends. I can't give you that here. Eventually you'd get bored and I just…" She trailed off, biting her bottom lip.

"What scares you?"

"I'm scared you'd start to resent me. Resent the life we built. Whatever that looked like."

"Okay," Nathan said. "I hear your point. Really, I do. I just don't have the same concerns."

"It's a little more than just a point," Kate argued. From where she was sitting, it was a disaster in the making. "It could never work. Not long-term. You'd get miserable and then I'd be miserable and then we'd both just be there, miserable and hating each other—"

Nathan burst out laughing, turning Samson sharply so he stepped in front of Shade.

Kate pulled the reins hard to stop them from colliding. "Are you done now?"

"Done?"

"Yes, are you done making excuses for all the reasons you think this won't work?" He looked at her with fond amusement.

"I don't know what you find so funny."

"You're not funny. You're adorable. You're also trying to sabotage this before it begins and if there's one thing I'm not going to let happen, it's that."

Kate frowned at him. She didn't know what to say.

"My life can move around," Nathan continued. "You're right about that. I don't *have* to stay in any one place if I don't want to. But I never had one place that I *wanted* to stay before. One place that actually felt like home. That's different now."

The space in Kate's chest swelled with a warmth that threatened to bubble up in the form of tears.

"So I'm not the problem here." He gazed at her, eyes

never leaving hers, and it took a moment for her mind to catch up.

"Wait, *I'm* the problem?"

"You are the problem, Kate Cardiff," he confirmed. He flicked the reins and Samson trotted ahead. "But lucky for you, I'm an excellent problem solver."

Kate dug her heels in hard, urging Shade and Tully to catch up. "Why am I the problem?"

"You're the one with the track record of running away." He was not cruel when he said it. He was just making an observation. But even that didn't seem to deter him. "So, if you want to go, if you want to run away from here, just tell me where, Kate, and I'll follow you anywhere."

Shade stopped moving. "That's it?" she said quietly.

Nathan pulled on the reins until Samson stopped. They stood so close their knees bumped. "Remember when I told you that I liked setting out on my own, forging my own path? Well, it's led me to you, Kate. So that's it," he answered back. "I'm in this. Whether we're here or on the other side of the world together. And even if a photography contract pulls me away, you know the great thing about those?"

Kate shook her head, a little stunned by his confession.

"They end, Kate. I get to come home. To you. So you just let me know where you decide that is and my bags are packed."

With that, a feeling of impossible bliss bloomed inside her chest. For the first time since falling in love with this man, she finally let go of all the worries she'd carried with her, because this was real.

Nathan was hers.

* * *

When Kate finally settled on what she wanted, she chose happiness.

For a long time, she hadn't been sure what that looked like for her. Animals were part of it, but not enough by themselves. Cal had once been something to her, but in the end, he wasn't the right one. Leaving home had been an adventure, but nowhere ever felt like home again after that.

Kate had always managed to find pieces of her happiness.

But never all of it.

And now, knowing it was possible, she wanted every crumb.

She'd been thinking about what Doc had said as they got the horses back to the ranch. While they tidied up the stables enough to get the horses settled, she mulled over his proposal. When he'd first alluded to retiring when she ran into him at Steele's, she hadn't thought anything of it. But now she wondered what would happen if she stayed? What if she took over his roster, sliding easily into the role he'd filled in this community since Kate was a little girl?

With Doc's offer, maybe it was finally time to stop running away and start running toward something instead. Nathan had said he'd follow her anywhere, but maybe here was exactly where she was meant to be.

Being on the ranch was what made her the happiest, and this could be the home base Nathan was always searching for. Now that she was thinking about it, she couldn't stop seeing it in her mind—her and Nathan building a life here together.

That was probably why she marched herself straight

to her dad's office as soon as they were done with the horses. Because now that she knew what she wanted, she was not going to let it slip away.

"Kate, are you sure?" Nathan said, catching her arm before she could burst through the double doors. "I meant what I said before. I'll follow you anywhere."

She was sure.

That was how she knew he was the one.

Nathan hadn't asked her to choose between anything. He hadn't asked her to compromise her life so they could be together. He just promised to be here, by her side, in whatever capacity she chose.

So she was choosing him *and* the ranch.

A life together.

"I'm sure," she told him, lifting her hand to entwine their fingers. She pulled his hand to her lips to kiss it. "This is what I want."

"Okay," Nathan breathed. A lopsided grin pulled across his face. *"Okay."*

"Wish me luck," Kate said.

Nathan pecked her on the nose. "You don't need it."

With that, Kate turned and pushed the doors open.

Her dad was there, sitting at his desk, poring over his books and his papers, trying to make the columns add up. Trying to move the numbers around to keep things floating.

Kate's heart broke for him, and she wished the wrinkles by his eyes were from laughing too hard instead of worrying.

But what if he didn't have to worry anymore? What if she could take away some of that stress?

"Kate?" Her dad looked up. He was tired, the circles

under his eyes giving him away long before the stiffness of his muscles as he stood to greet her.

"Hi, Dad."

"You get back okay with the horses?"

"Sure did. Everyone's safely in their stalls. We'll need to get the fences in the pasture repaired as soon as we can, though."

Her dad sighed. "We'll have to get some new lumber and probably have someone out to look at the damage on the roof of the house and the stables." The corners of his mouth were pinched. Kate knew he was wondering where all the costs were coming from until the insurance money came in.

"Dad," Kate said, reaching out for his hand. She held it between both of hers, feeling the roughened ridges of his knuckles. "I know you're having money troubles. You and Mom. I know you're worried about the future of the ranch."

"Kate," he said, trying to interrupt her. Trying to put off this conversation. To protect her and his pride.

"I want to help," she insisted.

He took a breath, letting it out slowly. "That's nice, Katie, but that's not your job. You're not the one that's supposed to fix this. It's on me and your mother."

"Dad," she began, trying to figure out a way to put all her thoughts in order. To make them make sense. She squeezed his hand a little tighter. "I'm not just Katie anymore. I'm grown up. I have a career and a life. I also have some money saved up."

Her dad pulled away, shaking his head. "Kate, I won't take your money."

"I *want* to do this."

"No," he said. "Not even a loan. You've worked hard

for what you have, just like your mother and I raised you to do."

"Then let me help you."

He turned away from her.

"Look," Kate said, giving it one more last-ditch effort. "I'm not asking you to let me break open my piggy bank to fix your problems. I'm asking you to let me be a partner in this. To let me buy into the *business*."

"What?" her dad said, looking over his shoulder at her.

"What if this isn't a loan?" Kate said, doing her best to hide the nerves trembling in her hands. Maybe her dad wouldn't go for it. She lifted her shoulder when he turned around again. "Doc's retiring. He told me so himself. He's got an entire practice set up in this town that needs a livestock vet." A small smile crept across her face as her dad's eyes widened. "That sort of happens to be my specialty."

"What are you thinking?" he asked.

Kate could hardly believe what she was about to say. "Cardiff Ranch *and* Veterinary Practice."

Her dad lifted his hand to his face, rubbing at the scruff from his beard. Kate grinned, knowing she'd got him. She'd spent a lifetime learning his looks. And this was the look of a man who had just stumbled upon a great idea.

"We're already going to have to do some construction after the storm, so it kind of feels like the perfect time to make some changes. And Nathan will be here to help, too, in between photography contracts."

"He will, will he?"

Kate couldn't help but match her dad's smile. "He's got all these great ideas for the website and for getting the ranch on social media so it gets the right exposure. And it turns out he's not a bad ranch hand after all."

There was a long beat of silence. Kate waited with bated breath.

"Well, I'm in," Rusty said, waltzing through the door and throwing his arm over her shoulders. Tara and Nathan stumbled in after him. Kate knew that Nathan had been waiting in the hall. Waiting to support her no matter how this conversation went. She just hadn't realized Rusty and Tara had joined him, silently eavesdropping.

"You are?" She'd half assumed that Rusty and Tara would have been on the first flight out of here as soon as they could arrange a contract.

"You are?" Nathan repeated, just as intrigued, though it seemed for very different reasons.

"Anything you need." Rusty grinned, looking around at them all. "I'm pretty handy. I even know my way around a toolbox."

Nathan shook his head, scoffing loudly. "One high school shop class does not count for anything."

"Four years of shop class," Rusty corrected him. "Four years. And I was especially gifted. Mr. Nixon said so himself."

Tara snorted, murmuring something about Rusty being an idiot. She turned around and the two of them walked down the hall, debating the merits of a birdhouse he built in the tenth grade.

"And what do you think about all this, Mr. Prescott?" Her dad turned to Nathan, hands falling to his hips.

Nathan lingered in the doorway with his hands in his pockets, trying to remain the silent partner. He quirked his brow, his thin-lipped smile breaking into a toothy grin as he said, "I think you're going to need to order a new sign for out front."

"Cardiff Ranch and Veterinary Practice," her dad repeated.

"Well?" Kate said, chest warming from Nathan's declaration. She looked to her dad for an answer.

It only took another second before he held his hand out to her, face splitting into a proud grin. "Welcome to the business, partner."

Kate laughed in disbelief, shaking his hand.

Then her dad pulled her in, catching her in a hug that was just as tight as the ones he used to give her as a girl, all traces of age and weariness gone. "Welcome home."

Epilogue

Kate woke up to one of her new favorite things: a very naked Nathan splayed out on the bed next to her. She basked in the warmth of his body and in the way his arm looped over her hip, fingers loosely clinging to her, like he meant to pull her close. To hold her and never let go.

Her fingertips traced loose patterns into his forearm, and Kate smiled as a dull rain pattered at the window. The clouds were interspersed with pockets of blue sky, and she wondered if the rain would disappear by the time they brought themselves to actually leave the bed.

She didn't mind the rain, though.

A lazy, rainy day in bed with Nathan was something she didn't ever think she'd be able to get enough of. Each day she grew more insatiable for him, and she couldn't remember why she'd ever worked so hard to keep them apart when they clearly belonged together.

As far as Rusty and Tara and her parents were concerned, they were both much better off now than when they were pining after each other.

Clearly, Kate hadn't been fooling anyone.

A buzz against the night table distracted her, and Kate rolled over to grab her phone, smiling as Sarah's name flashed across the screen. It had only been a few days since they last talked. Sarah had been shocked, hearing about the storm. Kate had filled her in on every detail.

Every single one.

And as much as Sarah had been shocked by the tornado, she'd squealed Kate's ear off when hearing about what happened after. She was no longer interested in the extreme weather event that could have killed her best friend or destroyed the ranch, but wanted to know exactly what happened with Nathan.

Kate did not disappoint.

For as much as Sarah teased and pried and threatened to kill Nathan if he ever did anything to upset Kate, she was genuinely pleased for her, and Kate needed that. She needed someone to share the overwhelming weight of happiness she felt.

Someone she could gush endlessly to, who wouldn't get bored or roll her eyes—as long as Kate made sure to throw in some racy details every now and then.

After trying to squash the feelings she had for him for weeks, all Kate now wanted to do was talk about him. Talk about how wonderful he was. How kind. How each day was a little more perfect than the last. This thing between them had reduced her to a romantic mess, but Kate didn't care.

She was going to live in her little bubble of bliss and no one was going to take that away from her.

"Hello," Kate murmured as she answered the phone, cognizant of the fact that Nathan was still dozing beside her. She didn't want to wake him.

"Morning, sunshine," Sarah all but sang. "Am I interrupting any sordid affairs? Any scandalous happenings? Anything rated R?"

Kate could almost hear Sarah's eyebrows wiggling. "No," she answered, much to Sarah's immediate disappointment.

"Well, that's no fun. You're no fun. *He's* no fun. And you can tell him I said that."

"We're being very tame."

"I can change that," Nathan hummed quietly beside her, eyes still closed but a perfectly wicked smile on his lips. "I can be *very* fun."

Kate bit her lip to keep from sighing.

She'd suspected he might have woken up and, like her, was just enjoying the peacefulness of the moment before Sarah called. But now that she knew he was awake, the rough, gravel texture of his voice stirred something in Kate, and she held her arm out, stopping the descent of his hands upon her body. If she let him, he'd thoroughly distract her from this phone call.

To his credit, Nathan behaved, but only mildly, his hand sneaking beneath the covers to rub circles into her thigh. It was a promise of things to come, and Kate's insides did a little flip in response. She flopped back on her pillow, wondering how long they could put off joining the others for breakfast.

"How's the job hunt going?" Kate asked before her thoughts could get carried away.

"It's not," Sarah said firmly. "I've decided I'm not going to take another contract anywhere right now."

"You're not?"

"I kind of like this extended vacation thing," Sarah said. "It's sort of nice to take some purposeful time off. I think I've needed it for a while, you know. Spend some real time with Parker instead of just the hours in between shifts."

"Of course," Kate said. "I'm sure he's glad to have you all to himself for a while."

"I've wanted to do some other things, too," Sarah said. "Catch up on some reading. Travel—"

"To your hot, sandy beach where the bartenders make all the drinks with tiny umbrellas? I'm not sure Parker's ready for that," Kate laughed.

"I know," Sarah sighed. "A few more years. I found this other place," she said. "It's cute. Cozy. Very family-oriented."

Kate quirked a brow. *Cute* and *cozy* weren't exactly words Sarah had ever used to describe her ideal vacation destination.

"It needs a little work. Went through sort of a rough patch recently. But it's got a barn and horses. Oh, wait, I've been corrected before. It's a stable."

"Shut up," Kate said, sitting up so quickly she got dizzy from the motion.

Sarah burst out laughing. "I wondered how long it was going to take you to catch on."

"Are you joking?"

"Why would I joke about this? Disappearing to small-town nowhere seems to have worked out well enough for you," Sarah teased. "Plus, don't you think it's about time Parker and I came for a visit? You *are* his favorite aunt."

"Absolutely," Kate said without hesitation.

"Then I can meet Rancher Hotstuff in the flesh," Sarah said. "Maybe even find one of my own."

Kate glanced over just as Nathan mouthed, "Hotstuff?"

She patted his arm before saying to Sarah, "You're really going to have to stop calling him that."

"Why? It's probably fitting, even though you refuse to send me more than a grainy photo of the man in some dark barn. Isn't he a photographer? Ask him to give you some tips."

"So funny," Kate muttered.

"I'm being serious. Or am I going to have to start begging your mother for information?"

"Oh, great," Kate winced. "That's the last thing I need. The two of you joining forces."

"The two of us are unstoppable when we put our heads together," Sarah said. "Give us a few days and we'd have the rings exchanged and the vows said before you even knew what was happening."

"I think you're getting a little ahead of yourself," Kate said, surprised at Sarah for even mentioning it, but more surprised at how nice it sounded.

"Parker could use a new uncle."

"Sarah!"

"What? You two have already survived one near-death experience, what's a little marriage thrown into the mix?"

"You are *so* not allowed to meet him," Kate decided. That was it. She was going to have to keep Nathan and Sarah on opposite ends of the ranch. She was also going to have to keep Sarah and her mother from being alone in a room together. One hour and the two of them would be plotting away.

"Oh, honey, bags are packed and we're leaving tomorrow. I've already cleared it with your mom. Apparently there's room in the house now that someone's moved into the guest house with her *boyfriend.*"

Kate shook her head, her fondness for her best friend outweighing her exasperation. Sarah was an unstoppable force when she put her mind to something. Nursing. Being a mother. Meddling in Kate's life. She was maybe even more unstoppable than the tornado that had changed Kate's life so drastically.

But Kate wasn't sure she really wanted any of it to stop.

In fact, just like the rain outside, she'd be quite happy if it just continued.

"Pick you up from the airport?" she asked, hearing the smile in her own voice.

Sarah laughed. "Sending flight details to your phone now."

* * * * *

COMING NEXT MONTH FROM

ⒽHARLEQUIN®
SPECIAL EDITION™

#2983 FORTUNE'S RUNAWAY BRIDE
The Fortunes of Texas: Hitting the Jackpot • by Allison Leigh
Isabel Banninger's fiancé is a two-timing jerk! Running out of her own wedding leads her straight into CEO Reeve Fortune's strong, very capable arms. Reeve is *so* not her type. But is he the perfect man to get this runaway bride to say "I do"?

#2984 SKYSCRAPERS TO GREENER PASTURES
Gallant Lake Stories • by Jo McNally
Web designer Olivia Carson hides her physical and emotional scars behind her isolated country life. Until a simple farmhouse remodel brings city-boy contractor Tony Vello crashing into her quiet world. They share similar past pain...and undeniable attraction. But will he stay once the job is done?

#2985 LOVE'S SECRET INGREDIENT
Love in the Valley • by Michele Dunaway
Nick Reilly adores Zoe Smith's famous chocolate chip cookies—and Zoe herself. He hides his billionaire status to get closer to the single mom. Even pretends to be her fiancé. But trading one fake identity for another is a recipe for disaster. Unless it saves Zoe's bakery *and* her guarded heart...

#2986 THE SOLDIER'S REFUGE
The Tuttle Sisters of Coho Cove • by Sabrina York
Football star Jax Stringfellow was the bane of Natalie Tuttle's high school existence. A traumatic military tour transformed her former crush from an arrogant, mean-spirited jock into a father figure for her nephews. But can the jaded TV producer trust her newfound connection with this kinder, gentler, *sexier* Jax?

#2987 THEIR ALL-STAR SUMMER
Sisters of Christmas Bay • by Kaylie Newell
Marley Carmichael is back in Christmas Bay, ready to make her baseball-announcing dreams come true. When a one-night stand with sexy minor-league star Owen Taylor ends with a surprise pregnancy, life *and* love throw her the biggest curveball yet!

#2988 A TASTE OF HOME
Sisterhood of Chocolate & Wine • by Anna James
Layla Williams is a spoiled princess—or so Wall Streeter turned EMT Shane Kavanaugh thought. But the captivating chef is so much more than he remembers. When her celebrated French restaurant is threatened by a hostile investor, he'll use all his business—and romance—skills to be the hometown hero Layla needs!

YOU CAN FIND MORE INFORMATION ON UPCOMING HARLEQUIN TITLES, FREE EXCERPTS AND MORE AT HARLEQUIN.COM.

HSECNM0423

Get 4 FREE REWARDS!

We'll send you 2 FREE Books plus 2 FREE Mystery Gifts.

FREE Value Over **$20**

Both the **Harlequin® Special Edition** and **Harlequin® Heartwarming™** series feature compelling novels filled with stories of love and strength where the bonds of friendship, family and community unite.

YES! Please send me 2 FREE novels from the Harlequin Special Edition or Harlequin Heartwarming series and my 2 FREE gifts (gifts are worth about $10 retail). After receiving them, if I don't wish to receive any more books, I can return the shipping statement marked "cancel." If I don't cancel, I will receive 6 brand-new Harlequin Special Edition books every month and be billed just $5.49 each in the U.S. or $6.24 each in Canada, a savings of at least 12% off the cover price, or 4 brand-new Harlequin Heartwarming Larger-Print books every month and be billed just $6.24 each in the U.S. or $6.74 each in Canada, a savings of at least 19% off the cover price. It's quite a bargain! Shipping and handling is just 50¢ per book in the U.S. and $1.25 per book in Canada.* I understand that accepting the 2 free books and gifts places me under no obligation to buy anything. I can always return a shipment and cancel at any time by calling the number below. The free books and gifts are mine to keep no matter what I decide.

Choose one: ☐ **Harlequin Special Edition**
(235/335 HDN GRJV)

☐ **Harlequin Heartwarming Larger-Print**
(161/361 HDN GRJV)

Name (please print)

Address   Apt. #

City   State/Province   Zip/Postal Code

Email: Please check this box ☐ if you would like to receive newsletters and promotional emails from Harlequin Enterprises ULC and its affiliates. You can unsubscribe anytime.

Mail to the **Harlequin Reader Service:**
IN U.S.A.: P.O. Box 1341, Buffalo, NY 14240-8531
IN CANADA: P.O. Box 603, Fort Erie, Ontario L2A 5X3

Want to try 2 free books from another series! Call 1-800-873-8635 or visit www.ReaderService.com.

*Terms and prices subject to change without notice. Prices do not include sales taxes, which will be charged (if applicable) based on your state or country of residence. Canadian residents will be charged applicable taxes. Offer not valid in Quebec. This offer is limited to one order per household. Books received may not be as shown. Not valid for current subscribers to the Harlequin Special Edition or Harlequin Heartwarming series. All orders subject to approval. Credit or debit balances in a customer's account(s) may be offset by any other outstanding balance owed by or to the customer. Please allow 4 to 6 weeks for delivery. Offer available while quantities last.

Your Privacy—Your information is being collected by Harlequin Enterprises ULC, operating as Harlequin Reader Service. For a complete summary of the information we collect, how we use this information and to whom it is disclosed, please visit our privacy notice located at corporate.harlequin.com/privacy-notice. From time to time we may also exchange your personal information with reputable third parties. If you wish to opt out of this sharing of your personal information, please visit readerservice.com/consumerschoice or call 1-800-873-8635. **Notice to California Residents**—Under California law, you have specific rights to control and access your data. For more information on these rights and how to exercise them, visit corporate.harlequin.com/california-privacy.

HSEHW22R3

HARLEQUIN
PLUS

Try the best multimedia subscription service for romance readers like you!

Read, Watch and Play.

Experience the easiest way to get the romance content you crave.

Start your **FREE TRIAL** at
<u>www.harlequinplus.com/freetrial</u>.

HARPLUS0123